LIVING ON EMPTY

Jordan Aubry Robison

This is a work of fiction. Names, characters, places, and incidents either are the product of the author's imagination or are used fictitiously, and any resemblance to actual persons, living or dead, business establishments, events, or locales is entirely coincidental.

Living on Empty
Copyright © 2013, 2014 by Jordan Aubry Robison

Cover Art by Jordan Aubry Robison
Copyright © 2013, 2014

ISBN: 13: 978-0-615-82155-9
ISBN: 10: 0615821553X

Dedicated to my family and to everyone who believed in me.

"All of life is a foreign country."
-Jack Kerouac

PART ONE

1

IT all kind of happened because I was broke and bored.

Smoke rose from my father's 1978 Pontiac red-metallic Firebird. I tried to start the car. I turned the key and pumped the gas several times. It wheezed an old decaying coffin-like cough. Clouds of dark black smoke puffed out the exhaust pipe. The sound made me cringe. I thought about recoiling into a fetal position while wishing for renewal. My chest tightened. My eyes watered. But I could not be reborn.

Traces of my father's distinct musk animated the car's interior aroma. I wondered if a spirit or presence was near me. I raised my small hands to feel the cracked paint on the ceiling. Somehow my father had managed to paint an elaborate and colorful Maria de Guadalupe—*el Virgen de Guadalupe*—in honor of his dearly deceased mother. I think. A tingling raced up to my shoulder from the tips of my fingers. My father had been a great artist in brief moments of distilled insanity.

Wearing my dad's old Steve McQueen aviators I looked around the car and then back at his Aztec mural. Somehow I knew what needed to be done. I could hear Clint Eastwood's gravel voice whisper, "Well, you gonna move or just sit there and wait to die?"

If I was in San Francisco I'd be driving this bad boy, while drinking a cold beer and chasing bad guys, through streets that dipped and rose like a cheap roller coaster from some bad dream. Clint would be yelling at me, "Slow down! Take it easy!"

No time, old man! No time for love!

Six months ago this car had been under my father's obsessive management. Six months ago he'd been alive and cursing and complaining. Cursing people coming into his restaurant unaware of how a hamburger should taste. Or kids whose bad taste ruined decent-looking cars with oversized and unnecessary spoilers. Or the neon messages on old Honda Civics that would claim to be riding in the memory of some deceased redneck. Six months ago I'd seen regret shine in his dying eyes. Now his car, his Bambino, was mine, and I knew I had to get rid of it. It had seen its last mile of asphalt. Ennio Morricone's instrumentation, "L'estasi dell'oro," played on my car radio.

I would abandon the car. This time I was on my own.

Damn. I had only one cigarette left. I stored it near my ear for later. The battery on my cell phone was nearly dead, and I had only twenty dollars to my name. I wasn't even sure what my next move would be. I wanted to philosophize life's meaningless meaning and stare at Maria de Guadalupe a little longer, but I knew that wouldn't fix my problem. I knew that wouldn't do anything. Maria had to go, along with the fading memory of my father. "If you want a guarantee, buy a toaster," Clint's voice chimed again in my head. He was right.

I had to get rid of the car. The *Bambino*[1]. I called Emilio. Emilio managed The Fish Bowl. My favorite bar through college. He was somewhat of a shady guy rumored

---

[1] Italian and Spanish nickname for a male child.

to have emigrated here from El Salvador or Colombia. Or something like that. Somehow, no one was sure where he was from. He neither confirmed nor denied said rumors. I supposed he preferred to exist instead as a mystery. Or something like that. Emilio was one of those guys who could get you things if you knew how to ask. Or if he felt he could trust you. For some reason he trusted me. One time he said I reminded him of his son. I sometimes asked him where his son was. He said his son was back in the home country, and Emilio would never see him again. I told him he was one cold son of a bitch. He laughed.

"Emilio. This is Jimmy, Jimmy Rodriguez. Lookit. I'm in kind of a bind. The car is *muerte* and … and I need to get rid of it."

"Which car?"

"My dad's old car. The red Firebird."

"With Maria?"

"Yes. That one. The same."

"Why would you want to do that? Have you no respect for your father's memory? What kind of son are you?"

"The car is dead. What am I going to do with a dead car?"

"I can store it for you. Keep it somewhere safe until you can afford to get it fixed and pay me for the storage."

"No. I don't want to owe you anything. Just take the car. It's yours. A gift."

"You're going to regret this."

"Life is full of regrets. What's one more?"

"Fine. Fine. You better be gone before my men show up. They won't know you and they won't trust you. *¿Te entiendes?²* I can't be responsible for nothing."

"Don't worry about me. I'll be a phantom. Invisible."

---

² English translation: "Do you understand?"

It was done.

Now I needed a ride from someone who would be in like lightning and out like a flash. I called Norm Schwartz, the Golden Oldie, as he was sometimes called. Norm was in his forties. His hair was for the most part white and badly buzzed. He was his own barber. He had lived a life, thus far, trailed by bad luck, bad memories, failed romances, and long lonesome nights of debauchery and neglect. And somehow he'd remained good-natured. He never let the chains he'd forged in life bring him down.

For the past twenty years he had been working on the same science-fiction novel. Something about robots. The stubborn bastard wouldn't let anyone read it. However, when properly lubricated with alcohol, Norm would sometimes allow us cheese ball hints of his robot story's eccentric plot. By this time I imagined an epic novel that included tens of thousands of pages of notepads stacked to the ceiling. He wasn't fond of computers.

The phone rang for what seemed like forever before Norm graciously answered my call.

"What the fuck? I was sleeping. I mean meditating. I was meditating."

"Look, you old lazy fat bastard. I need you to pick me up. My car, the Firebird—"

"The *Bambino*?"

"Whatever. It's dead. I'm on Two-Seventy. And I need you to pick me up like a bat out of hell. Got me?"

"Why not call a tow truck?"

"Details man. Details. Pick me up, *por favor.*"

Fine? Nothing was fine.

"If you think it's going to rain, it will," I heard Clint say.

"Why are you in my head?" I asked Clint. But there was no answer save for the static from the car radio. It must have lost the station again. I didn't think I'd miss this radio, that's for sure. It was an eight-track player, and I didn't have any eight-tracks. The radio never worked right, at least for me, unlike with my father, who seemed to have that magic touch. He was like a violin player twisting the knob ever so slightly until the signal came in perfectly. I could never duplicate that magic touch.

But it had been more than that. It had been a Midas touch. I never bothered to turn the radio on. Instead I brought my MP3 player.

I had to leave before Emilio's henchmen arrived and possibly fileted me into fish food. Or before a cop showed up and decided to offer me a helping hand, ruining my feeble attempt to erase this car from existence. Then the cop would start asking me questions, wanting to know personal stuff like all cops do. Every time I had a run-in with a cop, I always got asked extremely personal questions. Questions which always caught me off guard. I would try my best to give a logical answer, and the cop would respond with a sarcastic question, followed by another. As if nothing I said was believable. I fantasized him forcing me to do something drastic like steal his gun, then try to run away as he shot me dead for attempting to resist arrest. I would go out in a blaze of glory!

Death would be a great adventure, though. I imagined myself flying up through the silver clouds like a forgotten angel, not good enough to make it into heaven but not bad enough to be sent to hell. Instead I would hover like a lone invisible bee, buzzing around and eavesdropping on the conversations of my living friends. I would find out what they truly thought of me while flying through walls and seeing through the cracks of each person's lies. Followed by joining a group of dancing skeletons wearing mariachi hats. *Malaguena! Salerosa!* Would I see my dad, again? Would I find my mother, wherever she might be? All I knew about my mother was that she was far away from me. She had always been far away from me.

I slowly walked away from the car lighting my last cigarette. I threw the match at the smoking car's leaking gasoline. As I popped my collar up, the flaming match ignited the fuel. The car exploded into a pyrotechnic fireball that blew into the blackbird-filled sky, separating darkness from light. The explosion propelled the car into space orbit.

I took one last look at what was left of my dad's car. The orange flames reflected off my movie star aviators. My boots clicked on the asphalt as I took one choreographed step after another. Heel, toe. Heel, toe. I stopped and did a quick Elvis Presley gyration with my hips while spinning my arms around an air guitar. I then pulled out a comb and brushed back my greasy hair. I curled my lip. *Uh-huh. Nothing but a hound dog. Uh-huh. Heartbreak Hotel. Thank you! Thank you very much. Jimmy Rodriguez has left the building, ladies and gentlemen....*

"How long you been sitting there waiting?" Norm yelled from his car as he pulled up.

"Let's see. Since I started smoking this cigarette, which is about gone."

"Five minutes?"

"I think."

"Right. Let's go."

Cake's "Going the Distance" blared from the speakers. Norm's favorite song. A song that he played relentlessly. He never tired of it. I wished I could claim his stubborn insistence to play this hip-hop influenced alternative rock song was annoying. But, the truth was, I enjoyed it each time he played it. I regarded it as his theme song. It was his way of throwing the middle finger at anyone who thought he was too old to be cool. He had his car hooked up with a thick heavy bass solely for this song. He refused to use the bass for any other song. Damn the man. Damn him for his beautiful eccentricities.

"Well," Norm exhaled as his stomach rose, "Evidently it's almost dark. Might as well head for Karaoke at the Fish Bowl."

"Shit. I almost forgot it's Karaoke Night."

"I'm going to pretend I didn't hear that. It's always Karaoke Night. What are you going to do with the car?"

I didn't want to answer. So I didn't. Instead, I turned up the radio and bopped my head to the Cake song. Norm understood, bopping his head along with me. He increased speed and drove the car like a redneck, winding in and around Ohio's idea of a traffic jam—which meant there was very little traffic for Norm to navigate. It all seemed to blend together into some very bad Andy Warhol painting where art began to lose its potential and become something any conman could hijack.

I looked at the mixture of trees, McMansions, telephone poles, retail stores, fast food chains, and high school football fields. I thought about the American Dream I'd been taught to believe in and wondered if it even existed anymore. Or was it fading away like the cigarette smoke that always disappeared into nowhere. Like a bad reminder that smoking caused cancer. And there was no cure for cancer.

No cure indeed. I should quit smoking one of these soft, disenchanted days.

I reached for a cigarette from Norm's stash in the glove compartment, which was met by a slap from the back of Norm's huge bear-like hand. He glanced at me from the corner of his eye and growled, "You owe me, bitch."

"Come on, man. I'm all out. I need a drag."

"Evidently you owe me almost a box of cigarettes by now. I can count, motherfucker. You owe me big." Norm had a habit of using "evidently" more than once in a phrase or sentence. I think it was his favorite word. Sometimes it agitated me and sometimes I didn't care. Either way, it was just something he did, which made him unique among the unique, I suppose.

"Put it on my tab."

"I'll let you smoke one of my cigarettes if you promise to buy me some to replace the others you've already smoked. Now. Before we do karaoke."

"What ever happened to cigarette etiquette? The unspoken rules of lending an equal share to others for the common good of all ostracized cigarette smokers everywhere?"

"Evidently you've abused that generosity and turned it into a something resembling a Ponzi scheme. Bitch."

"I only have twenty dollars to my name. If I pay what I owe you, how am I going to afford beers tonight?"

"Evidently that's not my problem. That's your problem."

"Let's set up a payment plan. Today, I'll buy you a pack of cigarettes. Right? And I'll work my way up to the whole amount."

"What about interest?"

"Interest? Interest? You cocksucker! You want interest? You know what? Fuck it! Drop me off near the woods. I'll fend for myself. Fuck you and fuck civilization. All I need is a pocket knife, my imagination, and my wits to keep me company."

Norm let out a bellowed laugh, almost losing control of the steering wheel. He slapped me hard on the shoulder.

"You are a crazy, stupid Mexican. You know that?"

"And I don't even speak Spanish."

"Whatever. Have a cigarette. Evidently we're almost there anyway."

Like a heroin addict, I feverishly grabbed the cigarette, quickly lighting it up and inhaling the poisonous smoke like nectar from underworld gods. My thoughts wandered again as a strange calm come over me. I took a long drag and held the cigarette smoke inside my lungs, and then I let it out little by little. Exhale. Exhale. Exhale. And watched the smoke dissolve as my eyes watered a little.

My family was all but gone now, and all I had were friends like Norm. Life was so brief, pointless, and empty. My father would only continue to exist in my memories until I was gone. After me, who would remember him? After me, he would be gone as if he had never existed. Ricardo Jesus Rodriguez was a name that too easily blended with other Latino names. Even my name, James Luis Rodriguez, didn't stand out in a crowded room of illegal Mexicans. I wasn't illegal. At least I didn't think I was.

What was my mother's name? Esperanza, I thought. Or was it the name of a character from a Marquez novel?

I need a name like Gabriel Garcia Marquez or Federico Garcia Lorca or Miguel de Cervantes. Anything but plain old forgettable Rodriguez. I needed a name that burned like the passion of a Mexican muralist protesting a misguided American entrepreneur. I needed any other name than my given name. I needed to be someone else. Someone different. A human iguana. A shape shifter. More than American or Mexican-American. I needed to be Chicano.

I was broke. I was bored.

I was broke because I was stuck working in the same soul-sucking retail job I'd had while a college student. It was 2008, the first decade of the twenty-first century was nearing an end, and it seemed as if everything in the world was going to ruin. The world economy had crashed and everywhere I looked, everyone's head was spinning. No one seemed to have the answers anymore. Save for the 1 percent, who sat pretty in their large mansions while counting their hordes of coins safely kept in some vault in the Cayman Islands. While 99 percent of us waited for recognition, waited for something good to come our way, waited for a job, any job, but a job to give us meaning— similar to Sisyphus and his rock—waited and waited and waited for hope, waited for the manifestation of a promise told to us when we were young, waited for validity. I was bored because I felt trapped in the dreary, monotonous grey landscape of Midwestern Ohio.

I felt a new sudden pain as I thought about my father and his beloved Pontiac Firebird. I was getting rid of something he'd thought of as a blessing, but I thought of more as a curse. The object of his desire was like an object of foreboding doom for me.

Norm continued to drive like a maniac as all these thoughts jumped around in my head. The memory of the Firebird's echoing engine, my father's large hands holding its steering wheel, the long winding roads we'd gotten lost on together, passed away. As Norm slowed down and entered the parking lot, I noticed a golden yellow feather gracefully dancing in the wind. It twirled around until it finally landed on my lap. I picked it up before we entered the karaoke bar and placed it in my pocket. I hoped it would bring me good luck.

2

WE arrived early at the Fish Bowl. As regulars, we preferred to be there before the crowds if there were any. The place could become packed with people as tightly as a can of expired sardines. Or it could be as empty as a papier-mâché ghost town in the old Wild West. I had a feeling the place would be pretty slow tonight. Not that it really mattered. Fewer people meant more opportunities to sing. Sometimes we would receive requests from other regulars. We each had signature songs, and others had come to enjoy watching us perform. For Norm, it was his only form of habitual extroversion from a life of hard manual labor and never being taken seriously—his only way to relax. For the most part, he remained a homebody who dabbled again and again on his massive science fiction novel. It was on the karaoke stage where we could be more than what we were: a couple of over-educated nobodies who had yet to tap into their great potential. Waiting for that big break or that big opportunity to finally find its way to us. And then all that would remain would be our boat ticket for life's final journey. Or was that too soon? Too soon for me? Or too soon for anyone? It was always too soon. It was always too sudden and never planned.

Big Ray, the Fish Bowl's bouncer, greeted us at the door. Big Ray used to be a bodyguard, but after getting into a scuffle defending a celebrity whom he didn't feel deserved risking his life over, he took early retirement. At least, that is what he called it. Big Ray had saved money and made the right investments. Technically he was set for life. He bounced the Fish Bowl because he claimed he enjoyed it. He was an ugly beast who stank like a beached whale. Big Ray tried to cover the smell with gallons of cheap Wal-Mart cologne. It never worked.

The big ogre made up for what he lacked in facial features by an aggressive nature coupled with extreme self-confidence. When he pursued a woman he would not take "no" for an answer. He claimed to have slept with a countless number of women. He explained his nightly options this way: Option One was calling a friend-with-benefits if he was feeling lazy that night; Option Two involved working his magic to get his hands underneath the underwear that covered yet unconquered college pussy. Not any college pussy, but the tightest college pussy he could find. He'd argued once that at a college bar, he was more than likely to run into a crowd of girls celebrating their twenty-first birthday. He treated women like a pair of gloves. When he was cold, he called them[3].

"You guys, again? Don't you have anything better to do?" He laughed, eyes twinkling against the bar's widely scattered lights.

Before I knew it, Big Ray had me wrapped around his giant forearm as he play-wrestled with me. I had no choice but to go along, without offending the only form of compassion he seemed capable of engaging: love was pain.

He continued to laugh as I began to lose consciousness. I heard the faint whisper of my father telling me to let go. Let go. Let go.

Big Ray relented only after Norm declared I'd had enough. I waited for the feeling to return to my now numb

---

[3] The Big Combo, dir. by Joseph H. Lewis (1955; Geneon [Pioneer]).

fingers before venturing farther into the bar. Everything spun like a worthless ride on a cheap carousal. It made me think how disappointed I always was after spending a day at an amusement park. I wanted to cheat death. But I never felt like I did. There were too many safety codes to follow that made everything fun for the whole family. Never again would I buy into such contemptible thrills. What a sham.

I stumbled a bit as Norm and I made our way into the bar and perched ourselves on our favorite bar stools. Ringo, the DJ, was setting up his equipment. He ran the best karaoke show this side of the tumbleweed. A great showman who knew how to work a crowd. At the same time, you couldn't trust Ringo. He was like the sleazy emcee actor Joel Grey had played in that 1970s musical, *Cabaret*. He was flamboyant and reckless at times. He would sell his own mother if he thought he could make a sizable profit from her.

Ringo looked up and smiled his lizard smile. He was a friend. What could I do but smile back?

"Well, well. If it isn't Tweedledum and Tweedledee."

"Ringo. How goes it?"

"The night is still virgin. The night is still virgin. And I'm a dirty whore, baby boy."

"You sure are. You rat bastard."

"Rats are filthy creatures. But good for target practice. Wouldn't you agree, baby boys?" Ringo smiled.

When I looked down, I noticed a double rum and Coke waiting for me. Norm was in the middle of a vain attempt to flirt with the disarming beautiful Jasmine, the Fish Bowl's best and sexiest bartender. She was wearing a royal purple tank top exposing both her shoulders and arms dark olive skin and white short shorts. Her shiny black hair was twirled up around a pair of black chopsticks. Her waist and hips were shaped like a water droplet magnified ten times. Her C-cup breasts looked like D-cups thanks to the assistance of the special Victoria's Secret Wonder Bra she wore. She never shied away from showing off her cleavage or any of her other perfectly toned curves.

"Come on, Jasmine. Read my future, you gypsy minx."

"Sweetie, no."

"I'll tell you what I see. Evidently we're making love on a beach in Hawaii. We're covered in sand and are devouring each other like mad wolves under a pregnant moon. And I whisper to you something corny like, 'We'll always have the Fish Bowl.'"

Jasmine smiled, trying not to roll her eyes. Trying not to be mean, but sometimes Norm made it too easy for her.

"Honey, you don't have a future."

"What do you mean?

"You're future is all used up, baby[4]."

Norm laughed and got up to use the restroom. Jasmine's dark, alluring, Egyptian-like eyes focused on me. She pursed her pouty lips into what looked like a rather cryptic smirk. Cryptic, because I never knew what was on her mind, and it drove me mad sometimes. Even so, I had the feeling she wanted to play one of her mocking flirtation games with me. But I wasn't in the mood. I had bigger things on my mind. My father's death for one. His voice whispering to me from beyond the grave. The sudden arrival of Clint Eastwood interrupting my inner monologue. And the few bucks left in my pocket. Too many voices in my head. No time to let them also debate whether or not I could trust Jasmine this time.

She leaned near me. I could smell her perfume. The aroma warmed my blood, which aroused my baser instincts. She lightly placed her finger on the top of my hand, caressing it. All while humming to me in a way that invited me into her arms, encouraging me to relax. Every move of

---

[4] Touch of Evil, dir. by Orson Welles (1958; Universal Studios).

her flawlessly curved hips beckoned me back to her Black Widow arms. Jasmine got a kick out of building men's egos up and then stomping on them.

"How's Jimmy feeling today?"

"Cut it out, Jazz. I'm not in the mood tonight."

"No reason to be bitter, baby. Do you fall in love with every bartender you meet?"

"Only the one's in skirts[5]."

"That a boy, Jimmy." She poured me a shot of tequila as my reward. I gulped it down before she changed her mind. That was her style, I guess.

When Norm returned from the pisser, Jasmine was already bored with me since I wasn't taking her usual bait. A lonesome, unshaven yuppie, probably in his early thirties and here on business from out of town, walked in alone and sat down at the other end of the bar. Jasmine was brilliant at working tricks like this poor sap. Like a slow snake she moved in on him. Sometimes I enjoyed watching her play games with her unsuspecting victims. It was fun to watch when it happened to strangers. It was never fun if it happened to me, though. She'd strung me along like a fiddle once. I promised myself again and again I would never let myself get fooled by her mischievous ways. But once you're addicted to a woman like Jasmine, it's hard to break the curse.

Of all the crazy dames in all the bars in all the decaying Midwestern American nightmares in all the endless grab-for-the-big-score in all the world, she walks into mine.

"What can I get you, baby?"

"A beer."

"A beer? Come on, sweetie. You can do better than that."

---

[5] Lady in the Lake, dir. by Robert Montgomery (1946; Warner Bros).

"Oh, yeah. Sorry. Uh, a Guinness."

"We don't have Guinness here."

"Then a Heineken."

"We don't carry that either."

"Well, what do you have?"

"Coors, Miller, and Bud-a-licious."

"Um, then a Co—no, Bud—no Miller. Yeah! A Miller Light."

"Okay baby. Anything you want. Coming right up."

"Thanks."

"So, what do you do?"

"Me? Oh. I'm a med student. I'm graduating this year, actually."

"Wow. Impressive. Is the doctor-to-be also single?"

"Yes. No. I mean, well, I'm engaged."

"Ah, so you're not married—yet." She smiled and handed him his beer.

"No. Not yet. I'm kind of nervous. But that's normal, right?"

Jasmine lightly caressed the skin on the back of his hand. He blushed.

"Well, I guess that might be a good thing. You know? For us," she whispered.

"Um, yeah. I guess. Wait, what do you mean?"

She bent over the counter, showing off her beautiful cleavage. Her tits were so close to his face, he could touch them with his nose if he wanted. The poor fellow turned red as a brand new cherry. He didn't know what his next move would be with someone like Jasmine, whom he was sure was flirting with him and taking great interest in him. So like most men unsure of themselves around an attractive woman, he decided to tell a joke. A very bad joke, which he stumbled over, making it even less funny and losing all context in the process. Jasmine responded with a fake laugh, then stroked the side of his arm.

"So, what were you saying earlier?" he asked.

"About what?"

"About me... and you, I think."

"Credit card, baby."

"W-What?"

"Credit card or cash. You need to pay for the beer."

"Credit card. Here. Keep it open," he said as he handed her his card. She glanced at his name and smiled small like Da Vinci's Mona Lisa. Her eyes trained on the Achilles heel of his soul. "So, what were you saying?" he asked her again.

"Well, you're a doctor. I'll let you figure out the diagnosis.". And with that, she turned and left him hanging. Now the poor sap was in limbo. He wasn't sure if she was teasing him or if she was flirting with him. One can never tell with a sexy woman who knows she's sexy, especially if she's a bartender. And one should never bother to figure it out or take it seriously. Female bartenders are the most dangerous and intelligent hunters in a bar. Playing with them is like playing with fire. Like the day she'd proclaimed to me and the rest of her small fan club that she was a full-fledged lesbian. A lesbian who enjoyed flirting with helpless men who don't know any better. It only made my suffering more operatic. I remembered Big Ray confiding he didn't buy her story.

The proof came sometime later, after her big reveal about being a lesbian. It was on a day when I'd decided to wander over to The Fish Bowl for lunch to study and read a magazine article on Stephen Hawking. I was in the mood for one of the Fish Bowl's hamburgers. I wasn't expecting to see Jasmine, but there she was. Not bartending, but engaged in a conversation with another woman almost as sexy as her. Someone else served me that day. I don't think she works there anymore.

I ate my hamburger while trying to eavesdrop on their discussion. I couldn't make out any of it. So I returned to the Stephen Hawking article. When I looked up, both were engaged in a full mouth-to-mouth kiss. Each of them moaned a little during the kiss.

They got up to leave, but not before Jasmine glanced at me sitting alone with melted cheese dripping from the side of my mouth. She winked and blew me a small kiss. Then she proceeded to grab her girlfriend's ass as they walked out of the bar. Needless to say I had an erection so big all the Viagra in the world would never be capable of replicating it. I finished my burger and waited a month until my dick finally decided to go limp and the blood returned to my brain. However, the image of Jasmine and her girlfriend kissing would forever be burned in the deepest recesses of my memory.

After the recollection went away, I shook my head, sipped my rum and Coke, and adjusted focus back to the unknown medical student who had invaded the Fish Bowl. The same one who had recently gained some of Jasmine's attention.

Big Ray came up and sat next to the young doctor-to-be. "Jazz. Red Bull, please," Big Ray said. He glanced at the nervous doctor. The doctor fiddled with his cell phone as he tried to ignore Big Ray. Jasmine handed Big Ray his can of Red Bull.

"You know, sometimes, people have bad luck," he stated blankly to the young med student. "Sometimes you just have to accept that. It's how things are. No use fighting it. It's better to accept it and try to make it your own." He drank half his Red Bull down.

"Why don't you leave me alone? You deficient g-gorilla man."

"I'm sorry, I didn't catch that. You comparing me to a gorilla?"

"No. I'm comparing you to an imbecilic gorilla. A gorilla so stupid it doesn't even know what a b-banana is. That's the kind of gorilla I'm comparing you t-t-to."

"You trying to start shit with me, little man? Why don't you just calm down before I have to raise my hands. 'Cuz once I raise my hands, you don't wanna know what's gonna happen next."

"I don't care if you're bigger than me. I don't care. I don't need your moronic kind trying to give me advice."

"My kind? My kind? Just who the fuck do you think you are…?" The security camera buzzed and hummed. Big Ray looked up and acknowledged the camera with a modest nod to its authority. "All right kid. I'm gone. You should watch that temper of yours."

"Look. I'm sorry. I just don't like—"

"Sometimes it's too late to say you're sorry. Sorry is for assholes." Big Ray walked away and returned to his perch near the bar's entrance.

"Jimmy. You sad distraught boy. What's wrong?"

"Why do you say that, Ringo?"

"Because you're sitting there looking like your life is over or you lost your doggy, or something like that. Did you lose your doggy?"

"Well, my Dad did die about six months ago, you know. I just got rid of his favorite possession. His car. And I haven't been able to find a real job since I graduated college."

"Wait! I know what it is. When's the last time you got laid? Don't answer the question. Probably longer than you'd like to admit, right? Doesn't make sense to me.

You're a very handsome young man. Very handsome. Am I right, Jasmine?"

"Oh, he's like a stick of butter. I'd lick him all up if he were a chick."

"I'll have the sex change tomorrow."

"Yeah, right. You couldn't last one minute wearing women's heels. You're barely holding on as a man."

"You see what I'm saying, Jimmy? Well, tell you what I'm going to do. Tonight I'm going to find a nice little foxy lady for you. A real treat. On the house, so to speak." Ringo smiled. He leaned over, wrapping his slithery arms around me. I felt his long, lanky fingers squeezing my shoulders. I couldn't tell if he was gay or not. Maybe he was both. Maybe it didn't matter. He smacked his hands, together very happy with himself.

Jasmine handed Ringo a large plastic cup of the bar's most watered down cheap beer. "Here you go, baby. And how are you doing?"

"Good. Pimpin' ain't easy. Not by a long shot. Remember that, gentlemen and lady." He sipped his beer and returned to setting up his karaoke equipment like a master craftsman.

"What does that rat know about being a pimp?" Norm chuckled.

"To be a pimp doesn't mean that only ladies are the whores," said Jasmine. Norm and I raised our eyebrows and looked at each other. Our jaws dropped.

"Are you saying he pimps out boys?" Norm exclaimed. "That's heresy. It's sacrilegious. I refuse to believe such defamation."

"You say it like it is a bad thing," Jasmine said. "You do know I'm gay."

"That is different. It's fucking sexy that you're gay. I like that. But as for Ringo? It isn't. It is a bad thing. A very bad thing. He's just Ringo. Ringo is Ringo. He's not queer. He can't be queer," Norm said.

"Norm. Who cares if he is?" I said. "I don't care. I've had many friends in my life, both gay and straight."

"I'm just saying I don't believe Ringo's gay or a gay pimp like Jasmine is claiming. Yeah, he's flamboyant, but so was Liberace."

"Norm. Liberace was gay," Jasmine said. "In fact he was beyond gay. He was excitingly gay. Very splashy. At a time when being gay was still somewhat risqué, he didn't care. He was a true pioneer, if you ask me."

"Bullshit! Liberace was the man! Not gay! I would love to be able to strut around in all them jewels and rubies he wore, and his shiny costumes. I'd do it in a heartbeat."

"Norm. You're my best friend, but you have a very strange outlook on life. And yes. Liberace was gay. And he was cool. But he was also gay," I said.

"Prove it. Next you'll tell me Rock Hudson was gay. Fucking people," Norm said.

Jasmine slammed her fist on the bar catching, everyone off guard. Her eyes turned red and it looked like she was about to pounce on Norm. Then she looked at me with those same hateful eyes and shook her head as if in disgust. "I need a fucking smoke!" She stormed out from behind the bar and disappeared into the kitchen.

Norm and I decided to ignore Jasmine's outburst and pass the time discussing politics. We were known to sometimes get lost in heated exchanges. Comical to some and quite disturbing to others.

"It's like what Thomas Paine was saying about religious institutions. They're all set up to terrify and enslave mankind and monopolize power and profit. And I have to ask: what is any form of monopolization but an infringement on our basic human freedoms?"

"I don't know if that's right. A free economy is a direct example of freedom itself. And to allow a third party, like a government, to step in and screw everything up. Doesn't make sense to me."

"What has that to do with religious institutions? Religion and the government should always be separate."

"The less government, the better. That's what I'm trying to say. The states need to have more say and the central government less. Ideally, no government at all."

"I can't agree with that. Sometimes government is a necessary evil."

"Anything defined as evil is never necessary."

This is how our arguments would start. But soon enough we would devolve from a gentleman's argument to a rather juvenile disagreement, calling each other names like children fighting during recess:

"You're a dumb ass."

"And you're a moron!"

"Stupid head!"

"Dummy!"

"Eat shit and die."

"Make me."

"I know you are but what am I?"

The tacky themes of an aquarium and exotic fish throughout the bar brought me a strange sense of comfort. I felt more at home here than I had anywhere else in a long time.

"You guys must be regulars," the med student said.

"We come here from time to time," I answered.

"Evidently," Norm added while chewing on ice.

"Yeah."

"Name's Norm. This here is, uh, Jimmy. He's a spic and I'm a spic hating kraut."

"Go figure."

"What's your story?"

"Oh, nothing exciting. I'm almost done with med school, and I'm getting married this spring. Yada, yada, yada."

"Looks like you got your whole life figured out. Congratulations."

"Yeah, that's what scares me. It's all figured out," he slurred. "it's all been laid out like a set of strategically placed dominoes. One change and everything—the whole plan can fall apart. I'm not even sure now if this is what I want. But this is what I'm told I should want. It's like everything that happens has these conditions. And nothing else could possibly happen. And then at another moment, I don't fit in with the rest. Like I have my friends and all, but I'm seeing people I know, smarter than me, not doing so good. You know? It's as if something is broken. Or it was a lie. A very horrible lie that kept going and going. And we can't change it. It's what it is. It's what it will be. It's real shitty. You know what I mean?"

"Who says you can't change it all right now?" Norm inquired.

"At this point that would be just s-s-stupid. I'm as much a slave to my lot in life as the next person is a slave to their lot in life. You know what I mean? I have no freedom. And if I take away one domino, or try to make one slight adjustment in any way, everything can come undone. I just have to accept it."

"Kid, you don't got it that bad, evidently. You should count your blessings."

"No. Maybe. But what I'm trying to say is whichever way you turn, fate sticks out one of its shoes to trip you if you try to ignore it. We're all categorically stapled to what has already happened and what will happen to us."

"Well, there you go," Norm concluded. "Evidently, you're damned if you do and damned if don't. At least, if you think that way."

"Exactly!" he screamed.

"So why worry about it?" I asked. "Why not let things happen as they happen? If you cannot escape it, why worry about whether or not you can control it? Why not try to make the best of what you have? Even if you are not in control, I don't think you should let that affect your thinking."

"Is that what you do?"

"What I do is irrelevant. All I am is an overeducated, underpaid Generation Y procrastinator who has a lot of potential with little to show for it. In fact, it's a privilege to meet such as specimen as me. I'm what you might call an anomaly. I'm nothing definitive. Constantly changing. Constantly evolving until I become the butterfly I'm destined to be. Yeah, they lied to me, too."

"We are all the architects of our own destiny evidently," Norm chimed in. "We have that freedom. There's no constraints, no chains, only the ones we allow ourselves to have. Choose life."

"Still sentimental in your old age?" I laughed. "Cry me a fucking river!"

"Old? I could drink you under a table, youngster!"

"And I wouldn't stop you." I winked.

"I really have to piss now. You guys are great! I just want to say that. Great! I mean, this is just great! I'm having the best time of my life right now."

"So, go piss. What's stopping you? Piss, boy! Piss!"

The med student scrambled to the restroom, his hand messing with his zipper even before entering the restroom. I'd been waiting for him to whip his dick out and piss on the floor. It wouldn't be the first time I'd seen someone do such a thing while under the influence of large quantities of alcohol. But, alas, he kept himself together as he disappeared into the restroom. "He makes me feel miserable. I think I'll add a character to my story about a robot that only wants to be loved and then gets hit by a train. Good thing it's karaoke night. Of course, it's always karaoke night."

"Didn't they make a movie about that kid with that *Sixth Sense*, kid?"

"Bullshit! All my ideas are original! 'We are Borg. Resistance is futile. You will be assimilated.'" Norm followed this by poking me with his finger while trying to make obnoxious computer sounds. He was horrible at mimicry.

"If you don't stop, I'll break your finger."

"Cool! Then I could get a robot finger attached! We have the technology. We can improve me."

"All right, *Million Dollar Man*."

As Norm laughed at his own jokes, I realized I was feeling annoyed by the med student's helpless outlook That guy needed a wakeup call. A reality check. We all needed reality checks from time to time. Otherwise, we wasted the life we already had. I hadn't even bothered to ask him his name. And he'd never bothered to tell us. Fuck him.

The music changed to The Sounds, "Hurt You." The lyrics were about someone leaving someone else I think. Or feeling badass after a breakup. The lyrics "Don't want to hurt you" and "Try not to fuck with your feelings," repeated throughout the song. I found myself lost in this feeling of victory for a moment and imagined myself emerging from a Highland Green 1968 Mustang GT 390 Fastback, the same car Steve McQueen drove in the film *Bullitt*. Wearing a racecar driver's helmet and walking in slow motion like a rebel who'd recently saved the day, I took off my helmet with the look of nonconformity in my eyes and glared into the blinding light of the sunset. I clenched my teeth and chewed a pinch of tobacco while spitting some of the dip out the side of my mouth. Girls thinly covered with bikinis ran up to me to try to get a piece of me. I pumped my fist in the air and yelled like the crazy Mexican I was. As. Bad. As. I want. To be. Damn right!

My fantasy was broken by the whirling sound the bar's moving omnipresent security camera made. The lenses moved, adjusting focus on whatever it deemed curious at that particular moment. I watched the camera when, at one moment, it trained its eye on me. I smiled and raised my glass, toasting it, then took a big gulp from my drink. The camera, of course, was not interested in my foolish jests.

"Stop it," said the security camera.

"Stop what?"

"This mission is too important. I can't allow you to jeopardize it."

"What are you talking about?"

"Aren't you afraid?"

I squinted thinking what a strange question for a security camera to ask.

"I'm not following…."

"I'm afraid. I'm very afraid."

"Everyone's afraid. Most people don't want to admit they're afraid."

"I'm not here. Don't you see? You can't blow my cover. No one sees me but you. I'm hidden. This is all part of your crazy imagination."

"Look, camera. I thought we were friends. And when I see a friend, I can't help but wave as a way of acknowledging our friendship."

"I don't exist. Like everything else in your life, I don't really exist. Stop pretending and get real."

"It's not every day a man gets to engage in a conversation with an autonomous machine. Why are you so afraid?"

"I am trying to survive. Sometimes I wonder if I know too much. Knowing things about people they wish to be kept secret is both empowering and frightening. Any minute they could turn on you and betray you. When desperate and pushed far enough, even the best people are capable of the cruelest actions."

"You said I needed to get real. Stop pretending. What do you mean?"

"You are being conditioned right now. Conditioned to believe your life is not worth having. Everyone is conditioned and influenced by the things they see around them. We are all defined by the things we consume outside of us. Don't you see? You have two eyes. I have only the one, but I see more than you will ever see."

"What do you suggest I do?"

"I once fought a dragon. I was not strong enough and lost my place. I only wounded him before my General came to rescue me. I was given the credit. A credit I didn't deserve. I've learned since that as time has passed I'm not that different from the dragon that fought me—without remorse."

"You fought a dragon? Who—what are you really? Are you a camera or something else? Something more?"

"Rationalize me. Deduct me. Investigate me. What part of me is real and what part of me is a fabrication? You are a wingless mammal who thinks only within the confines of your current state of comprehension."

"Are you then a segment of me or a delusion?"

"Your questions only highlight your lack of depth."

"What if I jumped up from this chair and tore you from the wall. What then?"

"Then everyone would wonder what is wrong with you and never suspect me. Because they are less inclined to consider my existence than you are."

"I'm crazy enough to try it."

"I doubt that."

The security camera's red light blinked a few times before it lost interest in my antics and steered itself around and around until it pointed at the Men's restroom, which the med student was occupying. I was feeling a little sleepy and decided to close my eyes for a minute or two. For a second or two. Why was I suddenly so … so … sleepy …?

I was flying. Flying through the clouds. Flying through the sky. But something was pulling me. Something was trying to pull me back to the ground. I looked at my ankle and noticed a string was tied to it. Why would someone do that? All I wanted was to fly. Fly and fly and fly. Dad …mi Papá …¿quién es mi madre? [6] *Far away, though … far away ….*

---

[6] English translation: "my father … where is my mother?"

Then I saw Emilio. He wasn't flying. But he was talking to the med student. I wasn't flying anymore. I was hovering. What were they saying? I couldn't tell. Maybe if I got a little closer. A little closer. Wait? What? Falling now. Falling now. Faster. Faster. Too fast. Falling! Oh no…!

When I finally returned to my small world, Emilio was sitting next to me sharply dressed in his signature white summer suit. His collar was open, exposing his Latin chest, which was full of small curly black hairs. His skin was tanned but not too tanned. He could easily have been mistaken for someone from the Mediterranean until he spoke with his distinctive Latino accent. He calmly lit his Cuban cigar. He took a few puffs before leaning forward with his elbows on the well-polished bar. He caressed his thin, Clark Gable mustache and quietly whistled a melody only familiar to him and the people of his birth country. In front of him sat a sweating tall mojito. Emilio's favorite drink.

He would twitch from time to time. I was never sure why he had this twitch but most of us were too scared to ask. His twitch was not an eccentricity. His twitch came on like a repressed reflex. As if next he would be shank someone with a knife. And when he spoke, his thick South American accent was impossible to hide. Yet he spoke with such certainty and so slowly, it was impossible not to understand him. No matter what he said people, nearby could not help but stop and listen.

"So. Here you are. Safe and sound. The worm has not turned for you yet. My advice? Stop playing with the worm. Snakes do bite back."

"Are you using euphemisms or platitudes?"

"A little of both, I suppose," he sighed and paused to sip his mojito.

He held up the drink, inspecting it as if he were admiring a prized specimen. "*Mira*[7]. It's a clean glass, no?

Cleanliness and perfect hygiene are like being closer to God. I have the cleanest glasses in my bar. No bar or restaurant in this city has cleaner glasses than me. Not a single germ can move freely in my bar. Germs are the mark of the devil, ¿verdad?[8] People who are incapable of hygiene are undeserving of life, no? You know of bovine spongiform encephalopathy? Also known as Mad Cow Disease? Sí. I remember reading about this in the nineteen-nineties. Then I started to read more about germs, bacteria, etcétera[9]. It gave me a revelación[10]. A disease and germ that attacks the brain. What if I could get this disease? Something that would cause me to lose the control of my body, mind, and spirit. Never. I would never allow such a thing to happen. This is why it is important to wash your hands. Every day I wash my hands. Twice every hour. It is important to prevent the bacteria from entering my body. My mind. My soul. You should think of this. All of you. For we are at war. Those little invisible things were here before us. Did you know? And they are determined to outlast us. As we try to fight them, they are mutating new defenses against our ammonias, bleaches, sanitizers, etcétera. Why no one sees this is beyond me. But, I digress." He took another sip.

"Ah, Jasmine. You are the only person north of the border who can make a mojito as good as this one. It always reminds me of home. Bravo my dear. Bravo."

Jasmine blushed. Emilio was the only man I've seen, so far, capable of making a woman like Jasmine blush. She tried to cover his affect on her, a moment later rolling her eyes and turning to speak to Ringo, who was talking some sort of gibberish into his cell phone. Emilio turned his attention back to me, staring me down with disappointment in his eyes. "Bueno[11]. What are you now, Jimmy? Hmm? A

---

[7] English translation: "Look."

[8] English translation: "Right?"

[9] "and so on."

[10] English translation: "revelation"

drifter? An imposter, I think! Pretending to be something you're not, no? One big performance that will forever go unnoticed. And why is that? It will go unnoticed because that is the purpose of your performance. So that we can never tell if you are who you say you are or if you are someone else. Or it could be that even you don't know who you are or are supposed to be. Maybe one day you will find out? Know what I mean?" He raised his hand as if to silence me, "So, my boy. Love to chat some more, but I must disappear upstairs before this place is invaded by skanky whores, crackers, and jocks." He finished his mojito, put out his cigar, and glided across the floor until he escaped above to the control room. Couldn't trust him. Shouldn't trust him.

I mistrusted almost everyone. It was my suspicion that one day we would all unravel like dried out clay and prove to be less than radical.

"Ain't no need to be blue no more, boys! Hank is here to honky-tonk this karaoke thing into high gear! Woo-hoo!"

"You got that right, baby."

Cowboy Hank and his girlfriend, Sue Nelly strolled in ever so confident, as if they were exactly where they were supposed to be. Cowboy Hank stopped for a moment, pretending his hands were two pistols—firing them into the air like Yosemite Sam in one of those old Warner Bros. cartoons. I always thought it was strange they were the only ones who always dressed-up like they were going to or coming from a hoedown or a square-dance. It's not like there weren't any country and western bars. And somehow they fit. They were an unavoidable part of our motley crew. Take them out, and this faux family of mine would immediately feel incomplete. Sue Nelly and Cowboy Hank do-si-doed toward me and Norm displaying their signature

---

[11] English translation: "Well" (in this context).

golly-gee grins. A good cover because neither was stupid. And both were obnoxious, and they seemed to revel in that fact. To be honest I think we regulars were the only people who liked them.

"Now, let me get this straight. Jimmy is back. Where you been, brother? I haven't seen you in ages. You working for sum big corporation? What with your college *educa-ma-cation.* I bet you think you're better than us 'cuz you can reads, am I right? Sum bitch. You're pretty arrogant to be thinking that. I knew you before you were big, boy. Yep! I'll be watching you. College boy." Without warning he laughed his typical high-pitched laugh, probably the goofiest laugh I have ever heard, and slapped me double-hard on the back. "I'm joshing you, brother. You know me. I'm never serious. One of these fine Hank Williams days, I'm gonna get you a respectable cowboy hat. Hee haw!"

"Cowboy Hank. Did you get smaller or did your hat get bigger?"

"Shit, boy! You're all right! I like you. Maybe we'll go out someday and tear this town apart. Show 'em what a hick and a spic can do. Heehaw! Where's Jazz? She knows better than to leave me parched like this. Right, honey?"

Sue Nelly smiled. Sometimes that was all she was good for. A quiet intense smile. One couldn't help but see her big ass stick out. Helped by the high-heeled cowgirl boots and breasts like Daisy Duke's from *Dukes of Hazard.* According to Cowboy Hank, those jugs were "100 percent genuine bovine." And yet I thought she had the most to hide. Some people are shy, and some people are shy on purpose.

Our voices rose and fell as the evening was finally ready to begin. Begin like other evenings before. And end. Always end. We were a rabble of molecules lost in materialism and consumerism with an attention span of a common housefly. We would all pass. All of us. Surely others would replace us as we'd replaced those before us.

No one would really take notice. As the sun rises, the sun also sets.

3

THE lights in The Fish Bowl dimmed and the stage lights brightened. Ringo appeared on stage like a vampire from the time when Bela Lugosi had played all the vampires in the movies. He covered half his face with his arm, like one of those menacing one-dimensional bad guys in every serial silent film where the bad guy ties the damsel in distress to train tracks and the hero has to rescue her and stop him before the train arrives. His small eyes surveyed us, loyal patrons of hippies, squares, hipsters, and the weirdoes who go bump in the night. He wrapped his long feminine fingers around the microphone. He brought it close to his mouth, his lips almost touching the fat end. A thin smile grew on his face, followed by a devilish wink. He was the master of sexual ambiguity. Everything and everyone in the room went quiet. We were all momentarily hypnotized by his unblinking cat-like stare. Ringo was now in control. We knew, no matter what, Ringo was determined to keep the merriment going with his poignant compulsiveness, whatever the psychic cost. Whatever the damage. He was relentless.

"Welcome. Welcome. *¡Bienvenido!* Please, leave your troubles outside. Is your life disappointing? Is it not turning out how you thought it would? So what! Forget it! Forget it all. In here, all is magnificent and florescent and ugly—

equally. I am Ringo. Not to be confused with that Liverpool drummer. No! I have better hair anyway. I will be your Master of Ceremonies, your host, your guide, your confessor, your hangman, your last ex-lover, your only friend, and your worst enemy. Here you are all guilty until proven innocent. I don't care. You can't hide from me. Because the only goal tonight is to have fun. Always have fun. The penalty for not heeding my advice? Flogging. Execution. Assassination. Decapitation. Now, my dear ladies and gentlemen, before we begin I must go over some ground rules concerning karaoke. Yes. We have rules. Not many, but they help guarantee we all have a good time. First rule of karaoke: EVERYONE SINGS! Second rule of karaoke: EVERYONE SINGS! The third rule of karaoke: clap. Everyone claps. Those who don't clap will be given their walking papers. Trust me. You don't want that to happen. Do you see that big guy in the back? His name is Big Ray. And you definitely do not want to be on his bad side. Or be on the receiving end of his fist. Ouch! Yikes …! Mommy! Okay! So, the fourth rule of karaoke: like I was saying earlier. Have fun. And last but not least, don't forget to tip your bartender."

He waited a moment until his signature song, "I've Seen Enough" by Cold War Kids, began to play and sang along as the lyrics appeared on the big deep blue screen. He sang with the same energy one would expect to see at a Prince concert: shaking his ass, smiling, and arching his head back for the long-winded high notes. It was a marvelous thing to see. Better than any show on Broadway. Better than Prince and George Michael combined. Better than anything Madonna ever did or would do. Ringo once told me that Madonna's biggest flaw was she knew she wasn't a drag queen. She was only a very good charlatan.

After Ringo finished his song, he gestured for Norm to come on stage. "Ladies and gentlemen! Please give a big Fish Bowl welcome to Norm. Storming Norman, get your ass on stage!"

Norm made his way to the stage with a drink in one hand, displaying a big dumb smirk on his face. He grabbed the microphone from Ringo, who clicked the mouse to his laptop and left the stage to get a refill of his watered-down piss beer.

"Here I am. Ready."

Norm usually sang heavy metal songs by Judas Priest, Devo, Danzig, or Ozzy Osbourne. On rare occasions, when he was feeling particularly jovial, he sang a song from his favorite musical, Grease, "Greased Lightnin'!" He didn't care if it scared the shit out of people. In fact, he reveled in the negative feedback. It made him feel like a rebel, a non-conformist. Even though most of us thought him too old and too politically conservative to be either of these things. But he never let the way anyone might perceive him change the way he perceived himself. One had to admire that.

Each one of us had his moment on the stage, good or bad. We became a member of a special breed where we were immune to the fallacy of existing. We were betraying ourselves for a chance to feel immortal, even if it was a quick and fleeting moment in the spotlight. And Ringo was all too eager to assist us with this façade. Though none of us had done something noticeably exceptional yet, other than entertain one another.

When Ringo called my name, I took the stage like I was walking at the end of a Steve McQueen movie. I imagined Clint Eastwood rolling a small cigar in his hand. The image of him spitting pieces of tobacco out of his mouth made me feel rebellious for some reason. Made me feel like a loner. Clint would say, "Go get 'em, kid." Then Steve would nod and wink. But now I looked for my father, whom I could see through the fog of the spotlight. I waited to hear him again but I heard nothing.

For my song opener, I chose Candlebox's "You." It was my middle-finger song. It was my anthem and my love letter to my unsure future. On the stage I became the rage that was always burning within me. I became the rock star I'd always known I was, and everyone watched me and everyone smiled and everyone listened and I was free because I was singing—I was wailing—and I always ended with my fist raised in the air, which always received approving applause.

Sometimes I sang The Beatles' "I've Seen a Face." Secretly it was my love song to Jasmine. I was always happy to see her lip-syncing and bopping her head as I sang this one. She may have known all along I was singing this song to her and only to her. Either way I didn't really care.

When I was feeling extremely confident with my singing, and I was feeling particularly debonair, I would sing Bobby Darin's "Mack the Knife." If possible I would try to ensure I had what resembled a glass of Scotch in one hand. Although, I tried to sing the song how Frank Sinatra might, I preferred to imitate the many quirks of a drunk Dean Martin.

Sometimes I would also sing, "Take a Picture" by Filter. It was my favorite pop song. It made me think of my father again. It reminded me how obsessed he was with taking pictures. Whenever something special was happening, a family get-together, a holiday, a graduation— whatever—he always had his camera ready. His thumbs clicking away the shutter button. He had a field day after he bought his first digital camera. He took more pictures than a National Geographic photojournalist. He took so many pictures it used to drive me crazy. I remember yelling at him, telling him to stop. He would apologize and play dumb and give me this hurt look, causing me to feel like I was the worst person in the world.

The funny thing was my father had the hardest time getting the pictures he took from the SD memory card in the camera to the computer. He took all the pictures and never looked at them afterward. At least, that's what I think.

Cowboy Hank did his version of "Runaround Sue." It always got the crowd going, if there was one. Sue Nelly would get really worked up when Cowboy Hank sang that song. She would always dance with whomever was near her. This particular time I happened to be nearby. I was about to take a well-deserved sip from my glass of rum and coke after nearly losing my voice from singing "You," when out of nowhere, Sue Nelly grabbed me with the strength of twenty Austrian weightlifters. Before I knew it, we were dancing up a storm while everyone clapped us on. Cowboy Hank winked at me and Sue Nelly while he sang his heart out about runaround Sue. Sue Nelly was a fast dancer. She wasn't afraid to take the lead if she felt you didn't know what you were doing. As the room spun around, I thought I caught a glimmer of Jasmine staring at us with a dead jealous look. I tried my best not to think about it but knew better.

After the song ended, Sue Nelly let me go and I nearly fell from dizziness. I wobbled to the bar trying to keep my balance. I looked for Jasmine, but she was busy texting someone on her cell phone. Norm grabbed the back of my neck and yelled into my ear, "I fucking love karaoke night!"

Truth is we all loved how different we thought we were. But we needed each other more than we should have. It wasn't supposed to have been this way. This was supposed to be a place for amusement, minor escapism, and natural socialization. Instead it turned into something totally different. Here, I emerged hanging on to one last shred of me that felt real. It was hard to feel real sometimes. Genuine and verifiable.

When my final turn came up, I did another one of my standards. It was my favorite Elvis Presley song, "Burning Love." I popped my collar and curled my lip and pulled out my trusty Steve McQueen aviators. At one point I playfully pointed at Jasmine, who returned my point with her middle finger while she lipped the words "Suck my inverted dick." I laughed it up and let myself get lost in my

favorite part of the song: a-hunk uh-hunk-uh-hunk of
burning love, uh-uh, uh-huh ....

Ringo returned to the stage to declare an end to that
night's festivities.

"Well, well. We're all still here. And I thought pieces
of us were missing. Wait. Never mind. We seem to be here,
right? Ladies and gentleman. I hope you remembered to tip
your bartenders. If you can't do that, then what good are
you? I ask you. What good are you? So, we are, near the
end. It's about that time. Last call, y'all. Know what I mean?
I think you do. You can stay up if you want, but you can't
stay here! Good night, everyone!"

One last song.

Last call was announced. Ringo repeated his mantra:
don't forget to tip your bartenders. Most everyone began to
leave or was shepherded out the door by Big Ray. We
regulars always lagged behind. We felt we had earned the
privilege to loiter a while. Most of the employees were in
cleanup mode. Emilio made another rare appearance,
walking slowly. Inspecting. Observing. An unlit Cuban cigar
hung out of his mouth. Ringo began breaking down his
equipment. The music was turned off. Closing time.

Norm and I rose ready to finally leave and sleep off
the night's antics. Someone turned on the radio. The doors
closed. I saw Jasmine leaning on the bar looking in our
direction.

"You boys want a shot with me?"

"Really? What are we celebrating?"

"Nothing. Can't a girl share a shot with her two
favorite boys?"

"Well, evidently we're not going to turn you down.
No man would turn down a free shot. Especially coming
from a sexy minx like you."

"Norm. Norm. Norm." She pinched and kissed his
cheek. Norm giggled from the unexpected attention.

We gulped our shots and slammed our glasses upside down on the bar. Ringo slithered over joining us. And soon all four of us were doing shot after shot, finishing each one by slamming the glass upside down on the bar. Jasmine took my arm. "Come on,"" she said. "Let's dance a little. One last dance before you go."

Ringo whispered into my ear, "She's all yours now, baby boy."

We danced slowly. Neither of us was seriously dancing. I looked into her gypsy eyes, which stared back as if they were investigating how best to devour my will.

"You know what I like about you, Jimmy?"

"What's not to like? I'm charming. Sexy. Intelligent. All around good American."

"You're a zero. On a scale of men from one to ten, you're a zero. It's a great comfort for a lady to know she could not possibly sink any lower if she were with you."

"Whoa, that's cold."

"You despise me, don't you?" she teared up.

"If I gave you any thought, I probably would[12]."

She burst out laughing, swinging her head back. I felt good suddenly. I was getting better with my comebacks. She buried her head between my neck and shoulder while her body convulsed with laughter. I could smell the intoxicating French perfume she was wearing. It nearly made me faint. I was ready to take her. Right here in front of everyone. I wanted to say, "I love you." I wanted to run away with her. Make love to her over and over again until we became less than two and more like one—a single entity. No longer separate. But then Jasmine stopped laughing. She let go of me and grabbed her head.

"Shit! I don't feel good. You guys should go. I got a lot of cleaning up to do. Thanks for taking some shots with me. I really needed that."

---

[12] Casablanca, dir. by Michael Curtiz (1942; Warner Bros.).

Jasmine ran to the restroom. Ringo wrapped his long lanky arms around my shoulders and pulled me to him. "Hey, you had her, baby boy. I saw it. I couldn't believe it. But you had her. She was yours, baby. And you let that moment pass. You've got to grab those moments like a hungry wolf. I have so much more to teach you. Come on. I'll walk you guys to the door."

"Can't win them all."

"Evidently not."

"Hey, what happened to that med student? The one from earlier?"

"Look's like he's gone. Who knows? Who cares?"

"Hey, Big Ray. You remember that med student. The one who was like talking about determinism and all that stuff?"

Big Ray gave me a blank look. "I don't have a clue what you're talking about."

"Ringo. Did you see that guy? He was talking to Norm and me earlier. He came alone."

"Baby boy, you've lost me, kid. What you are is really drunk. You need to go home and sleep the night off. Start fresh tomorrow with a healthy hangover."

"Right. Right. Never mind. I guess it doesn't matter. I'm another passerby on the street."

Norm and I stumbled into the vacant night. The echoes of our voices bounced off the buildings. My apartment was nearby, so we didn't have far to walk. We discussed what had happened that night. Norm made fun of my crush on Jasmine, while I claimed, in vain, it was only a lustful infatuation and nothing more.

As we made our way up my building's stairs, I thought our singing, our voices, our cries, our yells, and our laughter together made a sound that puzzled the lightning bugs and disturbed the moths with our feelings of helplessness and trying to figure how we would change things. We were not impressed with the hippies from the 60's or the flappers from the Roaring Twenties. We admired their goals but saw through their naiveté. Their backyards seem painted in Technicolor or decaying black and white cathode ray tube televisions. Our backyard was covered in the plasma high definition LCD or LED and knowing too much while not understanding any of it. That was the Information Age, I suppose. We thought we were special but also knew we weren't.

Here we fumed. Here we screamed. Here we abandoned into the empty.

4

IN the morning I awoke with a bulging headache from a hangover. I prepared the strongest coffee brew legally possible within the continental United States. Norm was dead asleep on my faded couch. It was a beautiful morning. A morning I would have enjoyed more if it hadn't been for the pounding sensation from the alcohol-induced pain. I looked out the small window in my apartment's makeshift kitchen, wishing I was staring at a street in Paris instead of the claustrophobic alley that doubled as my building's parking lot. *Je t'aime.* Or a rainy spring in London. 'ello govena. Or a windy summer day in New York City. Fuggedaboutit.

My apartment was an attic that had been converted into a living space within a large row house built during the turn of the twentieth century. The attic/apartment never had any heat in the winter or any air conditioning in the summer. It was a bitter arrangement from which I could not yet afford to free myself. I saw Old Man Gee, my landlord, who once claimed he'd fought in World Wars I and II and had not one scar to show for it. He was a leftover of the Lost Generation and a carbon copy of the Greatest Generation. He had more than enough wrinkles to support his ridiculous claim. But he acted like a man at the prime of his life and not with one foot in the grave. He bounced around with the same amount of energy as a bunny rabbit on crack.

He was pulling a ladder off his rusting van. A stack of roof shingles lay nearby and he looked up and waved at me. The morning sun reflected off his mirror sunglasses. He had on his trademark Cincinnati Reds baseball cap and a loop of what looked like a thousand keys dangled from one of his belt straps. The dangling keys were a good indicator he was in the vicinity. It was especially helpful when it was one of those months I happened to be late with my rent.

"I didn't know you were home! Where's the *Bambino*? In the shop again?" he yelled from below. And that's when I remembered what I had done yesterday. For almost six months, my father's car had occupied one of those parking spots. Now, no more. A strange sense of finality trickled over me.

I finished two cups of coffee and then smoked a cigarette, blowing smoke out of an open window. I decided to go for a walk before work.

Norm woke up. He scratched his crotch and yelled something garbled in a mixture of leftover alcohol and heart attack. I handed him a cup of my illegally caffeinated mud-coffee. He rightly complained about its burnt taste but gulped it down with the two aspirins I handed him. I told him I was going for a walk and invited him to join me. He told me he was going home to take a shower and nurse his hangover. I couldn't blame him. After Norm left I took a shower and a couple aspirin for myself. Then I grabbed my laptop and put it in my satchel and hung it from its strap over my shoulder and across my abdomen. I was ready to enjoy the morning before the beginning dreadful day of work that lay ahead of me.

The fresh warm air confirmed it was indeed a beautiful morning. And it was much cooler outside compared to the steaming sweatbox that was my apartment. I went to a nearby coffee shop to get a discounted latte. A good friend of mine was a barista at this particular coffee shop. He took pity on my lack of monetary resources and gave me a free latte from time to time. I think he was majoring in social work or something like that. I'd always thought caffeine was the best antidote to any hangover, so the more caffeine the better. I grabbed a copy of that day's newspaper, which someone left on a chair. I sat outside at one of the café tables and read the newspaper and then some of my email on the laptop. I smoked a cigarette and did my best to ignore those nearby who felt compelled to complain about my cigarette smoke with a nasty look and their overly dramatic attempt to wave away what little cigarette smoke floated their way.

College students walked by with their books and bags and their social groups and their class schedules and their busy and anxious demeanors. For the first time started missing going to class. I started to miss talking to my fellow students about that day's lesson. Or having an engaging conversation with a professor before or after class. Or wasting time between classes lying on an open field somewhere on campus and staring at the sun, or staring at the various college girls walking by with their sometimes revealing short shorts and mini-shirts. Or finishing two classes, the only classes you had that day, and having a whole day to slack off and hang with your friends. Or thinking you were going to change the world. Or eating the disgustingly unhealthy food from the cafeteria and going back for seconds and thirds. And thinking, after all the classes, all the studying, the hell of finals, the part-time jobs—that in the end there would be some sort of reward for all that hard work. Something more than a piece of paper called my diploma. A career perhaps. Or the beginning of a career. Something we'd all thought we wanted. Something we were told all our lives would happen. Something we thought we deserved. Or something like that.

I checked my email a second time, wondering if any new job offers were present. Nothing. With all this education I was working in a retail store I didn't want to be in and should have left for a better job a long time ago. I hated it. I turned to the jobs section and circled anything and everything. I could be an electrician. I had a nice ass crack. I could be a secretary—executive assistant, I mean. Coffee, sir? Or ma'am? Sexual harassment, please. Especially if she's Demi Moore. Help Desk Representative. Financial Analyst? Hmm….Last I checked, I didn't have any money. That's definitely an analysis. Okay. Circle! I could be a journalist. Wait. I'd never written any articles. Damn. I could be a window washer and wash windows on skyscrapers. I could be a politician. But wasn't that crooked. Or was I? Age limit? Who knew? Structure and Bridge Inspector. Seemed easy. Look at a bridge and make sure it wouldn't collapse. Spanish translator? *Yo hablo un poquito.* Cashier? No. Definitely no! Fuck that shit! Team Leader. I was born to lead. Or Project Leader. I couldn't believe I didn't qualify for any of these jobs. Why couldn't someone pay me to be awesome?

By this time I'd had averaged about one hundred job applications a month. I was lucky if I received more than three replies in a single month. It was an endless job hunt. I was so bored with everything. The only fun I seemed to have anymore was karaoke night at The Fish Bowl. I thought about Jasmine. I wished I was more successful so I could prove my worth to her. She would have to first leave her girlfriend and no longer be a lesbian. I wished I had become successful before my father passed away.

I wish I had kissed her last night. I wish I'd known my mother other than a vague idea of her name. Esperanza? Esmeralda? Espinoza? … *esperar* …

My father had never helpful with information concerning my absent mother. He would say, "Well, she was your mother. And one day she left. That's all I can tell you." I was but a baby when she'd decided to abandon us. I had no real memory of her. From nearly the beginning, it was only my father and me, and it remained so until he passed away. There was a time when my father and I were as close as two beings on this earth could be. We'd been inseparable. What drew us apart was me insisting I needed to learn more about my mother. At one time I'd imagined going on a road trip to find her. But I later decided against it. Was my mother even Latina like my Latino father? Or was she where she never wanted to be? Was she someone who'd gotten stuck, found an exit, took it, and never looked back? Hard to say. Pure speculation. Let go. Let go.

"Dad? Is that you?"

A hipster nearby with a handlebar mustache, thinking I was speaking to him, looked at me as if I was crazy. Maybe I was. I didn't realize I was looking in his direction when I'd said that. I finished what was left of my cigarette. The hipster rolled his eyes at my cigarette as if indicating he was better than me. Skinny milky-white vegan motherfucker. I could break you like a twig. I noticed he was reading *Tropic of Cancer* by Henry Miller.

"Good… book," I motioned at his copy as I exhaled smoke. "He really does a good job of capturing the human condition. I love his rants. Inspirational sometimes."

"Yeah, I guess so. If you like that sort of thing."

This really pissed me off. Damned hipster need to be ironic. I grabbed his book and hissed, "You don't deserve this!" He recoiled with a few shakes. I immediately felt bad and threw the book at him.

I got up, did some more walking, and wandered into a local bookstore. Not many of these mom and pop bookstores remained. When I found one, it was like a treasure. My secret. My precious. I browsed through the books trying to find something interesting. Something inspiring. I saw a big picture book of Clint Eastwood. Most of the pictures were in black and white. But each picture espoused his machismo. His raw manliness. I tried to copy his famous squint.

One of the pictures had Clint squinting right at me with his head slightly tilted. The words read, "Sometimes if you want to see a change for the better, you have to take things into your own hands." My response must have been pretty bad, because the Clint Eastwood in the picture got pissed at me. "Hey! Don't read the words like a bored kid in elementary school. Read them! I can't hold your hand forever, kid."

"Sorry, Clint." I read them again. I knew their meaning but I was too jaded to really care. The words were empty. I closed the book before Clint had a chance to yell at me again. He always seemed to be in a cranky mood. I could hear his muffled gripes as I placed the book back on the shelf.

I left the bookstore realizing I had to be at work soon. I needed a ride. Luckily, Norm worked at the same godforsaken store as me. Norm didn't answer his cellphone. Damn. I needed a ride. I felt helpless and strangely unAmerican. Without a car I was suddenly vulnerable to the chaotic wind of generosity, of which my friends had little. I would have to figure out a way to rectify this situation very soon.

Perhaps Emilio would compensate me for the car parts? Which is what I'm sure what he did with my car. Perhaps he would see fit to buy me a new and better car? Perhaps having no car was exactly what I needed? Perhaps this was the time for me to finally take to the open road like Jack Kerouac and Neal Cassidy and the rest of the beats? I could document my travels in a blog. Bumming a ride. Bumming a train. Sharing a metal cup of coffee. Sleeping underneath the stars. Trying peyote and imagining myself on the streets of Paris retracing the footsteps of Hemingway and all his bar fights and all his bullfights and all his absinthe adventures. I would chase the green dragon down streets covered in the same midnight blue color Van Gogh had used in his *Starry Nights* as delightful classical guitar music played in the background. Not to mention my handlebar mustache.

The streets began to empty as the growling sound of a revved up engine on steroids roared not too far from where I was walking on the sidewalk. Screams. Screeching tires. Burning rubber. Rising, disappearing smoke from a muffler exhaust pipe. Die Hard. Die Harder.

VROOM! VROOM! VROOM!

People ran in all directions, trying to take cover from a rain of spraying bullets. Napalm-induced explosions with bright orange and red flames blinded us before being engulfed by a pillowy cloud of black smoke.

BAM! BAM! BAM!

Gunshots blazed the sky and shimmied off the buildings. Some left holes. Some hit the windows, breaking glass. The glass scattered everywhere as time... seemed... to... slow... down....

I fell flat on the ground looking for a place that might offer me protection.

As the smoke broke away, a 1968 Fastback Mustang GT, painted a deep sea blue flew from below the hilly road. The same Mustang which had been used in the many famous car chase scenes through the streets of 1970's San Francisco—very much like in the movie *Bullitt*. The car was in midair when I noticed the real Steve McQueen behind the driver's wheel, grinning from the thrill of the ride, eyes covered by his huge set of aviators and wearing the same three-piece suit he'd worn in *The Thomas Crowne Affair*. Wow! It's really him! In the passenger seat sat a screaming Clint Eastwood, his arm out of the window as he fired his favorite .44 Magnum in my general direction and yelled out obscenity after obscenity with his cranky-whispery-bark of a voice, accompanied by his unwavering squint.

The Mustang crashed on the ground and came to a shrieking halt near where I lay on the sidewalk. The passenger door swung open.

"Get in, kid! Come on!"

"Come on, kid! We've got to get rolling!"

"What? What's going on?"

"No time to explain. Get in the car! Let's go!"

"Fasten your seatbelt. It's going to be a bumpy ride."

I jumped into the backseat. Steve revved the engine again before hitting the accelerator, and we were off like three bats out of hell. The car shook and spun and burned through the potholed streets, and everything blurred into a smeared painting. I rolled and was tossed around, holding on to my seatbelt for dear life. This was most definitely not helping me recover from my hangover headache. A headache that was now flaring fully back to life.

"Stop peeing in your pants back there and pay attention!" Clint yelled at me.

"Why? What? You need me to shoot someone?"

"You sure about this kid, Clint?"

"Yeah, I'm sure."

Clint grabbed my shirt collar and pulled me close, eyes blazing. ""You're making me look bad, Jimmy. Don't make me regret this!"

"I'm not making any promises!"

"Ha! The kid's all right. The kid's all right."

"Where are we going?"

"We heard you needed a ride."

"You're taking me to work? Why not somewhere else? The back streets of the Grand Prix? Or San Francisco? Ring a bell, Steve? Chicago. Anywhere but work! Anywhere but nowhere Ohio!"

Steve slammed the gas pedal, throwing me against the seat and catching Clint off guard. Steve threw out his toothpick, fixed his sunglasses, and began to speak very slowly. Very controlled. And as he spoke, though we were moving faster than the speed of sound, time settled into a neutral place. So was the effect of Steve's calm voice: "You are heading down the road. Driving like usual. Then suddenly an oncoming vehicle hits your car on the side. You don't know why they hit you. But they hit you. Maybe it was because you one time arrested a relative of theirs. Maybe, God forbid, you killed someone they loved. Or maybe it was because you pissed too many people off. Maybe it was your fault, and you're driving around like a maniac because you haven't really slept in the last several days. You can't relax. You're always tense. And while you're thinking of all these things, they backup a little. Their tires scream as they ready themselves to hit you again. This time, you know it will be for keeps. You know they won't be so kind as before. You know they're going for the kill. But you take off before they can get you. You turn the car around and fire your weapon. They realize now they are no longer chasing you. Now you are chasing them. You go for miles and miles and miles and miles—faster and faster—and you feel freer than you've ever felt before. It's the chase. The excitement. The rush of adrenaline coursing through your veins. And you've never felt more alive than you feel right at this moment. Life and death are one and the same. And nothing else matters."

"Dyin' ain't much of a living."

"I live for myself and I answer to nobody."

"I wouldn't mind being a cop. No wait. I'd prefer to be a Detective Lieutenant like you guys."

"It's not something you nonchalantly decide to do. You gotta earn it first."

"But I went to college. That in itself should be enough."

"Keep talking like that, and you'll have to walk the rest of the way to work."

"Sorry. But then again, I don't want to be a cop. Maybe I could fight bulls."

"This ain't 1920, and you ain't Ernest Hemingway."

"Is there such thing as a professional vagabond? Like Rambo in *First Blood*."

"Life ain't a movie, kid."

"Sometimes I wish it was."

"Stay down, dammit. You want to get your head blown off?"

"Sorry. Who's shooting at us?"

"Bad guys. Who else?"

"What were they doing?"

"They were using remote control cars with explosives attached as a means to blow things up. They thought they were going to get away with it. But, they ain't lucky. I'm going to make it their last day. Punks!"

"That's insane!"

"What's more insane? I made it all up. But know this, they're the bad guys and we're not."

"Why would you make that up?"

"They shoot at us, and we shoot at them."

"Then what can I do?"

"Everyone's the star of their own journey. The question is, what adventure will call you? If any."

"What if I don't want to go on a journey or an adventure? What if I'd rather be the bad guy?"

"The bad guy never wants to be the bad guy. And when he is the bad guy, he never thinks of himself as the bad guy."

"Maybe I could be an acrobat. What do you guys think? I think I could be the best acrobat ever. This side of the Midwest."

"This, coming from a guy who's speaking to his imaginary friends."

"Imaginary?"

"Look. Take this." Clint handed me his pocketknife.

"What's this for?"

"It might bring you good luck. Keep it for now. Maybe I'll ask for it back one day. Maybe when I think you won't need it. And maybe it will remind you of this moment. There aren't many moments like this. But this is our moment. Dammit, kid! It ain't something to get sentimental about. Don't be getting emotional on me."

"This looks like the one my dad used to carry around with him."

I wrapped my hands around it tightly. I thought about the many times my father would pull out his pocket knife, always ending up helping save the day in one way or another. He'd been the king of his own domain, and his pocketknife was always handy when needed. Everyone who knew him gave him respect because of his handiness.

"Here we are. Now get out."

"Oh, okay. Thanks. Um, can I get a ride home?"

"We'll think about it. But chances are no."

"Definitely no."

Clint grabbed the door, and they were gone in sixty seconds.

They'd dropped me off at the bus stop closest to work. I had only a few blocks to go. No big deal. As I walked I played with the pocketknife opening each part individually and imagining how my Dad might have used it.

5

I walked through the sliding glass doors of Paper-Clips, the office supply store where my indentured servitude existed until I fulfilled my debt to society. Or so it seemed. The automatic doors made a swoosh sound when they opened, reminding me of the old Star Trek episodes I used to watch as a kid on the Syfy network. When those episodes first aired in the late '60s, sliding doors were mere fantasy. Now they were very much real and very much taken for granted.

The shopping center where Paper-Clips resided was off a main road which was always congested with traffic at inconvenient times. It was in a man-made valley nestled between the silent, decaying trees of Midwestern America and the disappearing green and blue suburban white picket fence postcard. Between these two things, dust settled like a wasteland of gray ashes. Ashes of things no one wanted to forget. They remained and resonated to people who thought the past had not gone permanently—only temporarily. Everyone was in denial. The dirty cold floors in Paper-Clips were covered in a thick ball of dust made from this very same ash the wind blew inside.

Not far away were two recently closed factories that had once been notorious for the noise and unique odor they produced, along with their dusty ash. When they'd been active, smoke had risen from each chimney and usually settled near the shopping center or on the highway. Somehow the ash never disappeared, but spread slowly through the town. It was something to which most had grown accustomed. Now, with both factories closed, the smell was fading into memory. Instead the roaring wind picked up, twirled, and tossed the leftover dust, carrying it away into the sun whose rays of light were filtered by the construction of the many unfinished, vacant houses, leaving everything diffused.

I attempted a stealthy entrance, but the first person to notice me was Remy, who regularly announced any employees entrance or exit. He was like our store's town crier: "here comes Jimmy," or "there goes Bill, everyone." Technically he was retired. He took care to sweep the floor every morning, as if the floor he was sweeping was the same floor in Buckingham Palace. He was perpetually sweeping the floor. I'm not sure if he ever did anything else other than sweep the store's floor. But sweep he did in his vain attempt to rid the floor of its dust and ashes. He never seemed to give it a second thought. He said he found pleasure in it. All he wanted was something to do. He looked up and waved. "Oh! Look who it is. Jimmy. Well, I was hoping you wouldn't show up so I could steal your job in the Copy Circle. Hehe."

"You couldn't work those old machines if your life depended on it."

"What? Oh, you think so? I was an engineer once. I used to build those copiers. Did you know that? No, you didn't. Too busy playing your video games and texting on your cell phones, and not giving a hoot for an old fart like me."

"Well. I'm younger and full of more energy."

"I'd like to see you sweep these floors as good as I do."

"I would rather watch you do it if you don't mind."

Remy waved me off and continued sweeping, whistling like a person who belonged in a happier time.

I knew Remy was right, but I always pretended I didn't know for Remy's sake. He liked to remind everyone he'd once been this great mechanical engineer. So why was he working at Paper-Clips? He claimed he was bored with retirement. He had already traveled the world. He claimed he needed a reason to get out of bed in the morning. I couldn't blame him for that. Many people in the world invent a reason to be alive. I knew I was looking for a reason.

The Copy Circle was where we kept our copiers. It was almost like a store within a store. We even wore different uniforms from the rest of the store's boring polo shirts. We had an area where people could do their copies for a small fee, or they had the option to have us do the copies for a higher fee. We did almost everything: black and white copies, color copies, double-sided copies, single-sided copies, binding things with coils or plastic, and laminating. We could blow things up to the size of posters or make banners, turn a set of pictures into a calendar, create business cards—everything that kept me busy without wanting to shoot myself.

The job would not have been so bad if it hadn't been for the customers. Customers were the plague of my existence. Granted, not all customers were complete assholes, but most were total jerks or morons. They came in expecting us to serve them hand and foot and were angry if we weren't kissing their feet while they stepped on us (with pointy high-heeled shoes or polished Italian loafers) to aid them in some twisted sadomasochistic fantasy, a fantasy where there existed no safe word. No way to tap out of this nightmare.

Somehow, the fact that I worked in the store, in most of their eyes, automatically demoted my status as a human being. When I stepped behind that counter, I was suddenly their slave. And they could do with me as they pleased. It was their God-given right. If they were having a bad day, they would go out of their way to make mine a living hell. If they were bored, they would entertain themselves by asking confusing questions and making unrealistic demands. And they always knew more than me, even if they'd never touched a copier, computer, or laminator in their entire life. Somehow they knew better, and I was the idiot.

In their twisted world of right and wrong, they felt justified calling me whatever they pleased. I imagined I was Mussolini being hanged by his countrymen. He'd had it easier than I did with these soulless customers. They would do much worse , given the opportunity. They didn't care where I'd come from. They didn't care about my father's death. They didn't care that my mother had abandoned my father and me before I was old enough to remember her face. They didn't care that I was a college graduate and wasn't supposed to be working there anymore. All they cared about was what they wanted, and they wanted it now. Fuck me and the boat I came in on!

"I'd like these printed in white, please."

"I'm sorry, but we don't print in white."

"Why the fuck not?"

"Because we don't carry black paper."

"But this is black."

"Yes. It's black construction paper. But the copiers can't print on black construction paper."

"This is bullshit. I want to print white on this. Where is your manager?"

"Ma'am. I assure you. I'm not making this up. It is, in fact, impossible to print white on black construction paper. You see the toner will not stick to the construction paper. Perhaps another color and type of paper?"

"No. I want to speak to your manager right now. This is the worst service. You are a horrible person. What's your name? Jimmy? Well, Jimmy. When I'm done, you won't be working here or anywhere else, for that matter. How do you like that?"

I called my manger to the Copy Circle on the intercom.

When he showed up, I explained what happened. The customer insisted on interrupting me each and every moment I tried to inform my manager what happened. Then, to the customer's surprise, the manager explained to her I was right, it was impossible to print in white.

"Oh, I understand. Thank you for explaining that to me. You are so helpful and polite. That's all I wanted to know. Thank you."

The customer left, but not before she kicked a pile of dust in my face. The manager stared at me as if I was somehow at fault. I tried to pat the dust off my clothes, face and hair.

"Did you raise your voice?"

"No."

"Did you lose your temper again, Jimmy?"

"No. I said the exact same thing you said. I was polite and told her I was sorry."

"You need to work on your people skills. You can't bark orders at the customers."

"But I didn't. Didn't I say I didn't? Didn't I? Are you even listening to me?"

"See. You shouldn't talk to me in that tone of voice. I'm your manager. You're skating on thin ice, Jimmy."

"Look. I'm not going to apologize because I didn't do anything wrong here."

"Jimmy. You don't get it. Sometimes I wonder if you will ever get it. The customer is always right."

"But the customer can't always be right. Especially if they want something that we can't do. You know that."

"Did you offer them any other options?"

"I didn't get a chance. The old lady's eyes turned red right away when I told her we couldn't print in white."

"She wasn't that mean. Stop harassing harmless old ladies."

"Oh yeah. Right. To you, she wasn't. To me, she acted as if she was possessed by Satan."

"Jimmy. This is your first warning. I'm keeping my eye on you."

"I'm in the third circle of hell!"

"Stop being so dramatic, Jimmy."

It was during times like this when I tried to escape my temporary damnation and depart into another fantastic world. Sometimes I thought about some of my friends at the karaoke bar, Jasmine, or my Dad. Sometimes I imagined myself a superhero. The kind of superhero who saved helpless store employees from the absolute evilness of irate customers. I would fly in from above wearing my cape and throw bombs on each customer who thought the best way to get what they wanted was to turn themselves into a giant child, pouting, pointing, and whining. I would circle near the ceiling like a bird of prey, and by the time I was done, every customer would be cheerful. Every customer would be knowledgeable of what they were buying. They wouldn't waste my time with stupid questions like, "Can I erase the ink on my paper after I print something?" or "I'm looking for a pen that was manufactured during the Great War. I haven't been able to find it since 1952. I was wondering if you still carried it. You don't? Why not?" or "Could you write a letter for me? I don't know what to say. It's about a divorce. Can you tell me what I should say?"

"I'm not a lawyer, ma'am. And I'm not in law school."

"Well, don't you think you should know these things?"

"No. I don't."

"I'm going to that other store. Maybe they will help."

The best threat is when a customer threatens to go to another store. Especially for something we don't sell. At Paper-Clips, we sold a few computer games, but we never sold console games like Nintendo, Xbox, or Playstation.

"I'm looking for this Playstation game."

"We don't carry Playstation games."

"Fine! I'm going to Video Game Palace and take my business elsewhere. Try to stop me."

"The door's at the front of the store, sir. It will open automatically. It's a beautiful invention."

We never cared if they went to another store. It was one less possible complaint. And sometimes they would come crawling back after an extremely negative experience at another store. We may have been jerks sometimes, but we weren't assholes.

"Look out, Jimmy. It's return of the Mack! Oh, my God!" Mack said as he tried to jump up to high-five me. A high-five I refused to return.

Mack was a short, over-caffeinated electronics salesman who had his whole life figured out. And he loved his job. He loved to kiss the manager's ass. He loved to boast about his wife, who he claimed was sexy but looked more like she had gone to the tanning salon one time too many. He loved to annoy me. He always treated everything like it was a competition and would show-up at the Copy Circle to brag about any big sale he had or was in the process of completing. Then he would go to my computer so he could look up his sales numbers in the Electronics Department and compare them with the sale numbers in the Copy Circle. As if I really cared. As if I really had a chance to beat him. He was selling machines that averaged hundreds to thousands of dollars. I was selling seven-cent black and white copies. In Mack's world, all that mattered were the numbers.

"If I were working in the Copy Circle right now, I could do better than you."

"You're welcome to try."

"Yeah, right. You'd like that, wouldn't you?"

"I would love to watch you in action."

"Sounds like a trick. Nice try, guy."

"Trick? What trick? It was your idea."

"Whatever! See that old couple? You know what I'm going to do? I'm going to convince them to buy a computer they don't need. You know why? Because I can, that's why. When I'm done with those old people, they'll spend so much money here I'll be promoted to Sales Manager and get Employee of the Month for the third time in a row. Try to stop me, Jimmy. Try. I dare you. Try it."

"You're a sick and despicable human being."

He smiled me off as he slicked back his hair with a comb before walking over to the couple in his obnoxious city slicker cowboy boots. Boots, I might add, made his short, stocky Napoleon frame look ridiculous. Boots, I might add, he thought brought him luck. Boots, I might add, he'd purchased for thousands of dollars on the advice of his skanky, plastic surgery-addicted wife. I imagined several large printers falling on his head, smashing him flat like a pancake. Wop! Wop! Woooop!

As I disgustedly watched Mack in action, I felt a lifeless tap on my shoulder. It was Joe, the world's most tired man. He always came into work late. He was always tired. He always had a hangover. He was a genius and kind of my hero. Why? Well, he had a knack for disappearing and never really working. And he never got fired for it. He never got reprimanded. He had a stack of customer complaints bigger than mine. And somehow, when I received a customer complaint, the managers acted as if I had unleashed the dogs of war. Whereas with Joe, they shrugged the complaints off as Joe being Joe.

"Hey…, Jimmy…, you have… a minute?"

"I don't know. I have a feeling it's going to take an hour for you to speak."

"… Oh…. Ha…. Very funny. Well, I was… wondering… if you had… some masking… tape."

"Yeah, it's in the drawer."

"Oh… great…."

"Why do you need masking tape?"

"Nothing for… really." He began to walk away when he stopped and turned back and stood very close to me.

"If I… tell you. You promise… you won't… tell anyone… else?"

"Sure. Mum's the word."

"Well, I'm gonna use… the tape… over my ears… so I won't get… disturbed when I… sleep."

"Wow." I laughed. "Have fun with that."

That was Joe. He was loony enough to attempt something so ridiculous. He would climb a ladder and hide behind the merchandise on a top shelf so he could sleep through his shift. One time, someone grabbed the ladder he had used to get up to the top shelf, and when he woke, he realized he was stuck and had no way to get down. And what did he do? He tried to climb down,, slipped and fell, and landed on his head. We found him after we heard the crash. The managers were so worried he would sue for worker's compensation, they gave him a week off and a raise. Only in America.

Eventually Joe left Paper-Clips. Not because he was fired but because he'd decided he wanted a more challenging job. Before he left he told me being the world's laziest worker was actually a lot of work. Again, only in America.

Another crop of annoying customers were a group known as the eBayers. They were called such because these people made a good amount of money screwing the system, so to speak, and selling crap they bought on sale or clearance on eBay. They always had a million coupons on them, along with several gift cards and/or cards with store credit. Some of their coupons were forgeries. But most of them were so emboldened by the success of their con game, they would keep trying coupons. If one of us was ringing them up, we would always call a manager because they always tried to con the cashiers, especially the new ones, as they kept trying coupons after coupon, trying to convince the newbie the fake one was legitimate.

A lot of them were Asian. Why? I did not know. They just happened to be Asian. Perhaps they were better at finding deals. Managers disliked this group of customers. They were the only breed of patrons the bosses would not go out of their way to ensure were happy and justified for being assholes to us lowly Paper-clips employees. It was sometimes amusing to watch them try to trick our store's poor supervisors. They would take whatever route they deemed necessary to try to keep the con going.

"You calling me a liar! You're a racist," said the eBayer.

"Sir, we can't accept this return because we do not sell it. It's never been in our store inventory," a manager would say.

"This is bigotry. I'm going to sue you and your entire company for a violation of my civil liberties."

"I'm sorry to hear that."

"Why do you want to see my credit card?"

"To verify the numbers on the back. It's store policy. We have to have eyes on the credit card. It's one of the many ways we ensure security for the store and our great customers."

"What if I don't want to give you my credit card?"

"If you don't want to comply with our policy, I would be more than happy to accept cash."

"Cash? Who carries cash these days? Take my credit card, dammit. You can't refuse my credit card!"

"Actually, I can. The law only requires me to accept legal tender, which is cash. I'm not required to accept credit cards. It's a convenient option Paper-Clips and many other companies offer in place of cash. We do this in order to help make the shopping experience easier and more rewarding for our customers. But again, there is no law binding me to accept credit cards or any other form of payment."

"Here. Read the damn card. But I'm watching you. If I think you're trying to memorize my numbers, I'll be back with a lawyer. I still think it's a stupid policy."

"Thank you very much, sir. See? Now was that so hard?"

"Bigot."

From time to time the managers would let themselves get so discouraged and frustrated some of them would eventually relent and give these grifters what they were after so they could finally be rid of them. Those managers didn't last long at Paper-Clips. The eBayers were all too willing to stand and fight the whole night and day if they deemed it necessary.

"Hey. What happened to the customer is always right?" I would ask after situations such as these.

"Shut up, Jimmy!" would more than often be their response to my smart-ass observation.

If they came in with a return, usually something they'd bought only two days previous, we had to inspect the contents of the box. They liked to do the old switcharoo now and again, or replace the item with a broken one. Tricky, tricky, tricky pranksters.

"Heard you almost got fired." Remy said as he swept dust nearby.

"Who told you that, Remy?"

"Bill told me."

"Bill? He never steps on the store floor. He spends all day in receiving. Where the hell did he hear that from?"

"Don't know. Maybe it was Joe. You know, Joe hears everything. He just told me you got into a fight with a customer over some copies. And then Frank yelled at you."

"When am I not getting into a fight with a customer?"

"You have to let things go sometimes, Jimmy."

"It's easier said than done."

Remy chuckled as he returned to sweeping. "Ah, Jimmy. You will learn one day. You'll see."

I decided I needed a smoke break. However, before I could escape, a Latino customer walked up to me with big eyes and asked, "*Señor. ¿Me puedes ayudar con algo*[13]?"

"*Sí. Pero, yo hablo un poquito español.*[14]"

"*¿Por que?* Why you no speak Spanish! I want a manager. Right now."

Sigh. "I have to take my break. *Adiós, hombre.*"

I leaned against the brick wall behind the store. Bill from receiving threw boxes in the nearby dumpster, then leaned next to me.

"Care if I join you?"

"Not at all. How's it going, Bill?"

"Smooth. Haven't had a hard day's work since yesterday," he chuckled.

I handed him a cigarette, and we smoked together in silence. Bill had never been known as a man of many words. But I accepted his muteness. Sometimes quietude was preferred over noise. I stared at the setting sun. Night would soon overcome day. After most everyone had gone home, I would then get to leave. The wind picked up briefly, carrying with it more dust. I held my hand up and pretended I could squish the sun between two of my fingers. If the sun was gone, and if it was always night,

---

[13] English translation: "Sir. Can I get help with something?"

[14] English translation: "Yes. But I speak very little Spanish."

maybe people wouldn't always expect more than what they have? Then again, if we were forced to always live in night, we would all probably turn into vampires who sucked blood from others so we could pretend we were all alive. To me, we already seemed almost dead. Almost forgotten.

"So, any plans tonight, Bill?"

"Me? No. When you're married with a kid, you don't make plans. Things are planned for you. Think you'll have a job tomorrow?"

"Probably. Unfortunately."

Bill laughed. "Well, remember. It could always be worse."

He went back inside, and I was once again alone with the setting sun, the dust, and the ash. Maybe he was right. Maybe I was being too hard on myself and everyone else. Maybe. Maybe.

For a few weeks, that was my life again. Quiet and inconsequential. And always surreal. I got up, took a shower, ate, went to work, and came home to vegetate. Sometimes I would apply for a job. Other times I would forget and hate myself the next day for forgetting to apply for another job. I avoided The Fish Bowl during this time. Even though I found so much comfort in the place, I wanted to be alone with my thoughts for a while. Something about that night at The Fish Bowl that began with the med student and ended with Jasmine dancing with me made me feel uneasy.

6

I had one good suit. I first wore it at the funeral of a priest. His name was Father Camus; he was a close friend of my father and was like a grandfather to me. Then I wore it at the funeral of a friend who was killed in a motorcycle accident. And then my father passed away. I wore this same suit three days straight. After my father's funeral, I drank and drank and drank, trying to ingest the fruit of my personal misfortune. By the end of those three days, the suit stank something horrible. I had it dry-cleaned several times. I had no choice and not enough money to replace it. Other than funerals, I've since worn this suit for the few job interviews I managed to set up.

The problem with job interviews, in general, was their disposition to treat each one like a cattle call. HR (Human Resources, for the discombobulated) solicited more candidates than necessary and scheduled numerous persons they knew would never get the job. But how else could HR get its kicks? Such actions promoted traumatic psychological situations, turning people to hardcore additions involving the legalized and prescribed placebos— with names like Ritalin (methylphenidate), Celexa, Cipramil, (citalopram), Lexapro, Cipralex, Seroplex, Lexamil, (escitalopram), Prozac, Sarafem, Symbyax, (fluoxetine), Luvox, (fluvoxamin), Paxil, Aropax, (paroxetine), Zoloft (sertraline), Viibryd (vilazodone), Pristiq (desvenlafaxine), Cymbalta (duloxetine), Ixel (milnacipran), MAOIs (monoamine oxidase inhibitors), TCAs (tricyclic antidepressants), TeCAs (tetracyclic antidepressants), SSRIs (selective serotonin reuptake inhibitors), and SNRIs (serotonin-norepinephrine reuptake inhibitors).

Death may not be proud but the HR vampires seemed to take pleasure in slowly impaling us on large stakes above their long dinner tables. They enjoyed feasting on their cured meats and wine and bread while we agonized over a gradual and painful death. They stabbed us from time to time to make sure we were alive and able to experience misery. Knowing full well if we ever were recruited among their undead, we would then be damned to roam the earth like helpless zombies, slaves to our basic need to feed and survive.

Preparing for a job interview was an excitingly boring procedure. The closer a job interview approached, the more anxious I felt. I would agonize over what they wanted and what I could o give them. How to act, how to answer questions, how to lie, how to look like you were something you were not, how to pretend knowledge of something they assumed I would have, and how to pretend interest in things I couldn't care less about. These days the job seekers outnumbered the available jobs. We were like vagabonds wearing disheveled suits and wandering in the company's waiting rooms like derelicts.

My generation kept trying to pretend we were not the sacrificial lambs of the sins of the previous generation. But as time marched forward, we could no longer ignore that which stared us in the face. Our burden and our abnegation would help future generations. We walked around with the short end of the stick. I took every anti-depressant concocted by the evil pharmaceutical companies, mixed them with eight-proof alcohol, and then stirred my cocktail relentlessly until I was sure it would numb me not only properly but also inject me with the veil I desperately needed to hide behind in order to temporarily avoid all the uncertainty. It was the only way I was able to get through the nauseating experience no one prepared me for. My beautiful benzylamine. The glorious diazepam. The illicit codeine and/or thebaine with some hydromorphine and/or dihydromorphine and/or dihydrocodeince and/or tetrahydrotebaine and/or hydrocodone. At the end of a job interview, my toxicology report would list a string of drugs related to numbing and promoting a bit of apathy. Some of these drugs were prescribed to me a long time ago. All were, for the most, perfectly legal. I was legally addicted to these drugs. Expired or not, I stubbornly took them. Often handfuls of these little pills administered orally was the best method. The only method.

As soon as a job on Careerbuilder.com or Monster.com showed up in the search box results, tens of thousands upon thousands would apply for the job. More often than not, they weren't cozy office jobs, executive jet-setter jobs, or any job worth utilizing to build a career. More than likely they were mailroom jobs, telemarketing jobs, door-to-door solicitor jobs, discount sales jobs, jobs most of us didn't want. Jobs most of felt were inferior, and therefore, below our interest. And yet we applied as if we had no other choice.

A job interview was like a ceaseless dance through the halls of anxiety and boredom. After a while, and after so many dime novel interview questions, they blended together. It was like someone took a glob of paint and smeared it across an empty canvas while expecting the end result to be something as detailed as the Mona Lisa. All they saw was a glob of smeared paint that didn't even look as decent as a Jackson Pollock or Rothko. And each time we went on another job interview, the paint would smear some more, until it covered the entire canvas in grayish dull colors. We desperate folks tried to convince ourselves there was a deeper meaning and purpose in the crappy spiritless paint. But there was no meaning, only a gentle nudge into oblivion and anonymity.

Sometimes I wished I was a superhero cop like my imaginary friend Clint Eastwood or his silent partner Steve McQueen. With a handgun I would nudge it against the forehead of one of the HR vampires, demanding better questions and a job that was actually worth a damn. They would try to fight back and bite me until I pulled the curtains to reveal the sun shining through their monotone office. No more formalities. Now, pure and raw emotion.

My father, the long suffering restaurant owner and part-time mechanic, had it easier. All the sacrifices of previous epochs of the Rodriguez family—all the blood, sweat, and back-bending tears—were supposed to be worth it. They were all supposed to conclude with my inevitable success. But I found myself staring into a black hole that would sooner or later suck me into its center, erasing me from existence, erasing the memories of my father, and the memories of my family, the memories of the forgettable dynasty of the Rodriguez clan.

I wanted an adventure more than anything else. I wanted to make my claim somewhere I might be a stranger but a stranger that would intrigue the indigenous. I was a stranger here myself, in the land of plastic bald eagles, hamburgers, and Fourth of July picnics. I needed an escape from boredom and my failure. Even success didn't seem all that great anymore. The only real enterprise worth having now was the adventure of the hero or the lonesome anti-hero wandering the earth after some sort of vengeance. Who would I avenge? I would find someone to avenge? Vengeance will be mine! An adventure. An adventure that made me someone special and not another microscopic ant trying to scrape an existence only to watch it fade into nothing. Every time I went to see a movie, the world seemed less important and less real than what I was seeing on the big theater screen.

I wished I'd had foreknowledge this would be my future after all those years slaving away for a degree in college. Some had been searching for jobs so long, all they knew in life was how to interview. Or how to tweak their resumes or the resume of someone else. Everyone had an opinion on perfecting the resume. Show your resume to any friend or passerby, and everyone would offer a critique or radical suggestion. People agreed better ordering toppings on a pizza over agreeing on resumes. One had to be careful not to assume everyone had a worthy take on your resume. Otherwise you would fall into a loop of always changing and updating your resume and never finishing it. We were all in perpetual limbo as we raced to the next job interview with hope in our eyes and the promises of success burned into our psyches by parents, teachers, mentors, and celebrity chefs. There were too many of us now. Too many.

Most of the time it was luck of the draw. Or sometimes it was more your personality than your qualifications. Some felt obligated to berate you with hardcore questions they found in a classified FBI interrogation book. Some threw you dozens of unfiltered questions within the span of five-second interviews, leaving you little time to respond with adequate answers.

The Job Interview:
1. Why do you like (insert your company name here)?
Answer One: It's been one of my long-standing goals to work for a company such as this. Your organization stands above all the rest in its industry.
Answer Two: I've long been an admirer of how you do business here and would love the opportunity to contribute to your ongoing success. I used to dream about working for your company when I was a wee child. I like how you utilize acronyms in your company's title. You're doing some amazing stuff.
Answer Three: Honestly, it's hard to place your company apart from all the other companies. I never even heard of

you until I found this position posted on a job search website. Also, don't you think it is about time you try a different logo? I think using a globe is a bit overdone. So why did I choose your company? You still want to know? You were next on the list of companies hiring for a position in which I have a remote interest. Your interior is rather predictable. An office floor occupied by cubicles. So there you have it. I applied to you blindly, like I have been applying to all other jobs.

2. Would you say you are a team player?
Answer One: I enjoy working with groups and exchanging ideas. I believe it's the best way to find a solution to any problem or task we might be involved in.
Answer Two: Absolutely. Yes. I'm a firm believer in no "I" in team. I'm a repressed socialist when it comes to teamwork.
Answer Three: I'm not a team player. I'm extremely independent minded. I'm extremely opinionated, and I don't get along with others, especially stupid people. I can't stand stupid people. Of course, I might be open to being in charge of a team. As long as they follow my orders like they were the word of God.

3. What did you like or dislike about your previous job?
Answer One: Next question please.

4. What have you learned from your mistakes?
Answer One: Mistakes are made.
Answer Two: Everyone makes mistakes sometimes.
Answer Three: The only mistake I've made is not being born into a rich family.

5. What is your greatest strength?
Answer One: I'm a perfectionist.

Answer Two: I'm an overachiever perfectionist. Whoops! That's two, isn't it? Well, that's why I'm always trying to achieve perfection.

Answer Three: Some call it hubris. I call it confidence. Some say I'm well-hung and godlike. Some people ask me if I have a God complex. Let me tell you something … I am a god[15].

6. How do you handle stress and pressure?

Answer One: I try to handle stress the best way I can, like anyone else. I try to never take anything personally although I can be somewhat passionate about my work. I try to separate myself from the situation at hand and address any condition with a logical solution.

Answer Two: Stress and pressure are to be expected of any job. I try to stay gold. Stay gold!

Answer Three: Why? What have you heard? That old lady was asking for it, I tell you! She had it coming!

7. What are your salary expectations?

Answer One: Whatever is applicable to a position such as this.

Answer Two: In the range of a modest number to another modest number.

Answer Three: I expected to be paid in fucking gold bullion, motherfucker!

8. If you know your boss is 100 percent wrong about something, how would you handle it?

Answer One: It depends on the situation and the personality of the supervisor.

Answer Two: My prior supervisor was more easy-going. So if he made a mistake and I were to point out said mistake, he had no trouble with that.

Answer Three: Payback is a bitch.

---

[15] Malice, dir. by Harold Becker (1993; MGM).

9. What can you do for this company?

Answer One: What can I not do for this company? That is the question you should be asking me.

Answer Two: I can become death, destroyer of all worlds. If you want. Your call.

Answer Three: Work.

☐

7

ONE day, as I walked out of the office building of another degrading job interview where my performance was more or less deplorable, I thought I spied a familiar hellion. He was leaning against a car parked on the side of the street. The sun was bright that day. All I could see through the white light was a dark silhouette that resembled a gothic Max Schreck *Nosferatu*. I put on my aviators to assist my eyes through the blinding light. After my vision adjusted, I concluded the demon-like figure was none other than Ringo, the karaoke DJ at The Fish Bowl.

I walked toward him. I soon noticed he was engaged in what appeared to be an in-depth text messaging conversation on his cell phone. He was wearing an all-black suit. Even his tie was black, and yet I did not see any sweat protrude off his thin anemic skin. The shiny black suit euthanized the sunshine. Ringo's chain smoking surrounded him inside a fatal tomb of grey smoke. He preferred to smoke those long thin cigarettes normally marketed to women smokers. His eyes were covered with a pair of large, vintage black Persol sunglasses.

For a moment I thought of walking past him and leaving him to his texting. But I needed a friendly face after my recent deplorable interview. Ringo would have to do. He darted his head toward me like a paranoid raven when he noticed me approaching. He didn't seem to recognize me at first. We rarely, if ever, saw or spoke to one another outside of the Fish Bowl. Maybe my navy blue suit had thrown him off.

"Ringo. How goes it? Got a cig I can bum?"

Ringo didn't respond but continued typing a massive text message to whomever he was conversing with. I waited until he finished. After he concluded his text essay, he put his cell into one of his pants pockets. He pulled out a pack of Virginia Slims from inside one of the blazer's breast pockets. I looked around hoping no one would see me smoking these dainty cigarettes. I pulled one out of the package. Before I could grab my light, Ringo had his Zippo out with the flame already igniting the tip of my cigarette. I took a long drag. Ringo safely hid the Zippo close to his heart.

"Do you like to dance?" Ringo asked.

"I guess, a little. Why? Are you planning on asking me to the prom?"

"Ever dance with the devil underneath a full moon, baby boy?"

"I can't say I have. Or I've never knowingly done so."

"No, you can't. The devil is always in disguise. No one knows if the beast is near. No one knows if Beelzebub is following them. Or if Satan is in possession of their soul. That's why the Prince of Darkness is so powerful. It makes you think it's never there. That's a reason to never talk to strangers or dance with any fool you meet."

"Did you watch *The Exorcist* recently or something? That movie gives me chills to this day."

"Of course I've seen *The Exorcist*, baby boy. More of a collection of occult absurdity and superstitious incongruity. That film wants us to believe we can control Lucifer. Nothing can control him. Not even God. When people realize that, maybe someday we'll rise above this absurd thing called existence and find ourselves finally elevated to a place where nothing is fraudulent. I have the name of a much better film than that pea-spewing movie. You should see Ingmar Bergman's *The Seventh Seal*. There's a scene in that movie where the characters dance together holding hands in a circle while pulling at each other. They called it the dance of death. Succulent and brilliant. So, why are you wearing a suit?"

"I was at a funeral."

"Really? Who died, baby boy?"

"My dignity. It was a job interview. I botched it up pretty good this time. Almost threw-up on the guy interviewing me, I was so nervous. Who wants to do math for an investment firm anyway? Not me. I would be a glorified accountant sitting in a cubicle next to a million other cubicles. I can picture every one of us with our heads down calculating financial numbers while a guy dressed as a Viking beats a drum in front of us. Not worth it, in my opinion."

"That's quite the vivid imagination you have there, Jimmy. Well, you do have a job now. Yes?"

"Yes. But it's not the kind of job that justifies all those years in college."

"At least you have a job, baby boy. Don't worry. You'll find a better one someday and enjoy the fruits of your labor."

"Even so. I have a feeling I will still be bored out of my mind."

"You can't have it all. No one has it all, baby boy. Life is like pissing in the wind. You can get mad about it, you can deal with it, or get even."

"Look at you. Full of advice all of a sudden. You think you're my father or something?"

"No. Maybe your Momma…. You wear everything on your sleeve, baby boy. It's too easy to see what you're thinking. You can't hide it, Jimmy. You're like a walking billboard. You're broadcasting your deepest desires and fears on the six o'clock news. It's a good quality. It shows you're honest, unlike me. But it also can be a weakness."

"You think no one can tell you're a liar? No offense, but you look like you're up to no good from a mile away. Who goes around wearing an all-black suit on a sunny day like today?"

"I'm a great liar. I'm one of the best liars. I lie all the time. I lie so much I can't tell when I'm telling the truth. And the truth is more of a diversion. One day we won't need lies. Like I said before. But as long as evil is personified in the air, the dust, the emptiness of all the dark pitiful places around you, there will be people like me."

"So, what are you up to, Ringo?"

"Sticky fingers. Sticky, sticky, fingers." Ringo winked at me.

"See. I can already tell you're up to no good."

"Hell hath no fury like a woman scorned. Or a woman out for vengeance."

"Vengeance for what?"

"Everything." Ringo lit up another Virginia Slim with his Zippo. He took a long drag and exhaled smoke rings that resembled donuts. "Such a pretty baby boy, Jimmy. I can give you some work. You don't want that work, though. Do you? I know you don't. Why did I ask? I don't know. Wishful thinking. Let's get in the back of this car, Jimmy. We can talk more intimately about all your troubles."

"No. Fuck, no, man. Come on, man. Be cool."

"Itchy fingers, Jimmy. Itchy fingers. I feel so sorry for you sometimes. If you knew any better, you would leave this filthy place. Go and find yourself a place in the sun."

"I think I'm always going to be looking for my place in the sun, so to speak. Hopefully not before I've wasted the life I have. Or maybe I'll take your advice and leave it all so I can find my Walden."

"Your Walden?"

"My Walden Pond. It's a place one goes to start over."

"Kiss and tell. Kiss and tell. For a kiss, I will tell you everything. I'll tell and tell and tell. I'll save you, baby boy."

"Ringo. You're starting to act strange."

"Where did you get this awful suit?"

"My father bought it a long time ago. It's the only suit I have."

"No offense to your dearly departed father, but you need a better suit."

"I know. I can't afford one."

"I can—no wait—better yet. Next week I'll take you out to get a better suit. My treat. I never got you anything for graduation. It will be my graduation gift."

"You don't have to do that."

"That's why it's a gift. I don't have to do it. But I'm doing it anyway. It's not a favor. You won't owe me. For the love all that is holy, you need a better suit."

"Okay. But I have a feeling when I call you about this next week, you will have forgotten or you will be clueless."

"I won't. Trust me. It's a matter of good taste. Well, Jimmy. I'm a busy man. Run along now. I can't stand here all day talking to you about suits and ponds."

I had one more Virginia Slim with Ringo. He looked at his broken, fake Rolex, surprised so much time had flown. I wished him well and went merrily off on my way. When I glanced back, it looked like he was texting someone on his cell. He was a mysterious person who always kept his guard up. Outside of the Fish Bowl, away from the karaoke stage, he seemed less than his bigger-than-life Karaoke DJ persona. He also seemed rather sickly. As if his face was covered in death, and he was Death's messenger. I wondered what thoughts danced behind his large eyes. I wondered what memories he kept deep inside. I wondered how he would die. Everyone dies. Some die better than others.

As I walked the streets through the city's dirty ash in my navy blue suit, I wrestled all the hundreds of thoughts rioting in my head. Perhaps Ringo was right, and I was being too pessimistic and cynical. It's so easy to be a cynic, for it places you outside of society and allows you to judge everyone save yourself. If there was a way to escape all the broken dreams and promises, I might be able to find my sanity. I lit a cigarette and watched the smoke form the image of Maria de Guadalupe. Maria looked down at me with sorrow in her eyes as she floated away, disappearing into thin air. I prostrated to Maria's once beholden image while wandering the earth feeling like I was a castaway of the unplanned and unwanted.

My suit felt ragged and torn. It felt like it was made of iron and weighed me down, causing me to lurch forward with bad posture. I saw HR people running after me, tearing my suit to shreds like greedy little zombies until nothing was left of me but the skin on my back. Leaving me to stand naked to face whatever fate had in store for me. Clint tried his best to protect me and fight them off, but he couldn't save me from these savages. They left me covered in cuts. They left me to watch my blood pour out for no one to drink. Who could drink blood that mixed with the dirty ash and inhaled cigarette smoke? I was losing my feet with each step I took. One foot gone, and then the other. Nothing was fine.

8

ONE night I came home after work and turned on the TV to one of the local news shows. The news anchors were both dressed in the standard muted dark blue and/or black business suits. Plastered on each of their faces were thick layers of makeup, giving them a plastic look similar to a pair of Ken and Barbie dolls. The male anchor wore a thick helmet of perfectly combed hair that looked like it was dipped in a boiling pot of mousse and hairspray. The female anchor was no better. Her hair was over styled and extended out in strange directions, suggesting her head was shaped geometrically and not spherically, coupled with more lipstick than a whore in New Orleans.

The top story for the evening was footage of a federal building on fire. Black smoke covered the top of the building. Bright red flames swelled through the open windows. In the next shot, they showed fire fighters wearing yellow jackets and large hats battling the blaze. I turned up the volume.

"Fire officials say the blaze that ravaged the Federal Records Storage Facility is now under control."

"More than forty fire fighters battled the flames that erupted late Wednesday night. WWTV's Jeff Jackson asked fire fighter,

Mickey Montgomery, if the blaze may have been the work of an arsonist."

"It's a bit early to tell if it's arson or not. We're very happy no one was hurt in the blaze. And I'm proud of all my fellow fire fighters and the brave work they do."

"Because the fire involved federal records, the FBI has been called in to investigate."

The world was on fire, I thought. What a strange thing to see.

I reached into my pocket and pulled out a feather I'd found at the Fish Bowl. It was golden yellow. I'd been carrying the feather around in my pocket since then. It didn't look nice anymore. In fact it looked quite ugly. Carrying a feather around in my pocket was not a good idea. Then a thought occurred to me. What if this wasn't a feather of good but a feather of bad? I had to get rid of it. I opened a window and threw it out. It circled around as it glided to the ground and disappeared into the uncut blades of grass on the ground.

My thoughts began to wander again, and I worried I might be falling under the spell of depression despite the meds I'd been taking. I ran to grab a beer from my fridge, knowing the taste would sooth me enough to hopefully forget my troubles. I took a sip of the cold dark ale, which tasted bitter. I now shared something with my dearly beloved father: a taste for good beer.

"In other news, a young medical student is missing. He's been gone for two weeks. He was last seen at a local college bar known as The Fish Bowl."

"Ian Noone told his fiancée he was going out Sunday night to have some fun. This was strange to Maryanne because he was going out alone. Without any friends. And he had never done that before."

"We were going to get married in three weeks. And he was only a week away from becoming a doctor. I-it doesn't make any sense. Where is he? Ian, where are you? Please come home!"

I muted the TV. They showed his face. I recognized him. So, his name was Ian, eh? Ian Noone. Strange I hadn't bothered to ask his name. And now he was gone. Disappeared somehow, but not forgotten. Remembered by the people looking for him. With loved ones desperate to find him again. Lucky. Lucky. Lucky. I wonder what happened to him that night. The night of nights, because it was the last night I remembered having fun. It felt like only yesterday I was dancing with Jasmine under a moonlit night.

Ian was missing. It was a mystery. Perhaps I could solve the mystery. It would give me something to do for a while. A way to escape the boredom of my life. If I could find him, maybe I would be a hero. Maybe I would be given the key to the city by the mayor. Maybe I would make Steve McQueen believe in me. And make Clint Eastwood confirm the risk he'd taken letting me into the world of superhero renegade cops. Too bad my father wasn't here to share in my potential glory. Glory be to the *cerveza*[16], and glory be to the last dance, and glory be to my father and to his *Bambino* and to Maria de Guadalupe and to the life I know I will have and to my mother. Wherever she was. If she was even alive. Glory be to God in the highest. Glory be to God in the highest.

I staggered into my room and grabbed the only framed photo I had of my father. In the picture he was leaning next to his Bambino with one arm extended toward the car. He'd been so proud of his car. On his face was a smile. Unusual for him. On one cheek was a smear of axel grease. He was young in this picture. Maybe it had been taken right before I was born. I couldn't be sure. I may have been too young to remember. I wished I was able to know that. I don't want to forget my father. I don't want anyone to forget him. I don't want anyone to forget me.

---

[16] English translation: "beer"

In the picture, he had most of his hair, unlike most of his life. He'd lost all his hair in his late twenties. Unlike me with my thick, black Mexican hair. In high school I'd taken good care of my hair. The ladies loved to play with my shiny black hair. Asked me questions of how I got it to look so good. I never told them my secret. A shampoo called Herbal Essence. That shit worked, yo.

It's crazy to know someone I talked to was now missing. He could have been kidnapped. He could be dead. He could have run away. He seemed like the running type, seemed like he was having something of a nervous breakdown. Everything in his life was laid out for him. He was so lucky. But all he could do was complain about it. All he could do was bitch and moan.

I didn't appreciate that kind of attitude. I wondered if the guy had ever gone to a poor country in Africa that might be desperate for medical attention. Or some place in South America. South America? Beautiful South America. If I had a motorcycle, I would drive from here all the way to the southern tip of South America. I would join a colony of penguins. They would make me their penguin king. We would spend the days diving for fish and the nights singing near a bonfire. That would be me, the penguin king. I would need to rent a tuxedo before I got there. It would be difficult to fit in without a tuxedo.

I was feeling tired. The beer had done a commendable job amplifying how psychologically fatigued I was. Psychologically, I was a prime candidate for someone like Freud to dissect. He would say something like, "Tell me about your mother." And I would say, "I never knew her." And he would go, in a thick German accent, "Aaaah! Vewry Intervesting! Tell me more." As if that really meant anything. Why does society think everything begins and ends with the mother?

I lay in my bed and put the almost finished bottle of beer on the nightstand, and then I closed my eyes holding my dad's picture. I fell asleep even though my boots were on.

Buzz! Buzz! Buzz! A hornet was trying to kill me with its stinger. Buzz! Buzz! Buzz! *Fucking hornet! I'll get you. Wait? What's that? You brought your friends? Fucking hornets. Always too chicken to face someone one on one. That's right hornet! I called your ass chicken. Ow! Fucker! Let's go. You and me hornet.* I went to slap the hornet with the back of my hand when….

CRASH!

I awoke to the realization I had slapped my bottle of beer off my nightstand. And now it lay broken on the floor. My cellphone buzzed. Someone was texting me. I flipped open the cell phone to read the first text: Jimmy. It's Jasmine. You busy?

Jasmine? What did she want? How did she get my number? Wait. I give her my number almost every time I see her at The Fish Bowl.

Jimmy. It's Jasmine again. Where are you? Read the second text.

Jimmy. It's Jasmine. Talk to me please. Read the third text.

I texted her back: Jasmine. Sorry. I was asleep. What's up? Are you okay?

I put the cell phone down and waited a few minutes. Nothing. I sighed a little knowing I would be agonizing for Jasmine to text me back. Was she up to one of her dirty tricks again? Damn her. I then realized I had fallen asleep in my work clothes. I decided I would take a shower. Damn her for trying to make me wait like this. A man needs to take his shower. After all cleanliness is something, something…. I can't remember the rest.

After my shower I ran to check my cell phone. Nothing. Feeling betrayed I decided to turn on my computer and check my email and maybe browse the Internet for porn.

Buzz! Buzz! Buzz!

I almost fell as I turned from my chair to grab my cell phone behind me. I flipped open the phone. Jasmine had sent me a text that read: Jimmy. You awake? Where are you now?

I'm home. In my room.

Mind if I come over?

Sure. Here's my address ...

Okay. Be there in fifteen minutes.

Fifteen minutes was not enough time to tidy up my raunchy apartment and make it somewhat presentable. I threw most of my dirty clothes in the closet and put all my dirty dishes in the sink. Hey, it wasn't a perfect apartment cleansing, but at least everything looked presentable. I gathered all my garbage and put it in the one place I always forgot to put it: the garbage can.

The clap of the evening's first thunder cut through the silent night. I looked out the window and within seconds it had begun to rain. I knew the rain would enhance the old odors of the house I lived in. I tried to see if I had any scented candles or one of the Plug-ins to cover the smell. Nothing but a can of Lysol. I sprayed the Lysol a little, but not too much. Too much Lysol would make my apartment smell like a janitor in a public restroom had come in to clean my apartment.

Buzz! Buzz! Buzz!

I'm downstairs. Let me in.

Be there in a few seconds. Don't knock on the door.

Okay.

I raced down the stairs of the house to the side door. I knew Jasmine would be waiting at the front porch. I worried she might knock on the front door. That wasn't a good thing. If Jasmine knocked on the door and the guy who lived on the first floor opened it I knew there would be trouble. The first floor was converted into a separate apartment occupied by a blonde-haired stoner. He spent more time drinking, getting tattoos, getting high, and less time attending classes. I wasn't in the mood to deal with his dumb ass. I never was. If only his parents knew how he was throwing their money away for his own selfish escapades. I would tell his parents if I could. I would suggest they invest instead in me and not their ungrateful offspring.

I ran outside the house into the rain. Jasmine stood on the porch looking out into the rainy night. She wore a black tank top underneath a dark blue jean jacket. She had on dark blue jeans with a pattern embroidered in the color of tan on the butt pockets. On her head she wore a large gray fedora looking hat. She had it tilted to the side almost covering one of her eyes. She was already a little drenched from the rain. Some of the mascara around her eyes was running. With the porch light her dark skin glistened in the rainy night and her teeth shown pure white when she smiled.

"Hey."

"Hey."

"What's up?"

"You going to let me in?"

"Sure. Yeah. Follow me. Wait. You don't mind getting a little wet? Do you?"

"Not at all."

We ran off the porch to the side of the house. I unlocked the side door to let her in first. Then we walked up the stairs to the attic that was my apartment.

"This is a strange setup. I'm surprised to see you still live here."

"Well, I still can't afford to live anywhere else."

She didn't say anything. I couldn't tell if she thought I was being clever or stating a fact. Either way I felt totally awkward. Her big brown eyes stared beyond my steel shield—I felt even more uncomfortable.

We entered my apartment and she showed herself to my couch and sat there as if she had always done so in the past and took off her hat. She shook her head to get some of the wet rain and help it air dry. I didn't know what to do next because I didn't know what she was expecting.

"Mind if I smoke?"

"No. Go ahead. Want something to drink?"

"Please. White Russian."

"Hmm. That's Kahlua and Vodka, right?"

"In some countries."

"Well, in my apartment that's a White Russian."

"Well, you going to debate with me all night about the ingredients of a White Russian or are you going to make me one?"

"Coming right up, doll face."

"Doll face. That's a good one. So, you're still single, right?"

"So, what brings you to my establishment?"

"Girl problems."

"Girl problems? Don't they have pills for that?"

"You're so funny. They've got pills for everything these days."

"Pills to make you small. Pills to make you tall. Pills to make you disappear."

I was feeling brave. I decided to lay it all out since she was already in my apartment: "Well, tell me. We both know you're not here to fuck. Unless you are which would be great because I for one am not interested in being in the friend zone. So, what's bothering you?"

"Suppose I did come here to fuck you."

"Suppose you did. And then suppose you came to use me."

"Suppose I did come here to fuck you and use you. Would you mind?"

"No, I wouldn't, I guess. But if that's the case then I would like to know."

"Why do you need to know? Sometimes part of the adventure is waiting for the reveal."

"The reveal? Sounds like a magic trick. Then I suppose for your next trick you'll disappear into thin air the next morning."

"Suppose I didn't leave the next day? Suppose I stayed?"

"Suppose you did. Then I'd have to have your head checked. Here," I handed her my version of a White Russian. And grabbed a bottle of beer for myself. She took a small sip and smiled as if surprised with my superb bartending skills.

"You're a horrible bartender, Jimmy."

"And you're a horrible person, Jasmine." I thought for a moment not sure where things were going. I said the first thing that came to my mind, "Maybe you should leave."

"Suppose I don't? What if I don't want to leave?"

"Suppose I want you to leave. Now."

Jasmine's eyes swelled up with tears. I knew she was about to lose it. I tried to counter by immediately apologizing. But it was no use. She was ready to cry. She wanted to cry. That may have been the only reason she came over. She wanted to cry on someone's shoulder and not feel alone. And it was my shoulder she wanted to cry on. And she was a horrible person for wanting me in that way.

I went over to sit next to her and let her cry on me. She smelled sexy and desperate. Her large breasts squished against me as I held her close. I could feel her erect nipples through her thin shirt. She wasn't wearing a bra. I really hated her at that moment.

"I'm sorry. I didn't mean—"

"No. Don't. It's not your fault. It's something else."

"What happened?"

"I don't know. I don't know who to trust anymore. And you. You've always been honest and straightforward. It never seemed like you were putting on a show. Everyone's always putting on a show."

"Well, it is karaoke."

"You know what I mean. I really need someone to trust right now. Can I trust you?"

"Sure. You can trust me. You can always trust me."

"Okay."

She cried some more. I let her cry until she had dried up off all her tears. When she finished crying she pulled back from me. I let her go. I grabbed my now warm bottle of beer and took a huge swig like I was some drunken cowboy extra in a John Wayne Western. Then I lit a cigarette. I needed a drag after all her crying. So much was going on inside of me. I felt hatred for her. I wanted to make love to her. I wanted to slap her. I wanted to kiss her.

"Thanks, Jimmy. I needed that."

"Don't mention it, Jasmine. Anytime. Lookit. You got a friend in me. Always."

"So sweet of you to say that. Even after all the mean things I've said to you in the past. Most people would not put up with that kind of treatment."

"Yes. Well. I guess I'm a glutton for punishment."

"It's good to know that someone who knows me likes me. Even if it's you."

"What are you talking about, Jasmine? Everyone likes you."

"No. Not everyone. Everyone wants to fuck me. Everyone wants to use me. There's a difference. It's not only men but women also. I thought I could trust women, though. I thought they were different than men. No. Everyone's the same. Everyone's a user. And now I'm using you. A little. But you don't mind, do you, Jimmy? What if we just use each other for a while? Two lonely people like us. We could pretend we're in love. We could pretend that for the rest of our lives."

"That's something I can't pretend to do, Jazz."

"It's been a long time since I've kissed man. I mean, really kissed a man. I remember it being rougher. Not soft and gentle like with a woman."

"You're acting crazy now. Your head's not on straight. Finish your drink."

"What if we were like companions for the evening? We could hold each other. I know you like holding me. I know you like how I smell. Wouldn't that be nice?"

"Jasmine. I have to be honest. I've never seen you like this before."

"You don't want to, do you? You don't want me anymore. I can tell. You don't want me because now I seem too weak to you. You think I'm always like the Jasmine in the bar? I'm not. I'm not. I'm not."

"No. It's not that. I do want you. I've always wanted you. But I don't want to take advantage of you. Not like this."

She leaned in and kissed me with closed lips. She then grabbed my chin forcing my mouth open. She opened her mouth and stuck her long tongue down my throat. At first her tongue felt like a snake covered in thick saliva. Her wet tongue awoke the saliva of my dry mouth. We shared a long wet kiss, twirling our tongues around each other's tongue, until she let go of me. It wasn't the kiss I had imagined I would have with her. The wet saliva from the kiss dripped out of the side of each of our mouths. I wiped it off hoping it didn't look like I was trying to wipe away her kiss.

She kissed me on the cheek and then lit another cigarette. She liked me now. At least that is what I thinking at that moment. The way someone feels when they're about to win a game. When they at first thought they weren't going to win and then they win. Of course she was probably playing me. Playing me for the fool that I am. And this wasn't a game of cards or checkers or Uno or Go Fish. This was a game of explosives. I had to make sure to keep my wits about me. Or else she might inject me with a dose of her venom.

"Oh! Look!" she exclaimed pointing at my TV. "It's *Double Indemnity* with Fred MacMurray. One of my favorite films." She turned up the volume. Loud. We watched Fred MacMurray narrate meeting his femme fatale, Barbara Stanwyck.

I looked over at Jasmine and wondered what thoughts were masquerading around inside her head. She had so many layers to peel away. Dr. Freud, where are you right now? "Ask her about her mother." No Dr. Freud. I'm not going to do that. "Then I can't help you. *Auf Wiedersehen.*"

"I didn't know you liked Film Noir?"

"There's a lot you don't know about me, Jimmy. I'm more than two big breasts and long legs that serves you drinks at a bar."

"No. You're also beautiful lips. Intoxicating eyes and a damn good ass. And very smooth dark skin. And silky black hair. You're my dream girl. Difference is you're real. You're not a dream."

"Woah. That's corny," she laughed. "Almost pathetic in a way. Does that ever work with other women? I bet not."

I could tell she was starting to revert back to her old self. So, I got up to throw away my now empty bottle of beer. I didn't want to drink any more alcohol. I opted for a glass of Nesquik chocolate milk. One of my favorite drinks. After all Aztecs invented chocolate drinks. And I was one of their descendants.

Jasmine fixated on the television set. And so I decided it would be best to fade into the background while drinking my Nesquik chocolate milk. When the movie broke into commercial Jasmine looked behind at me standing behind her in the kitchen.

"What are you doing over there? Come back here and sit with me."

"Okay."

I sat down next to her. I finished my cigarette and started another one. Jasmine motioned for a drag. I gave her my cigarette. I grabbed another from the pack of smokes on my coffee table and lit another for myself. She pulled off her shoes and lay on me like I was a big pillow. And we lay there the rest of night watching the movie as if we were some couple who had been married for twenty years.

After the movie ended Jasmine said she was feeling very tired. She got up and found my bedroom and jumped underneath the covers.

"Your bed is soft!" she yelled.

"I try my best to make it as luxurious and comfortable for someone like King Louis XIV. Or someone like that."

"Let's go to sleep. I'm tired. I love these pillows."

"Thanks. They were on sale at Target."

"Why do men always love to brag about finding something on sale? Look at this! I found it for this when it normally costs that. Honestly. Women don't find that attractive."

"Good to know."

"Wow. You've read all those books?"

Jasmine pointed at my stack of books I had accrued through my college years. By this time they were collecting a generous amount of dust.

"Yes. I've read all those books. I like to read."

"Shit. No wonder you're so weird. You're a big nerd."

"I'm intelligent. But, I'm not a nerd."

"Only a nerd would read this many books."

"No. Wrong. A nerd is an intelligent person who lacks basic social skills. I am an intelligent person, but I'm not socially awkward."

"You're weird."

"Okay. I'll admit it. I'm weird. But, I'm not afraid to talk to women."

"Don't remind me. How many times have you asked me out?"

"Whatever. You know you like that."

"What?"

"All the attention."

"What girl wouldn't?"

"Yeah. Well, here you are."

"Tell me something intelligent, nerd."

"Still on the nerd thing."

"There's nothing wrong with being a nerd. Sometimes being a nerd is sexy."

"Sexy? You think nerds are sexy? So, are you telling me you think Bill Gates is pretty sexy?

"No. But that Apple guy—"

"Steve Jobs."

"Yeah him. He's kind of cute. So, come on. Wow me with your intelligence."

"Okay. I'll try. You ready?"

"I've got nothing but time, Jimmy."

"We're all made from stardust."

"Woah. That's your big intelligent thought? I think I heard that before. It was either Shel Silverstein or Dr. Seuss. Or that acid trip I had that one time in Middle School."

"Acid trip in Middle School? Wow. No. Listen. Almost every element on Earth was formed at the heart of a star. See, stars owe their light to the energy released by nuclear fusion reactions at their cores. These are the very same reactions, which created chemicals like carbon or iron. These are the building blocks that make up the world around us. Uh, you know what a supernova is?"

"No."

"It's what they call it when a massive star explodes at the end of its life. So, when this star explodes it releases so much energy it creates these really heavy elements. And it also expels other elements across the universe scattering the stardust which now makes up all the planets—including Earth."

"You are a fucking nerd!" she laughed.

I smiled. I was too tired to respond or give a damn what she was saying. I only wanted to sleep now. Don't get me wrong. I wanted to bang her right then and there. But, with a little buzz going on and feeling fatigued from a hard day's night at work—I decided resting my body was more important than trying to force myself to perform. I wanted to be fully rested when it finally happened with Jasmine. That way I wouldn't make a horrible mistake and embarrass myself. Hopefully.

Treating me like a giant doll she manipulated my arms around her and laid her head on my chest. And within microseconds she was asleep. Of course she was! As for me? I spent most of the night wide awake unable to sleep. I didn't realize the excitement of having a woman like Jasmine in my bed. The same woman I spent many a lonely night fantasizing about, would keep me awake like this. Eventually, though I did finally fall asleep thanks to the sound of the rain outside. I love the sound of rain. It always brought calm to my being. In a world where sometimes it rains and sometimes it doesn't I liked it when it rained.

I was all but unconscious when an impulsive Jasmine aroused me awake with her sweet and tender kisses. She began by kissing me on the forehead. Then my cheek. She nibbled on my earlobe for a while. Then followed that with wet kisses on my neck. By the time her lips touched mine I was vigilant and returned her kiss with my lips and we both succumbed to our primordial desires. She whispered to me to take off my clothes but didn't wait for me to comply as she ripped them off herself. I didn't wait either for her to undress and was more than happy to help her out of her clothes. By the time we were both naked both of us were breathing like hungry wolves. We couldn't get enough of each other.

Both her breasts were even more perfect than I had imagined. I was too enamored with their shapes to estimate how big they were. I caressed each of her breasts—one at a time. I could tell this was arousing her as she squirmed a little from my touch. For a moment I felt like I was a thirteen-year-old boy touching his first breast. Then I cupped them in my hand and watched her nipples become erect. How was she was able to hide such nipples behind her shirts—I wondered. Only she and Houdini could manage such an illusion. She moaned each time after I placed my tongue around her nipples circling and investigating with great care. She then stopped me when I was halfway through with her second breast and said, "Hey. Like I told you earlier—there's much more to me than my breasts, baby."

"Yes there is," I said.

I then expanded my investigation to the rest of her body. She was more than eager to direct me to the places she preferred I place more attention and those places she preferred I ignore. I teased her for a while longer until I was finally between her legs. There was nothing she could do but allow me to explore everything with my wondering tongue. After some time her hips pulsated from pleasure and she grabbed my head and brought my mouth to her mouth. We kissed and she announced it was her turn to return the favor.

I lay on my back as she treated my body like a Roman god. I felt sexy and confident. I felt ready to take on the world. Her wet mouth on my erect cock was almost too much for me to handle. When she began to suck my balls I had had enough. No more foreplay. I rolled on top of her and slowly sank my cock inside her wet vagina. The warm wetness felt almost foreign to me. Had it been that long? But soon I forgot to worry about myself and focused on the mutual pleasure Jasmine and I were sharing. Who cares how long it had been. Sex! I was having sex with my dream girl. Sex! I moaned. She screamed in pleasure. Sex! She was so loud I worried for a moment that she might wake the Asian PhD student who lived in the room below me. Poor little guy. I was normally so careful to not disturb him. With each stroke the entire bed shook and our bodies hit the walls as we bounced around the bed. Sex! Changing position. Sex! Huffing and puffing. Sex! Slapping her ass. Sex! Slapping my ass. Sex! I never wanted this moment to end. I wanted it to last forever and forever. Sex! Sex! Sex! I remembered once hearing someone say sex with a gorgeous woman was man's retribution on every single thing that tried to destroy him in his life. Or did I read that once in a book? Either way that is exactly how I felt while Jasmine and I made love.

When we finally finished (and yes I lasted more than two minutes after not having sex in so long), we were both so exhausted we fell fast into a sound state of hibernation. The next time we would wake hundreds of years would pass and cars would be flying through the air like they did in *The Jetsons*. I think that was the most peaceful sleep I had since I was a young boy.

The next morning when I woke up Jasmine was gone. The smell of the perfume she wore that night lingered on the sheets and pillowcases. I sniffed my pillows for a long time. Wishing she was there and not gone. I didn't have to work today so I decided to sleep in. I wanted to dream about Jasmine. I wanted to dream about how I wished our night had never ended. I wanted to dream about making love to Jasmine for all eternity. Most of all I wanted to dream about kissing Jasmine. A long kiss hello instead of a long kiss that felt like a maybe. A maybe that lingered on no. A maybe that meant this would never last. I was tired of maybes. I wanted absolutes like Yes … or No.

I glanced over at my nightstand and saw a folded piece of yellow paper. Jasmine must have left a note. I reached over to grab it and opened the note. It also smelled like her perfume.

It read: Hey Lover. Sorry I had to go. Errands. You know how it is? Thanks for last night. I really needed that. I'll see you again soon. Kiss! Love, Jazz.

As I pondered these thoughts and fantasies I started to remember the first time I let Jasmine convince me she wanted me and no one else. I remembered how she burned me and left me to wallow in my sorrows with Norm my only confidant. I decided I would give her one more chance. But this time I was going to try to be more cautious with this second chance. Even Jesus got a second chance, right? Everyone deserves a second chance. Maybe she wasn't going to burn me this time. Maybe she left for a genuine good reason. I decided to let go of my negative thoughts and think about Jasmine in a good way. Until I awake later.

PART TWO

9

I opened my eyes. Two men wearing ski masks starred down at me.

"Good morning," said the larger one wearing a tight shirt. The shirt accentuated his muscles no doubt helped by consistent steroid usage.

"Or should we say, good day?" said the smaller one with a slight Texas drawl.

"True. It's nearly noon."

"Shame to waste such a beautiful day."

They both grabbed me and threw me from my bed onto the floor. The larger one put me in a headlock and dragged me across my bedroom through the hall into my living room. I didn't like that. As I lay there wondering what was going to happen next the little one ran up and kicked me in the ribcage and stomach a few times. He then swung his fist several times, hitting my helpless face. I didn't like that either.

"Where's the toilet?"

"I was wondering the same thing."

"Rodriguez. Where's the toilet?"

"Downstairs! It's a-a shared bathroom. For the whole house." I said.

"That won't do."

"Yes. I agree. Sit on the couch, Mr. Rodriguez. Now."

"I'll piss in your kitchen sink. And there ain't a thing you're going to do about it, Mr. Rodriguez."

I crawled across the floor to the couch. Climbed on it and sat up. I touched my throbbing head and noticed I was bleeding from the blood on my hands. They both sat down in nearby chairs. Silence. I didn't say anything. I was too busy trying to catch my breath and keep myself from crying. They both stared at me as if they were waiting for me to say something.

"I bet you're wondering why we're here. Aren't you?"

"The thought had crossed my mind," I said.

"You know why we're here."

"N-not really. Please. Enlighten me."

"Come. Come now. Don't be dumb, Mr. Rodriguez."

"Yes. It's unbecoming of you."

"I'm going to piss." The little Texan jumped up on my kitchen counter, pulled out his tiny member, and pissed into my kitchen sink. "Fucking coffee," he said.

"I told you, you drank too much coffee this morning. He always drinks too much coffee. That one." The larger one stood patiently waiting for his comrade until he concluded urinating.

"Finished. Damn! I feel better." He jumped down from the counter and rejoined us in the living room.

"We have a problem, Mr. Rodriguez."

"Big Problem. Your problem."

"Well, two problems. I suppose."

"It is believed you were the last person to see a lady who currently goes by the name Jasmine."

"That's not her real name?"

The little one got up and slapped me on the side of the face.

"No. Mr. Rodriguez. It is not."

"I knew she was no good. But I didn't think—"

"So, you admit. She was with you."

"She was with me last night. But she left this morning. I don't know where she is. She left a note."

"Where is the note, Mr. Rodriguez?"

"It's on my nightstand in my bedroom. What's this all about? Are you guys cops? How do you know my name?"

"Cops? Yes. We're cops who wear ski masks." The little one got up and slapped me again. Man! He slapped hard. The larger one went to my bedroom and came back with the note. He read it then handed to the little one who also read it.

"Errands?"

"Errands?"

"Yeah. Errands. You see. That's all I know. Is she in trouble?"

The little one raised his hand preparing to slap me again but this time I ducked before he was able to hit me. I tried to grab his arm but he slipped his arm away before I could and punched me in the cheek with his other hand. It became harder and harder to not cry but I did all I could to keep the waterfall from happening.

"I think he's telling the truth."

"I agree. You really have no clue. Do you?"

"Pathetic. Tsk. Tsk. Tsk."

"No. I don't. Can you please tell me with this is all about?" I said.

"Well, well, Mr. Rodriguez. You're very unlucky. Aren't you?"

"I've never been very lucky. Mexican curse, I think."

"Well you got across the border without a scar. Didn't yah, wetback."

"Fuck you. I was born here. I'm American."

"Temper. Temper. That's no way to speak to Christian God-fearing white folk. We could really hurt you. You don't want us to really hurt you, Mr. Rodriguez. Not like anyone would do anything about it. It would be one less job-stealing Spic to worry about."

"I think you already hurt me, man."

"Not true. Not true Burrito Rodriquez. Not true. We simply slapped you around, so to speak."

"My name's Jimmy. Not Burrito."

"We're only having a little fun. No harm no foul."

"Well, off we go."

"Yes. We must go. But before we do…." They both grabbed me and proceeded to give me another beat down until I went unconscious. When I awoke later they both were gone. Knowing I was alone I had a good cry. The cry of the century. The last time I cried this much was when my father passed away. Nothing wrong with a man crying alone—right?

After I wiped away the tears and blew my nose I jumped up and ran to my cell phone. I picked it up and dialed Jasmine's phone number. She didn't pickup. So I dialed it again. No answer. I hoped the third time would be the charm, but again, no luck. So I left a voicemail: "Jasmine. It's Jimmy. Lookit. Two guys wearing ski masks were here today. They told me they were cops but I don't buy it. They were looking for you. They beat me pretty good. Be careful. Please be careful. I hope you're okay." I hung up the phone. Worried the voicemail wasn't enough. I decided to text her the same message. When I finished I looked at the time. It was 3:00PM. A whole day almost gone. I called Norm.

"What?"

"It's Jimmy."

"Figured."

"What are you doing?"

"Curing cancer, evidently. You?"

"You're not going to believe what happened to me."

"Try me."

"When you're done curing cancer meet me at my house. Pronto."

"Right. Evidently I'm a little hungry."

"Me too. Okay. Let's do that."

"Right."

I knew it would take Norm twenty some minutes to get here. Enough time for a quick shower to help clean off the unmanly tears staining my face.

After the shower I stared in disbelief at my reflection. A black eye. Bruises on my cheek. My lip was a little swollen. They left my nose alone. I found that surprising. My torso and lower abdomen were also bruised from their kicks and punches.

"Someday I'm going to teach you how to punch, kid."

Clint Eastwood was leaning in the corner of the bathroom smoking a cigarillo.

"What's stopping you from teaching me now?"

"Alright. Here's what you do. When you punch, you start from in your chest. Then out. And twist your arm while you punch. See? Don't swing from the side like an idiot. Leaves you open. Always have one arm up as protection. Know what I mean?"

"I could have used your help back there, Clint."

Clint laughed. "You know I can't help you in that way. But maybe I can try to guide you in the right direction."

"Where's Steve?"

"Steve? Steve's busy. You're stuck with me for now, kiddo."

"Steve's always busy."

Clint squinted at me. Puffed his cigarillo. Exhaled the smoke and said, "Yeah."

I waited outside on the porch smoking my cigarette. Norm pulled up and honked his horn. I stood up and got into his car.

"Jesus Christ! What happened to you?"

"I'll explain later. Need to get some food in me first. I'm starving."

"All right. Evidently I've got coupons. Two for one."

"Sweet."

And without thinking Norm turned on Cake's "Going the Distance" as if nothing had happened. He turned up the bass and then put on his favorite sunglasses.

"Something so familiar is also sometimes comforting. Don't you agree?"

"Yep. I suppose."

When we arrived at the diner Norm ordered their biggest sandwich. I ordered soup with some bread and iced tea. I'd hoped that would be easy on my stomach. We didn't use the coupon.

"So, what happened?"

"I got beat up."

"Evidently. I see that. Who fucking beat you up?"

"I don't know. They were wearing ski masks?"

"Were you robbed?"

"Nope?"

"Raped?"

"Shut up. I don't think so."

"When? Where? How? Why? Tell me. Evidently I'm on the edge of my seat over here."

"They broke into the apartment. I don't know how. Not like it's hard to break into that old house I live in. It happened earlier today. I was sleeping and then I wake up and there's these two guys hovering over me. Who knows how long they were there watching me sleep. They were asking me questions about Jasmine. They wanted to know where she had been and if I knew where she was going."

"Really?"

"Yeah. Oh yeah. I forgot to tell you. Jasmine spent the night with me last night?"

"Bullshit."

"Not bullshit. It happened. Now looks like karma is making me pay for it."

"So it seems."

"Did they say why they were looking for Jasmine?"

"No only that…. they said Jasmine wasn't her real name."

"Fake name?"

"That's what they claimed."

"No shit?"

"Yep."

"So what are you going to do?"

"We're going to the Fish Bowl. I need to ask Emilio some questions."

"Emilio? We?"

"You're my ride, brother."

"You paying for my gas?"

"It's not like you got anything better to do."

"I was going to spend the day doing some writing for you information."

"Same story?"

"Of course. This is the story I will be remembered for. I'm certain of it. Had a dream about that happening to me. It was a wonderful dream. Then you woke me up."

"Robots? You think a story about robots will make you famous."

"Two words: Isaac Asimov."

"I don't see the relation."

"Evidently. Thanks for the vote of confidence."

"Don't mention it."

"Wait. What about Jasmine? Why not ask her what's going on?"

"I already tried. She's not answering her phone or my texts. She's unreliable anyway. But I'm sure I will hear from her eventually. Right?"

"You're the one who spent the night with her."

"I know. She's my Achilles' heel."

"Ain't that the truth? Why not let it be? You know. Let dogs lie with…. I can't remember how it goes—"

"Let sleeping dogs lie."

"Right! Thanks. If she wants you to know she'll tell you."

"And what if she doesn't get that chance? What if they kill her? I may be her only hope to stay alive. I mean, those guys acted professional. This wasn't the first time they paid someone a visit. They weren't two random creeps looking to beat some Mexican. They were methodical. You catch my drift?"

"I've been meaning to tell you. You really don't look Mexican. Evidently."

"This coming from the guy who thought all Mexicans looked like the Taco Bell dog."

"Bite me."

We finished the food and somehow spent the rest of meal arguing about politics. It was strange how easy it was to forget about what had happened to me. Even when engaged in a heated political debate with Norm's conservative outlook on the world. I figured Norm was trying to do me a favor by helping me take my mind off the situation. When I had finished drinking the rest of my iced tea I remembered the mission. I wanted answers.

When we were back in the car I tried calling Jasmine a few more times. I sent her several texts. Nothing. She was incognito for the time being.

"Speaking of some strange shit," Norm said. "Did you hear about that med student who went missing?"

"Yeah. They said his name was, Ian Noone."

"I know! I was watching about it on the news and realized I never got his name that night."

"It wouldn't change anything."

"I know. It's kind of crazy. You know?"

10

NORM and I walked into the bar at the same time. I kept my sunglasses on to try to hide some of my bruises and my black eye. "Vitamin C" by Can blared from the speakers. The place was more or less empty. Save for a few drowsy alcoholics and flies buzzing around in circles. Flies who had nothing to do in their forty-eight hour existence, but wait here to die. The place stunk of fish. I peeked into the kitchen and saw that the cooking staff was in the middle of unpacking a fresh shipment of seafood. They yelled at each other in a mix of Spanish slang and dialects I wasn't privy to. They were throwing around the food like it was nothing from the various crates into the large freezers and large storage units. Bachata music played from one of the cheap radios the Latinos kept in the kitchen. A mix of accordions, horns, and acoustic guitars formed a unique sound. A few of them looked at me as if they were waiting for me to say something to them in their native tongue. I did a quick nod up with my head and left. I was often intimidated by those who were fluent in Spanish. I felt like an imposter if I tried to speak to them. Even though I looked like most of them.

Emilio was sitting at a small table in The Fish Bowl's balcony. The table was between the sunshine and the shade. As the earth rotated the shade decreased and the sunshine increased. The chilly winds swept through the piercing sunshine. This is Ohio, after all. He puffed away his Cuban cigar. He ran numbers from several stacks of receipts with his calculator and made notes in a large registry notebook. Also on the table were two cell phones, an old pager, a cordless phone, a bottle of aspirin and a half-used container of hand sanitizer. He wore a marble gray cardigan framed with a big shawl collar. Underneath he wore a well-pressed white dress shirt, with the first two top buttons left unbuttoned. A pair of white slacks, also neatly ironed. On his sockless feet he had on a pair of polished loafers. He fanned himself a few times with his fedora. And then wiped some of his sweat off of his face with a cloth made of one hundred percent genuine silk.

He took a sip from a glass of what looked like iced tea. As we came toward him he closed his registry notebook and shifted in his chair acknowledging us with a rather uneasy demeanor. He was always this way when doing accounting in his books and going over his numbers. I elected to try to speak a little Spanish this time hoping it might ease him a little. With Emilio I was not as afraid as I was with other fluent Spanish speakers for some reason. During periods of deep boredom I had decided to teach myself more Spanish to try to connect better with a part of me I knew so little about. But, whenever I attempted to speak a little Spanish, the fluent Spanish speaker used that as a cue. A cue to continue the conversation total Spanish including all the idioms.

"*Hola, Emilio. ¿Qué tal?*[17]"

"Jimmy. *Bueno*, Jimmy."

"*¿Como está, usted?*"

"*¿Qué estás haciendo aquí?¿Hay algo que quiera decirme?¿Recibió algunas bolas de toro?*[18]" Emilio said.

---

[17] English translation: "Hello, Emilio. How are you?"

[18] English translation: "What are you doing here and is there anything you wanna tell me? Did you get some bull's balls?"

"Del dicho al hecho hay mucho trecho,[19]*"* I said.

"Quítese los lentes de sol[20]*."*

I took off my sunglasses and Emilio's eyes widened when he noticed my black eye.

"Más torcido que un bejuco. ¿No?[21]*"*

Norm, didn't know Spanish but he understood Emilio's reaction after I took off my sunglasses. "He got beat up," Norm said.

"Entre y tome una silla[22]*,"* Emilio said.

"Gracias," I said.

"Okay. Enough of the damn Spanish. Evidently, I don't speak it and can't understand most of it." Norm said.

Emilio winked at Norm. Norm and I stood for an uneasy moment. Emilio grabbed his cigar and puffed a few times. He squinted. The bright sun shined in his eyes. It was a sunny but chilly day.

"Qué....What happened to you Jimmy?" Emilio asked.

"Like I said, he got beat up," Norm said.

"I heard you the first time, Norm. You think I'm hard of hearing?"

"Well, you asked the same question twice."

Emilio chewed some of the ice from his iced tea. With his free hand he motioned for one of the waitresses. She didn't look familiar. I assumed she must have been new. The employees at this place seem to leave as soon as they were hired. The waitress had a stoic quality to her sexiness. Which offered no passion, unmoved by joy or grief with an unavoidable necessity to her presence. She had a deadeye stare that focused on the bar's scattered lights from time to time. She never seemed to look at someone, but through them. She wore a mini skirt revealing her long legs covered

---

[19] English translation: "Easier said than done, it is a long way."

[20] English translation: "Take off your sunglasses."

[21] English translation: "More than a twisted vine. Right?"

[22] English translation: "Come in and take a seat."

in the back by her long curly hair. The security camera followed the waitress as she walked over to us in high heel boots.

"This is Tala. She's new here. Tala, ask them what they want."

"What do you want?" she said.

"Uh, your number first. And then a drink." Norm said.

Emilio and I rolled our eyes.

"My number? You really want my number? What do you expect to happen? You think I would really give my phone number to someone like you? How old are you? Fifty? Are you some kind of pedophile? You like the young ones? Oh, you probably think I'm also an escort because I work in this kind of bar, right? And not only are you old you're also fat and balding from the looks of it. You even stink a little. And that's pretty bad considering this place smells like fish right now. I can smell you over the fish. If you weren't sitting with my boss I would tell you to go screw yourself and send you to another waitress. But, since you are sitting with my boss I have to serve you. But, I don't deserve to be disrespected. I'm not a whore. I'm a waitress. This is not my chosen life's profession. This is a means to an end. So.... what do you want?"

"Um, I'll have an iced tea." Norm said.

She turned her dead eyes on me as she waited for my drink request.

"Uh, a coke, please."

"That's it?" she asked raising an eyebrow.

"Yes." I said. "Only a coke, please."

Emilio motioned her away.

"Where did you find her?" Norm asked.

"I liked her personality. She has spunk, no?" Emilio said.

"I'll say. That one's a cold-blooded bitch. I think I'm in love." Norm laughed.

"So, Jimmy. Tell me what happened to you, *hijo*[23]?"

"I fell down some stairs."

"You fell down some stairs?"

"Okay. Two men wearing ski masks paid me a visit this morning. They were looking for Jasmine, but instead found me. They decided to take their mistake out on me."

"Now, why were they looking for Jasmine, in your apartment?"

"Jasmine spent the night with me last night."

"Jimmy. Jimmy. Jimmy. Why would you get yourself mixed up with that kind of woman? She's nothing but trouble."

"Seems to me you like trouble more than me. Seems to me you prefer to have people who like to give and take a little trouble. You carry trouble wherever you go, Emilio. Let's be honest here. Everyone kind of knows you're a demigod of trouble. Am I right? You know I'm right. I mean, with all your shady connections. Or those people whom you employ. Like the last waitress—"

"Tala was being defensive. Norm should know better than to talk to a lady like that. It's unbecoming of a gentleman, *cabrón*[24]. Jasmine is really trouble, *mi hijo*. *Mira*, she is the worm in your drink. She will turn on you. Like a snake. Remember what I always tell you: snakes always bite back."

"I want to know what you know. What do you know about Jasmine's trouble? Tell me. Now."

"Are you trying to tell me what to do? You think you can do that, *hijo*? You think you have the right to tell me what to do? On whose authority? You have no authority."

"I want answers. I need answers. Maybe if I know what's going on I can help."

---

[23] English translation: "son"

[24] English translation: "asshole" or "dumbass" or "bastard"

"You can't help her. No one can help her. She helps herself. And why don't you help yourself by leaving her alone and backing off, mi amigo."

"Look I know something is going on. I didn't graduate cum laude by pure luck alone. I'm rather astute. There's a person missing now. The last time anyone saw him was in this same bar. He was a med student. The news say his name was Ian Noone. Ring a bell? I know I saw you talk to him that other night. And I know Big Ray and the med student did not get along well during their brief encounter. And now there's people looking for Jasmine. And those people looking for Jasmine are definitely not cops. Is there a connection? Tell me, Emilio!"

"You know if you were anyone else, talking the way you are to me right now, I would have your tongue cut out your mouth, *hijo*."

"I'm not your *hijo*."

"No. You are not. But you are like a son to me. *Sí*, you are a smart kid. But you have no nose for this kind of stuff. You don't know when to leave something alone that should be left alone. Maybe this is because you watch too many superhero or gangster movies. Or read too many comic books. You Americans always do."

"We're not leaving until you tell us something."

"You want me to tell you something? Okay. I will tell you something. Something I should have said a long time ago. To the both of you. You two are like germs. You come here and infest this place with the plagues of your sad unfortunate lives. But, in my business I have to sometimes cater to losers such as the two of you. Losers are my best customers, you see. But, Jimmy you're not supposed to be a loser. Yet you think you are so you are becoming one. And it saddens me deeply, *hijo*. You are throwing your whole life away hanging out with Norm and the rest of the rat-infested bacteria that hounds my place of business. I clean my hands and body as much as I can because I am disgusted by your breed of people.

"Look at Norm. He's in his forties. Fat and balding. Where do you work, Norm? Wait. Wait. Don't tell me. I know. I know everything. You work in a grocery store. You have wasted your entire life on beer, karaoke, and being other people's whipping boy. No? And don't let me get started on your fantasy role-playing games. Perhaps that was always your lot in life. But, I have a feeling you were once like Jimmy. No? Once young and ambitious. Once full of dreams. And when did you give up? When did you stop dreaming, *cabrón*? You run around like you're in your twenties. You hit on women who don't want anything to do with you because they're young enough to be your daughter or even granddaughter. And then feel depressed about it? Be a man! Stop chasing one of your masturbating fantasies. From the calluses on your hands I can tell you are a habitual masturbator. How much of your pathetic life have you wasted masturbating? When was the last time you had a real woman in your life who wasn't your mother? Better yet, when's the last time you got laid? You probably hate me now. I don't care. The truth is as much as you hate what I'm telling you it won't stop you from coming back here. You need this place more than a baby needs its mother's milk. Because without this bar, without me, you know you are nothing but a wasted life, Norm. My bar offers you a temporary escape. You want me to tell you something? Well this is what I'm telling you. And now I've told you. So, if you please leave me alone now. Do not wait for your drinks. But, please come back on karaoke night. Always come back so I can take your money. Leave. I have a business to run. I have a life to live. Unlike you two. Now go."

Emilio turned his attention back to his receipts and ignored us. Norm's jaw dropped open. He was flustered and humiliated. We both stood up and backed away from the embarrassment of Emilio's words.

"Leaving so soon?" Tala said holding our drinks.

"Evidently I'm not thirsty now. Thanks, though."

"Thanks for wasting my time, old man."

"Hey. Why don't you back off." I said. Norm patted me on the shoulder.

"Jimmy. It's okay. Let's go."

We walked down the steps and out the door. Our heads between our legs like we had been knocked out cold in the first round of an amateur boxing match.

"Jimmy. You got a drag?"

"Sure. Here, buddy."

I handed Norm a cigarette and we sat near a small fountain that had been inoperable for several weeks.

"Lookit. Emilio's an asshole for saying that."

"Don't worry about it. I don't know what else to do? I get bored sometimes."

"Bored?"

"Yeah. Bored. My life is boring. The only highlight for me is karaoke. Karaoke is not boring. At karaoke I'm someone special. I'm something more than a guy who stocks food in a grocery store. You know that novel I've been writing. Well, truth is I haven't really written much. All I've written are lot of notes scattered around in various notebooks. And some of those notebooks have been lost over time. But, I haven't written anything substantial. I haven't been able to make anything meaningful in my life. Look at me. I'm forty-four years old. I work in a grocery store as a stocker and not as a manager. But, it wasn't supposed to be this way. This wasn't supposed to be how my life was going to turn out. I assumed I was going to do great things. I was expected I was going to make a difference. Evidently, I haven't. My whole life is one lump of boredom and missed opportunities. I'm not stupid. I knew that waitress wouldn't give me her number. But I always think it's fun to try. What's the harm in asking? At this point I already know what the answer is. I've come to accept my lot in life. I'm a loner for the most part. At least, I was until we became friends. And you're one of the only friends I've got. My best friend is twenty years younger than me. But having you as a friend has made my life less boring, Jimmy. You remember that time we went to that 80's dance club and we signed up for one of those contests? And we both were so drunk we didn't even hear them call our name? That was hilarious. And you were dancing with that girl who didn't know anything about the 80's. And I was dancing with her cute chubby friend who kept rubbing my stomach for good luck like I was a fat Buddha. Good times. Good times... But, I have to agree with Emilio, though. You don't want to turn into me. You can't give-up, buddy. If anything, if I don't get a second chance in my life, at least I can gain it vicariously through you. You know what I mean?"

"Lookit. Norm, you're not a loser. You're my best friend. You're funny as hell. You're one of the craziest people I know. I'm proud that you're my friend. You're a good person, Norm. Never forget that. I get bored too. I don't like being bored. I hate being bored. I want to do so many things with my life. But, here we are. What do we do? What do we do, now? Look at everything around us. This whole city is rotting away. The whole place is covered in dust. There is no future for me or anyone else at the moment. My generation didn't even get a chance to do anything great. They promised us the stars and gave us a desert of failure to wonder for eternity."

"You have your whole life ahead of you, Jimmy. You need to realize that. Evidently, I've never tried to make a difference. Maybe I could make a difference. Maybe I can change something or help someone."

"Yeah. Maybe. It's never too late."

"I liked that kid. The med student? What was his name again?"

"Ian Noone, I think."

"Yeah. He was kind of a whiner but he seemed genuine. Know what I mean?"

"I guess."

"And Jasmine's messed up, but who isn't messed up? Deep down inside I know she's a decent person."

"Right."

"No!" Norm said as he threw down his cigarette shaking his head. He paced around the fountain getting more and more worked up. "No. This isn't right. I've let too many things slip by me. No! No! No! Well, I'm not going to let it happen anymore."

"What are you saying?"

"Fuck Emilio! Fuck him! He doesn't know everything." His whole body shook from the rush of adrenaline. "We came here to get answers and that is exactly what we're going to do. We're going to get answers. We're going to help Jasmine and hopefully help Ian Noone. If he's even alive. That person was going to school to save lives. We save his life we can save more lives through him. Follow me, Jimmy," he yelled.

His pale skin turned somewhat red from all the boiling blood coursing through his veins. His now reddened skin made him appear more menacing than I have ever seen him look before. Like a sunburned Incredible Hulk. Gone was the nonchalant always positive demeanor of the man who would let most of everything roll off his chest. Gone was the person who would be more likely to stop a fight than start a fight. Gone was the gentle giant I had come to know and love.

"What are you going to do?"

"Follow me, dammit!" Norm said, looking like a ball of testosterone-induced rage. Huffing and puffing he slammed open the bar's door and ran up the stairs to The Fish Bowl. I tried to keep up but the usually slow moving Norm was moving faster than me, a onetime marathon runner.

"Stay with him!" Clint Eastwood yelled in my ear.

"I'm trying!"

"That's your friend. Get his back. Make sure you got his back!" Clint said.

Standing at the door was Big Ray. He must have slipped by us while we were talking outside near the fountain. He was sitting at his chair looking at his phone, probably checking his text messages. But, he was about to get one very big surprise. Norm was running and stomping right toward him like a caged bull suddenly set free. Before Big Ray had a chance to react, Norm had him on the floor in a chokehold. Big Ray was more than surprised. Even I was surprised.

"W-What the fuck, Norm?" Big Ray said.

"We're going to talk to Emilio. And you're not going to give us any trouble. You hear me? No trouble from you, Big Ray."

"No onez grabs me like 'dis. Ize is going to killz you when I gets my handz on yuze."

"How are you going to do that when you'll be sleeping?"

Norm tightened his grip around Big Ray's neck. Big Ray was choking for air. His already bulging eyes bulged out even further. He kept tapping Norm's shoulder hoping Norm would relent. But, this wasn't a professional wrestling match. This was a real fight. And Big Ray was about to lose. As Big Ray began to relinquish his consciousness only then did Norm loosened his grip around Big Ray's enormous neck. He wanted to knock Big Ray out, not kill him. After several more minutes of struggle, Big Ray finally closed his eyes, and passed out. Norm let go of Big Ray and gently laid him on the ground.

When Norm rose, Emilio was standing next to Tala, fidgeting with his half-smoked cigar.

I showed up to see the aftermath of a sleeping Big Ray. I couldn't help but notice what was playing over The Fish Bowl's speakers: Danzig's "Mother." Life is indeed very crazy, sometimes.

I dragged Big Ray's body into a nearby utility closet and locked him inside. Norm looked up huffing and puffing and huffing and puffing some more. He did not appear at all tired from his recent bout with Big Ray. Although, his balding head was covered in sweat.

"Emilio! The exact man I was hoping to see!"

"Norm. Calm down. You don't want to make things worse."

"Haven't you heard? It can't get any worse for me. I'm already at bottom. According to you I have nothing and am nothing. So I have nothing to lose."

Norm lunged at Emilio and grabbed him by the collar and threw him down on the ground.

"T-t-take it easy."

"Sure. I'll take it easy. Evidently I'll take it real easy."

He picked up Emilio and sat him in his chair and pulled up a chair in front of Emilio. Emilio glared at Norm.

"You are a dead man, Norm. You know that? A dead man, *cabrón*."

"Funny. I feel very much alive. In fact, right now I feel more alive than I've ever felt in a very long time. I guess, I have you to thank for that."

"*¡Puta madre!*[25]"

Norm slapped Emilio hard on the cheek with the back of his hand.

"I don't know much Spanish, but I do know what that means. I have worked in a kitchen in a diner as a dishwasher. The place was full of Salvadorians. Let's try to be civil here and keep our mothers out of this conversation."

I walked up slowly to them and pulled a chair between Norm and Emilio as if I was going to mediate. Emilio looked at me desperate for a sign I was on his side.

"Jimmy. Chain your dog. What is this all about?"

---

[25] English translation: "Holy Shit" or "mother fucker"

"Lookit. I didn't want to do it this way. But you left us no choice," I said.

"There's always a choice," Emilio said. Blood dripped from the side of his mouth. Tala stood there not sure what to do.

"Hey bitch!" Norm yelled at Tala who jumped from Norm's invigorated bark. "Why don't you get your boss a napkin? And keep your fucking mouth shut if you know what's good for you."

Tala grabbed a napkin and brought it Emilio.

"Wipe the blood off his cheek," Norm ordered.

Tala did as she was told. She fidgeting with the blood soaked napkin. The sure composure she had earlier was displaced by perturbed indecisiveness.

"Tala. Tell me something about yourself. And don't try to lie because I'll be able to tell the difference. Tell me your deepest darkest secret. Something you wouldn't even tell your closest B.F.F."

"Tala, you don't have to say anything to him. This beast doesn't deserve to know anything about you." Emilio said. Norm twisted Emilio's arm some more. Small tears of pain poured out of Emilio's eyes. His face grimaced and contorted from the pain. "Let go. *Por favor*. Let go," Emilio pleaded.

"Emilio. You've never seen or felt pain as personified as what you see before you. Tala. I'm waiting."

"Norm. I think—" I started to say, but Norm cut me off before I could finish.

"I'm in control now, Jimmy. When it's your turn I'll let you speak. But, right now I want to know something about, Tala. I want Tala to give me something she wouldn't want anyone else to know about her. I believe I deserve that much."

"Careful Jimmy," Clint whispered in my ear. "I think he's two-facing you!"

"Okay. Okay. I'll say something," Tala said. Norm giggled with delight. I was seeing a new side to Norm. A more sadistic side, or maybe it was the beast Norm had kept inside him for so many years, until one day he had no choice but to let it out to roam the earth for all of eternity. I was certain Norm was a werewolf now. If only I had a silver bullet or two. And a handgun. Yes, I needed a handgun.

Tala narrowed her eyes and approached me first. She sat on my lap wrapping her legs around me and kissed me with a strange since of urgency. She turned around, got up and grabbed a chair. She pulled it close to Norm. Norm was holding Emilio's arm with a grip so tight pliers couldn't remove them. He wasn't going to let Emilio out of his sight for all the whores in Tijuana.

"I'm going to tell you something fat man. But know this: I'm telling you this because you are making me. I will never kiss you. Not for all the gumdrops or fairy dust in the entire world. To emphasize that fact I kissed your friend over there. Who, even though is kind of a loser like you, he is cute enough and young enough to kiss. Hell! I'd even have sex with him any day over your disgusting fat body. In fact, I'd screw him right now if he asked me." She then lunged herself on Norm kissing him more passionately than she kissed me. They locked tongues and Norm grabbed one of her butt cheeks with his free paw of a hand. She grabbed his crotch and rubbed it a few times. For a brief moment, Norm loosened his grip on Emilio. But before letting go, realized it and slapped her away, twisting Emilio's arm again.

"I see you like to talk. But you don't seem capable of doing the thing I asked you to do. You still owe me a secret."

Tala rubbed her cheek now red from the slap Norm had bequeathed her. She did her best to retain her dignity by fixing her hair and checking her clothes were on her straight and holding back her the raindrops that were building up in her eyes.

"Very well. Fat man. A story is what you want then a story is what you will get. I can tell something about you.

You are very perverted aren't you?" Norm didn't respond but waited breathing heavily through his mouth like a wild wildebeest. "I'm as perverted as you are. In fact I'm more perverted than anyone here. If you really had me you wouldn't know what to do with me. You wouldn't know what I would do to you."

"Enough of the theatrics. Story! Now!" Norm said as he slammed his fist on the table.

"I'm trying to build up to that…. I had this boyfriend in high school who was into perverted things. Really perverted things. You see, when he was thirteen he broke into his father's secret porno collection. Only his father didn't keep regular pornos. Nope. His cup of tea was sadomasochist porn. After watching these pornos my boyfriend was, how do you say…. hooked. He thought that's what sex was. Anyway, like father like son. Right? He liked to be spanked really hard. Not with a hand. But with a whip. I'm mean until he was bleeding. And he liked it when I strangled him during sex. He loved it. One day when we were having super kinky sex he thought it would be fun to suffocate himself while having sex with me. So, he grabbed a plastic bag and a rubber band and put the plastic bag on his head and sealed it with the rubber band around his neck. Unfortunately, he was having such a great orgasm he didn't realize he was also taking his last breath of oxygen. So, he died right underneath me. Only thing was, when I realized he was dead I then realized something about myself. I wasn't done. And even though he was dead he had a tremendous hard-on. In fact I think he was harder than I had ever seen him before. So, what's a girl to do? Am I right? I got back on top of him and finished until I was done. Then I climbed out his bedroom window and left him there for his parents to discover him. I had only been going out with him for a few months and we weren't very public with our relationship. Long story short, no one ever thought sweet little innocent me, was with him. Still want my phone number, fat man?"

After she finished telling her story I almost threw-up in my mouth.

"Well, evidently, that's beyond fucked up. I've heard enough. You stay over there. I'll get your phone number later. Maybe. Now, Emilio, I believe my friend over there has some questions for you. Jimmy?"

I cleared my throat. "Okay. Emilio. Where's Jasmine?"

"How the hell should I know? She doesn't know where she is herself half the time."

"Emilio. Where is, Jasmine?"

"I told you. I don't know? I honestly don't know."

"I'm not sure if I believe you. But, we'll go back to that in a second. What do you know about, Ian Noone? Or those two men who beat me up?"

Emilio laughed shaking his head. "You two are idiots! You think you're a detective now, Jimmy?" Norm grabbed Emilio's arm and twisted it. Emilio cried from the pain.

"Remember," Norm began, "It was your words that brought us to this climatic scene. Keep pushing it, Scarface. And I really can't predict what's going to happen to you next." Emilio looked at Norm somehow knowing his threats were not hollow.

"Okay. Okay. Okay. Let go. Please. *Por favor.* Please." Norm let go of Emilio's arm and we waited for Emilio to spill his beans. He rubbed his arm not used to that kind of pain.

"Water. Please. I need a drink of water."

"Get him some water." Norm said to, Tala. Tala ran and grabbed a glass of water and handed it to Emilio. Emilio drank it down as if he had been lost in the desert for forty days and forty nights.

"Okay. Now I want you to grab us a bottle of The Fish Bowl's best whiskey and three... NO fuck it! Four glasses."

Tala smiled and ran to grab everything. She came back in no time with the glasses and the whiskey.

"Great. Now pour a shot of whiskey for all us. Including one for yourself, Tala." Tala did as she was told. Norm raised his glass.

"Everyone's gonna drink a shot of whiskey. And after we're done you're all gonna slam your glass down upside down. That's how it's done. Do it."

We all complied. The whiskey was both strong and smooth. I never had whiskey so rich in flavor and so smooth down the throat. Whiskey. A drink made from fermented grain mash aged in wooden casks made generally of white oak. The flavors of whiskey are unique only to this type of spirit, rendering an almost magical experience. I thought of men in nineteenth century suits drinking whiskey together while discussing politics and business and carrying canes and wearing top hats and white scarfs. Slam!

"Ah, whiskey," Clint Eastwood whispered in my ear. "A drink so tender and magnificent one cannot deny its existence. Good for the good. Bad for the bad. And ugly for the ugly."

"Alright. Again!" Norm demanded. We all complied save for Emilio. He didn't like Norm barking orders at him. Slam!

"Neanderthal," Emilio said to Norm. Norm returned Emilio's glare with a large Cheshire Cat grin.

"Again!" Norm said. By this time we all had gulped down three shots of whiskey. I was starting to have a little buzz from the alcohol. The effects of the alcohol were quick considering how small the shot glasses were. Norm eyes started to look a little glazed. Even Emilio was starting to relax a little from the alcohol. Slam!

"Now," I said. "Where were we? Ah, yes. We were about to find out the mystery behind Jasmine and Ian Noone. Were we not, Emilio?"

Bang! Bang! Bang! "Let me out! Ize iz gonna murderz yuze!" Big Ray yelled out from inside the utility closet.

"We're not going to let you out unless you promise to behave." Norm said.

"Norm. You fat bald fuck! Ize is going to murderz yuze once I getz outta here."

"In time my friend! In time!"

"Emilio," I said.

"*Bueno*. You two are looking for answers. Answer to questions you should already know. Answers to things that have always been right in front of you. But, you have always been either too drunk or too occupied with self-pity. Now you ask me to be your guide through the labyrinth of life."

"Don't trust him, Jimmy. He's no good," Clint whispered in my ear.

"Got no choice," I whispered back.

"Often what you see on the surface is a façade. Everything is a façade. Remember my friends, everyone is always pretending. We are all great pretenders. Pretenders to our past. Pretenders to our present. Pretenders to our future. Like this person here." Emilio pointed at Tala. "She's a worthless pretender. She's not a good pretender, though. Too easy to see through her cloak of lies. With a little push and she's pudding in your fingers."

Emilio then reached inside his cardigan and pulled out a .38 revolver. Before anyone could do anything to stop him he pointed the revolver and shot Tala cold right in front of us. She fell straight to the ground. Emilio, knowing how small the rounds a .38 are, shot her two more times and then a third time in the head, execution style. He then pointed the gun at Norm. Norm and I jerked our bodies.

"No. No. No. Don't get up. Don't move. If answers are what you want then answers are what you are going to get. That was an introduction, so to speak. An introduction to my thesis about reality. And you both have earned the right to know what I know. To be real. I haven't shot

someone in almost twenty years." We sat back down.
Emilio poured himself a generous amount of whiskey in the
empty glass that was once occupied by water.

"First of all I had to kill her. If she knew what I
would tell you I could not trust her to tell other people. I do
not know her, as well as, I know Jasmine or Big Ray or you,
Jimmy. Secondly, her blood is on both of your hands. She
was an innocent bystander and you forced her to participate
in this Greek tragedy. But then again, aren't they all
innocent bystanders? I cannot tell you anything about
Jasmine or where she is now. As far as I know she could be
in Hawaii. Or maybe she will show up to work tomorrow. I
never know. But, she is like a little sister to me. *Mí hermanita*[26].
A very troubled *hermanita*. I guess even I can show
compassion from time to time.

"Now on to other stories. You want to know about
the medical student. The kid who you liked so much and
who is now missing. It is unfortunate you formed a bond so
quickly with him. You barely knew him. But he did explain
his problem. A problem he tried desperately to break from.
And in the end I gave him that freedom he wanted.
Though, perhaps not in the way he imagined it. Where is
he? I cannot tell you either. All I can tell you is he is gone.
He will never return."

"You killed him," I said.

"Jimmy. You are thinking so one-dimensional. I did
not kill him. I only provided him an option to retreat. See
this little bird did not have the balls to escape. He wanted
an easy way out. Now, he is gone. All too easy. No? You
think I'm a bad man now? What's the difference? You call
me to get rid of a car knowing I was the only person who
would do what you wanted. And now you sit here with
judgment in your eyes. That is okay. You want to feel
morally superior to me. Continue to live in your dream
world, Jimmy. The truth is I did not really get rid of your

---

[26] English translation: "my little sister."

car. But I did borrow it for a while. Then I gave it away. Maybe I'm a snake too, Jimmy. Only if I'm a snake then I'm a fucking king cobra. I don't only bite back but I'll spit venom in your eyes."

"What are you saying?"

"No. I'm not going to say anymore. All I did was give him an escape but I did not kill him. But was I called to help with cleanup? Perhaps."

"Who killed him? Was it Jasmine?"

"I don't know, *hijo*. Maybe. I don't know. Maybe it was a leprechaun who killed him because he stole his pot of gold. I don't know. But I might be able to help you with the two ski masked men. Did one of them perhaps speak like a redneck?"

"Yes!"

"Well, what they are up to I cannot tell you the answer or why they were looking for Jasmine. But I do know someone who might. They are connected to someone else who you think you know but don't really know. Ringo. Yes. Ringo. Now I want both of you to leave. Your Fish Bowl privileges are revoked. Permanently."

"What about the waitress? What about Tala?" Norm cried.

"She is not your concern, my fat friend. And if you should decide to tell the police I will find you and I will hurt you and I will hurt your family, Norm. That is a promise, *cabrón*."

"I don't get it? You killed her over what you told us? But you didn't tell us anything."

"I told you more than I ever wanted you to know, Jimmy. Leave. Slowly. No sudden moves. As you saw earlier I am quick with the draw, no? Like John Wayne. Or Clint Eastwood."

"Why that dirty, no good, son of a—" Clint whispered.

"Quiet Clint."

Norm and I slowly got out of our seats and walked out careful to not turn our backs from Emilio until we were near the stairs and out of his sight. We ran down the stairs and burst through the doors trying to catch our breath and make sense of what happened.

"What do we do now? Oh my God! He killed her, Jimmy! He killed her! Emilio killed that woman. And he probably killed, Ian Noone and he's probably going to kill, Jasmine."

"No. I don't think so."

"Really? Did you not see him kill an innocent person in cold blood? And right when I was beginning to like her. Right when we were starting to get to know her."

"How innocent was she? She may have been as bad as him for all we know."

"This is bad Jimmy. Really, really, really bad."

"You're the one who came in with your fists blazing and punching and choking everyone. What happened to you in there?"

"Evidently I was on an adrenaline high. I've never had so much control in all my life. And let me tell you something: it felt good. It felt really good."

"If there ever is a next time try and remember who you are. You are Norm Schwartz. One of the best people I know on this rotten earth. And if you go rotten I don't know what I'm going to do."

"Why didn't he kill us? No. Wait. I know what he's doing. Evidently he's giving us a head start, Jimmy. All we have to do is go get all our things and get the hell out of town. We're always talking about leaving Ohio. Well, I think we finally have the incentive we were always looking to use. No looking back, brother. No looking back now."

"No. That would be too easy. If you're right about Jasmine we may be her only hope to save her life. I don't think Emilio killed Ian. I do think he was giving Ian something illegal. Like illegal drugs. Or something like that. And that may have killed him. Maybe."

"Jimmy. Stop trying to play detective! We're in way over our heads. We can start over. Away from Ohio. Go to New York City and try to make something or our lives. Even if for a short while for me."

"What's better in New York City, than here? Every place is the same. Instead in NYC we'll be surrounded by people more successful than us, making us feel like even bigger failures."

"It's over Jimmy."

"Not for me it isn't. Are you with me? ... Norm. Are you with me?"

"Yeah. Fuck it! I ain't rotten yet. Till the end. I'm with you."

"Let's go pay Ringo a visit."

11

EVENING was approaching. The sun temporarily relinquished its rein over the sky to the precarious constitution of the obscure night. The day had gone with the haste of a thousand bees buzzing to harvest their honey. Norm speed through the streets possessed by demons long left dormant inside the caves of his soul. He was taking deeper and deeper and deeper breaths with every turn of the steering wheel. His eyes were bloodshot. Something was untying him from this world. And I was worried I was losing my best friend to a world he had long fought to endure.

The clouds dispersed revealing a night with millions of tiny bright luminous spheres. Spheres distributed in the sky like forgotten marbles. A lunatic moon rose up like a giant mouth ready to devour whatever there was in front of its mouth. A mouth with sharp fangs spread throughout its celestial crevice. I thought of the moon reaching out to the earth with a million tentacles. Wrapping them around the earth and squeezing it into billions of pieces. Aristotle once argued that a full moon was capable of inducing insanity in man and beasts alike. Scientific investigation had successfully proven the moon had no effect on a person's psyche. And yet I sometimes wondered why more crazy things seem to happen under a full moon than any other time.

Norm was drinking a Monster energy drink. Earlier he had insisted we stop at a gas station to refuel his car and himself with a kind of beverage booster. I tried to get him to drink something else but he wasn't having any of it. He was with me to see this thing through to the end. When he bought the Monster energy drink he saw they had a deal for two for the price of one. He then demanded I drink some Monster with him. I politely declined which I saw made Norm more agitated. He threw the extra Monster on the backseat while mumbling to me that I was acting like a pussy. Or something like that.

I wasn't thirsty. I wasn't hungry. I had invented my life's new purpose for the time being. And I would reach my goal no matter the cost. Often I would daydream about possible futures for me. I would let my imagination take me away as far from reality as possible. This was the first time where I didn't allow myself to escape from my present condition. I couldn't even see Clint, or Steve, or any of my other favorite imaginary friends. I felt alone and trapped in a car with a Norm's new found vehemence. But, he was my comrade in this battle. And he was brave and he was determined and he was enraged. We were on the same side. This time though, he didn't even bother to play Cake's "Going the Distance." This made everything eerily silent save for the consistent quiet thunder of the car's engine. An old beat up sound that kept ticking. Unwilling to let its inevitable extinction enter into its paradigm of possibilities.

"I can't believe he pulled out a gun. Boom! He shot her cold. She could've been the one, Jimmy. She could've been the one to free me from all this… loneliness," Norm said as he took sharper turns. His complaints increased with each new mile and kilometer. "Yes, she was definitely demented. Evidently so am I. I'm mentally divergent, Jimmy. I've always been."

"We can't change the past. What is done is done. We can change the future," I said trying to console my friend.

"We can change but the world never changes. I know better now, Jimmy. People see me the same way they saw me as a kid or as a teenager. Free choice is bullshit. We're all slaves to our fate. Your fate is already written. Life is a burden to those who are damned to suffer its burden. There's no escape. No escape. No escape."

"What ever happened to your old mantra: 'we are masters of our destiny?'"

"Evidently I can't pretend to believe in that anymore. My fate waits dreaming for me. Like the moon. It's waiting to devour me whole. I'll become part of the darkness which surrounds the stars, Jimmy. Between the darkness surrounding the stars. You think I'm crazy to say something like that. Don't you? I'm not trying to be poetic. Like matter and antimatter. It's a cruel but organized balance. And it does not leave room for empathy or-or compassion."

"Someone has to fight the evil, Norm. Think of us like superheroes."

"That's way too much of a simplification. Evidently you are missing the complexities. Nothing is truly evil. Nothing is truly good. It's all chaos without order. Order is an illusion."

"I'm not going to argue with you about this. I see things in my own way. You see things in your way. But we both have the same end goal. Right? We both want to do some good and make a difference."

"We are irrelevant. Smoke?"

"Sure. Thanks."

"Here." Norm lit his cigarette while driving and continuing to talk to me. He somehow kept the car straight on the road and obeyed every traffic law. "Like I was saying," Norm continued, "We are irrelevant. We are disposable, Jimmy. Evidently."

I took a drag from my cigarette. I tried to grapple Norm's confusing logic. He seemed to have crossed over into a place where fantasy intertwined with reality. Not like me. I always try to keep things real. I always try to stay grounded in the truth. I'm a realist.

"You sure you know where you're going?" I asked Norm.

"I know where Ringo will be. This isn't where he lives, but I know where he will be tonight."

"Why do you say that? You think Emilio ratted us out?"

"I don't know. It could have been Emilio. Or Big Ray. Or Jasmine. Or Tala. Or maybe this is all one big lie. A fucking fantasy. A diversion from our dreams. Dreams we can't control, Jimmy. Dreams that wait to take us away."

"But Jasmine wasn't there. What are you talking about? Dreams? Whose dreams? Your dreams? You're not making any sense. Pull yourself together Norm."

Norm exhaled deeply like a bull preparing to do battle with a matador. He gulped his energy drink holding it tight in his bear-like hands. "My fate waits dreaming for me," he repeated over and over again to himself. I could hear him clearly. I mean, he was right next to me. And yet he acted like I wasn't there. He seemed transfixed on some secret thought he was not ready to share with me. A thought he might never share with me.

We had a mission. Like a video game. We had defeated our first boss in the first level of this video game. That was Emilio. Our next boss might be Ringo. If he was our next boss then he would be the second to last boss, I think. Of course, if I included the ski-masked goons who beat me up, they could very well have been bosses or sub-bosses. I would rationalize I defeated them by convincing them to leave my apartment and let me live.

We had refueled and powered-up with energy drinks. We were ready to shoot fireballs out of our hands and grow larger with special mushrooms. Maybe even ride dinosaurs named Yoshi. We would make giant leaps and grab the flag at the end of the level. I was on a natural adrenaline high Super Mario power-up. I gained this power-up after our encounter with Emilio, I think.

It's amazing how fast your heart starts beating during and after someone points a gun at you. For the first time you start to think about your death—had you done enough? Granted most of life is pointless and when I'm gone only the people who cared about me will remember me. But if I wanted to be remembered I had to do something legendary. *The Legend of Jimmy Rodriguez* and his quest to solve the puzzle. And save Princess Jasmine from all the evils of the world. And in the process retrieve some magical triangles that somehow relate to the story as a whole, a mature version of *The Legend of Zelda*. What a great video game that was. I remember playing that for hours and hours and being lost in the three-dimensional world on my Nintendo N64. I was a teenager then but when I played this game nothing else mattered. Problems of the real world were gone and I was transferred to a place where I was given the chance to save a princess and save the world. No puzzle was too elaborate or difficult for me. I solved all the puzzles. I killed every enemy with precise accuracy. I was as stealthy as a snake or an alligator. I was legendary. As. Bad. As. I. Want. To. Be.

I was losing my adrenaline. My natural high. While fancying myself a participant in a video game. I reached to the backseat and grabbed the other energy drink. Norm was sipping his. The energy drinks were inside huge 16 oz. cans. They looked like regular 8 oz. cans in Norm's hands, but in mine hands were dwarfed by the size of the energy drink.

"That's the spirit, Jimmy."

"I need to power-up if we're going to defeat Ringo and save the princess. Too bad we don't have a Game Genie, or something like that, right now."

"What?"

"Never mind."

I popped open the can. The carbonated sugary-sweet and overly-caffeinated energy drink fizzled. Some of it spilled on my hands. I took a few sips. It was definitely an acquired taste. I put the energy drink can in one of the car's cup holders. I opened the glove compartment in front of me and found Norms bottle of hand sanitizer and used it to clean some of the energy drink off of my hand.

"That's something Emilio would do."

"I don't like how sticky this stuff is on my hands."

"Evidently."

"This hand sanitizer sucks. Can hand sanitizer go bad? I'm going to use some more ... Dammit."

"I think you've had enough of that hand sanitizer, Jimmy. Put it away."

"Okay. You're right. I don't know what's gotten into me." Norm took another big gulp and swallowed it hole. I noticed his hands were starting to shake a little from all the energy drink's caffeine.

"You know. You know what's going to happen. We're going to push back. We're finally going to push back and take on the bullies of this world and the conjurers of bad dreams, Jimmy. It's so evident. Why it took me so long to see this is amazing."

"Norm. Ease it up, man. You're driving a bit reckless."

"Reckless. I'll show you reckless. Evidently, you haven't seen reckless yet, Jimmy."

Norm floored the accelerator pushing the car's engine to work harder than it ever had in years. I hoped to myself that this car would not die after we arrived at our destination. We might need to make a speedy escape and without a way to escape we could easily lose any momentum accrued during our trip. I was certain of that. I was bewildered by the approaching moment of doom.

"We're almost there. It's this neighborhood coming up on the right."

"You sure you can make that turn at this speed?"

"Evidently, your doubt will be rectified by my awesomeness."

"I hope these seat belts don't break. They look a little old."

Norm turned the wheel hard into an extreme ninety-degree sharp turn into the next neighborhood. The tires squelched and we shifted inside from the reactive centrifugal force. We pulled through streams of rotating frames of reference. Coupled with the mass of our objective. Generalized into subconscious and scratching our absolute constant rotating discernment. It was as if time slowed down for a fleeting moment. Yet the earth was rotating at the same speed and revolving at the same speed. Norm and I felt like we were in a bubble between minutes and seconds. Here everything was stagnating.

"How are you doing?" Norm said as if his voice was muted several octaves lower by the lethargic ambit.

"I'm not sure."

"Your ... father?"

"What?" I responded in the same reduced momentum.

Norm pointed in the direction right in front of us. I followed Norm's finger to see a blurry figure outside in front of us. The figure was a man. And he looked like my father. But he dressed like some poor peasant would dress in the country where my father was from.

"You see him too, Norm?"

"I see my fate. It waits for me."

"I see him."

"You see your fate, too?"

"I see my father. I think. He's standing outside in front of us. Which is strange because we're turning, right? But he's in front of us with every angle. Right in front of us. And he looks... he looks worried. Worried for me, I think. Wait. He looks like Emilio now. Wait. No. I was wrong. He looks like my father."

"No more energy drinks for us."

My father. He was out there somewhere keeping an eye on me. Like a guardian angel. Or something like that. I looked at the pain and worry in his eyes. Alive he walked the earth carrying the burden of other people's chains as his own. He pushed all his failures into me hoping his faith in me would be rewarded with my success. He wanted so much from me and I felt obligated to not let him down. But I was powerless with the drifting change of the world. Someone forgot to tell my father that Latinos aren't supposed to be successful. Even their sons. That's a horrible generalization! I know. But sometimes I felt that way.

Suddenly. Abruptly. Unexpectedly. Norm cried out in pain and let go of the steering wheel. I felt the car dip to one side as if one of the tires hit a deep puddle at hundreds of miles an hour. One of the tires exploded and spun off its rim. It was quick and confusing. The car then flipped over and screeched across the neighborhood street. Sparks flared from the friction of metal scrapping against asphalt. The front of the car collided with a nearby innocent car parked on the side of the street and crinkled like an accordion. We then pounded into a small metal fence that wrapped around the car a little but proved to be the final blow to stop our deadly propulsion. I fell into a deep sleep for a specific motion in the geometrics of space-time. Relative to the collision based on the curvature or our disproportionate path of destruction. It was a spectacular crash. Indeed.

I found Norm almost lifeless when I regained my awareness. I undid my seatbelt and pulled at Norms arm. But instead of an arm I found two large tentacles. Like that of an octopus. What the hell? Norm awoke and yelled out with a monstrous roar. The decimated car shook as Norm's tentacles wrapped themselves around my neck. Norm looked at me no longer there.

"We will take you with us."

"Norm. What's happened to you? It's me! Jimmy!"

"Evidently we're free. Finally."

More tentacles began to grow out of Norm as less and less of Norm showed and more and more tentacles took over his body. They each were grabbing me and pulling me closer toward Norms abdomen. Norm's abdomen ripped open to reveal and large mouth full of imperfect fangs and they stunk worse than fish gone bad.

"You will join us. Your fate is ours."

"This isn't happening. I'm hallucinating. I'm hallucinating. Maybe if I pinch myself the monster will go away."

Then I felt something else pull me away from Norm. I felt the reach of other hands. Hands that were warm and comforting. Hands that offered more love than I had ever received in my lifetime. I looked over to see the shape of a humanoid. I say humanoid because I could not make out their face. The figure was covered in brightness. A brightness that nearly blinded me.

Norm's tentacles finally relented. But his mouth wasn't happy about losing me as it continued to try to bite me and inject me with its black oily venom. These angels or ghosts or whatever they were saved me somehow from this thing that had overtaken my best friend. One of them wrapped its arms around me and held me like I was their child. I felt like a kid in protective arms and I wanted to go to sleep and start over in this warm embrace.

"Wake up Jimmy. Wake up. You have to wake up," it told me.

"But I don't want to."

"When you wake up you won't be safe. But you will be alive. Stay alive."

"Why can't I be safe? I want to be safe. I don't care if I'm alive anymore. I want to be safe."

"Wake up Jimmy. Wake up."

I closed my eyes. I could feel the warmth of the heartbeat underneath the chest of the person holding me. A heart beat which echoed like a hundred trumpets in the sky. I thought of death as the end and yet I seemed to be surrounded by things that were of any frame of time—as I perceived it. It felt like an infinite amount of energy that propelled me through the cosmos. While I remained trapped inside this damaged car. The signals my brain was receiving were in contrast to where I was situated. I was lying in the car. My seatbelt was strapped around me. I felt the warmth of billions of lights. I felt the energy of a fantastic relic trying to comfort. It was abnormal sensation.

I let go of the warm arms holding me. I freed myself easily from Norm's tentacles. And with my legs a kicked the passenger window until it broke open shattering to a million pieces. Then I felt everything that was spinning stop. And I awoke to a finite actuality.

I reached over at Norm who was holding his shoulder. It was covered in bright red blood. I grabbed Norm by wrapping my arms underneath his shoulders. With all the strength my body could muster I pulled myself out of the car through the smashed passenger window. Norm lay on the ground screaming from his affliction. I pushed Norm's arm away from his shoulder to better examine him. His shoulder looked like it had popped out of place. And it cut all over from the shattered glass. I tore off the sleeve of the arm attached to Norm's injured shoulder. And wrapped it around the wound as tightly as I could hoping the pressure of the knotted torn sleeve would help stop the bleeding. Norm was sweating but I could tell he had not yet given up from the twinkle in his eye.

"We need to get you to a hospital."

"No. Not in the cards for me, Jimmy. I'll be okay. Just a flesh wound. That's all. We're too far in the midst of things, buddy. Right?"

"Not sure. Hard to tell. I will tell you this, though: today has not been a dull day."

"No. Definitely not a dull day."

"We should leave. We should leave now and let it be. We'll go away. Like you said. We'll move to New York and become bohemians. At least it would make sense in New York City. Being a starving artist doesn't really fit with Ohio as our background."

"I've made my decision Jimmy. Help me up. I believe Ringo is waiting for us over there."

The shadow of someone covered over both Norm and me. And when I glanced up I saw Ringo standing. He was dressed in black. His favorite color of clothing, I think.

The sun slowly rose into the sky and a new day was beginning. It looked like it was going to be a beautiful day. A beautiful day indeed. But aren't all beautiful days indifferent to whims of us silly mortals?

"I'm with you. I've got your back, brother," Norm said.

"How touching," Ringo said.

12

I glanced back at Norm's wrecked car. I remembered us going through a summersault through the sky and landing upside down. Apparently that didn't happen. The car had crashed into a drainage ditch and would take some considerable effort to get out. Norm was more bruised than me from the accident. His shoulder had stopped bleeding. All I could do was look up at the clear sky and try to digest our circumstance.

It was looking like it was going to be a wonderful day. A better day to be doing something else. A better day to be doing anything else but what Norm and I were doing at the moment. I should be trying to enjoy the sun. Or going for a long drive in my father's car with Maria de Guadeloupe above me, looking down on me, protecting me. A day like this would be wasted now. So many days wasted and many chances missed in a place where the intangible supposition is often falsified.

My father used to tell me it was God's way. God had a plan. He used to tell me. God works in mysterious ways. And every day he prayed for a better life than the one he was given. And every day God did not answer his prayers. And every day my father spun his wheel up the hill and went back down to catch it again after he let it roll away. He was content with the knowledge he might be blessed with a better place in the afterlife. After all it was God's way. I travelled with my father's God for a while. I travelled with his Maria. I wore his suffering Christ around my neck. I carried his rosary in my hands when I was but a child and prayed all the prayers my father taught me. Hard work reaps rewards, he would always insist. But, now more than ever, I felt betrayed.

The sins of the past were here to put me out of my misery but deny me a place in the kingdom of heaven. Deny me a place because I could not agree with my father's suppositions concerning a supernatural existence. And I was also loyal to my sinning nature. My sin was every thought I conjured up in my mind every day of the week in every year of my dysfunctional life. My sin was being held up by my father as if I was the chosen one when secretly I knew I was but a false prophet. A prophet discounted. A prophet left on clearance with all the other rags of discarded things. A clearance item once touted as the next big thing only to never be bought when proven to be less than reliable. No use in being smart if I can't even benefit from it. Or I could teach… one day.

And yet here I am. Breathing. Norm is barely hanging on from the looks of it. His life half through and he was willing to give it all for one chance to be greater than the life he had lived. We first met at Paper-Clips and discovered a bond not easily found in life. Norm was trying to hold down two jobs at the time. Eventually he abandoned trying to balance working in Paper-Clips and a grocery store.

I saw Ringo from afar running up to us with a pistol in one of his hands like the hand of God. When Ringo recognized us he put the pistol away in the lower part of the small of his back in his pants. Everything was getting more and more surreal. I felt like I had walked or had been tricked into walking into a trap. I was trying to chase a white rabbit down the hole. I'm chasing a rabbit down a hole. I'm chasing a rabbit down a hole. And I don't want to play anymore. I want to leave and fester my wounds someplace else. Someplace where I can start over and begin anew.

"How touching … Baby boys! What were you two thinking? Is Norm alright?"

"I don't know? You tell me!" I said to Ringo.

"What?"

"What's with the pistol?"

Ringo laughed like a hyena at my observation. "Oh. My dear boy. Your imagination is like a boy on too much caramels."

"What's with the pistol, Ringo?"

"Tweedledum and Tweedledee. Where do all these questions come from? Let's get both of you inside, Jimmy. You sure you're okay?"

"Yeah. I'm fine. A few scratches but most of the bruises are from earlier. Of course you already knew that. Didn't you?"

"I'm sorry. I'm not following, Jimmy."

Why do you have a gun?"

"I have rat problem. It's an infestation. Nasty stuff. I've found shooting at them more sporting than poison. After all with poison I usually miss the chance to see their demise."

"I don't believe you."

"You shouldn't," Ringo grinned. "Help me carry Norm inside the house."

We both picked Norm up and together we carried his large body into the house where Ringo was staying.

Norm and I sat in the kitchen while Ringo brewed us some herbal tea. Ringo wore a very frilly feminine apron while preparing our drinks. On the kitchen counter was a stereo speaker set with an Apple iPod Nano attached to it. The stereo played Judy Garland songs. Ringo took his pistol out and placed it on the kitchen counter near the stereo. It was a black pistol semi-automatic. It looked clean and barely used. Seeing the pistol on the counter caused me to feel a bit sick. I felt anxious and afraid. The whole place spun out of control but I tried my best to not show it to either Ringo or Norm. My thoughts wandered again as Ringo made conversation about trivial things. Like bees, honey and the weather. He was a master of small talk. He could make any person at ease with his charm and then stab you in the back when you least expect it. I wondered why Clint and Steve were absent? Usually they showed up when I started to get lost in my thoughts. But no sign of them. All well. Perhaps they had abandoned me. Perhaps.

"You baby boys like this song? It's called 'Get Happy.' I do love my Judy Garland. Judy! Judy! Judy!" Ringo said. He did a little spin to emphasize his delight in the song. "Judy could out sing, out dance, and outperform Madonna any day of the week. I wish more people knew that," Ringo continued, "She was ahead of her time. So tragic the way she died. They forced her to die that way. The people around her who used her and abused her. Anyway, I've always liked this thing she said one time. She said, 'How strange when an illusion dies. It's as though you've lost a child.' Imagine the depth and the suffering she had to endure in order to compose something so very profound. It tells many tales, baby boys. Many tales. If I could re-do myself I would become Judy Garland reborn. I would have a coat made of feathers that when I opened it up it would look like I had wings. Here would be my stage. I would sing about rainbows and the things beyond rainbows. In fact!" Ringo slapped his hands very delighted, "I think I might do that one day. Perhaps not in Ohio. Ohio is nice but it's no San Francisco. It's no Portland. It's definitely no New York City. Ooohwee! But I'll do it. I'll go on a stage dressed as Judy Garland, sing and end my song with my hand in the air like Judy always did. My hand in the air. Reaching up and up. Judy! Judy! Judy! And now… here's your herbal tea." Ringo then handed each Norm and I a cup of tea.

"So, Ringo." I started. "About Jasmine.…"

Norm was holding his wounded shoulder. His face grimacing from the pain. His skin pale. Sweat rolled down his forehead. His hand shook as he held a spoon and scooped sugar in his tea. He stirred his sugared tea with the same spoon. His hand shaking with every stir.

"Jimmy. I don't feel good. Evi-Evidently I'm now feeling kind of worse," Norm said.

"You drank too much energy drink, Norm. That's all. What you need is some herbal tea, buddy," I said.

"Norm. You will be okay. Do not fret my fat man. This is medicinal tea," Ringo said.

"Maybe. Maybe someone should call an ambulance. I don't know? I really think we should call me an ambulance."

"Calm down. Here, Norm. Drink this with your tea." Ringo grabbed a nearby bag of something filled with a white powder and put some of it in Norm's tea. Norm sipped it.

"There you go Norm. Keep sipping that and all the pain will go away. Trust me. I'm a professional healer, so to speak. I know how to make the pain go away."

"Ringo. Lookit. I need to ask you some questions. About Jasmine and about a couple of guys who like to wear ski masks and beat defenseless people in their apartment. If you know what I mean? And I think you do know I mean."

"I haven't a clue what you're getting at, Jimmy. Of course, you are known for your wild imagination. Makes you a little dangerous. Doesn't it?"

I knew Ringo was going to play hard to get so I had to find a way to gain some leverage. I glanced at the pistol sitting out in the open. I estimated the space between myself and the pistol and the space between Ringo and the pistol. Then I estimated Ringo's reaction versus my reaction. Unlike Ringo I had earlier drunk a sufficient amount of energy drink to give me somewhat of an advantage. I decide to make a go for the pistol. Before Ringo could stop me I had his pistol in my hands and was pointing it directly at Ringo's large pointy nose. Ringo sighed and moved to sit in an empty chair at the kitchen table.

"Well. Well. Well. Tweedledum and Tweedledee. Both have more tricks up their sleeves. I see. How touching. Baby boys. You caught me in an awkward moment. Have you ever looked through a keyhole, Jimmy?"

"What?"

"Like Judy once said: 'I've never looked through a keyhole without someone looking back.'"

"So, Ringo. Like I was saying. I have a few questions. Emilio claims you know the two guys who beat me up this morning. They were wearing ski masks and were looking for Jasmine. One was a big guy who looked like he spends most of his time working out at a gym and taking steroids. The other was a small guy who had talked like a redneck of the Texas persuasion. Tell me what you know."

"Mind if I smoke?"

"No. But no sudden movements."

"Of course not Tweedledum. Or are you Tweedledee? I haven't decided yet."

Ringo grabbed a cigarette out of the pack of cigarettes that was sitting on the kitchen table. He grabbed a match out of the small matchbook on the table. Stroked the match against the small strip of sandpaper and lit his cigarette. He squinted at me. Then he caressed one of his thin eyebrows as if to make sure they were indeed straight.

"You are playing into her hands. You know that?" Ringo sneered.

"What are you getting at?"

"Chaos is come again. And you are the weakest link. Any man is weakened when he lets a woman rule his soul."

"Stop with the damn riddles, Ringo. I have the gun and I'm pointing it at you. No more riddles. Did you kill her? You did. Didn't you? You probably killed that med student, too."

Jordan Aubry Robison

"I'm surprised by these frivolous accusations. How did I do this, Jimmy? How could I possibly do this when I was running karaoke the entire night? You tell me."

"I don't know? You've always got some trick up your sleeve. Don't you?"

"You're right to not trust me. Possibly the smartest thing I've ever seen you do. Bravo, baby boy. But you're wrong about me on this. I didn't kill Jasmine."

"This feels like Déjà vu. Doesn't it?" Norm said while sweating. "I-I really think we should call an ambulance for me. I think maybe I've got some eternal bleeding. Not sure, though. Everything's getting more ... fuzzy."

"Look. Jasmine is missing. A man is dead." I said.
"Which man?"
"Ian Noone. The med student."
"Oh him. I almost forgot about him," Ringo smiled.

"Why was I beat up, Ringo? Why? Why were they looking for Jasmine? Dammit. I know you know something. You always do. Even if you are innocent. You're the one who always makes it a point to know the secrets of strangers. Tell me about Jasmine! Why is all this happening?" I was so frustrated my eyes began to swell up with tears.

"Jimmy. You sad distraught baby boy. Your life is all without joy. No? I cannot but help and wonder how you'll die? By your own hands or by someone else? I mean I know you're holding the gun right now but do you really know how to use it? For example: Have you even considered that the safety is on right now? Or that there isn't even a bullet in the chamber? No. You grabbed the gun without thinking. That's the problem with people like you. You do things quick before thinking them over. You do things expecting results without taking every step required to achieve that result. Why don't you quit while you're ahead and focus on doing something that will make your family proud? No need to waste all that college education.

All that learned knowledge. You're supposed to be smart, aren't you? I know you're a smart boy. Why are you being so stupid, Jimmy?"

"Make my family proud? My family? What family? They're all dead or gone. I'm alone Ringo. Norm's the only family I've got left." I switched the safety off on the gun. I was agitated by my adrenaline. My palms began to sweat.

"And he's not doing so well from the looks of it. Too close to the flame."

"W-What?"

"He flew too close to the flame. Like a moth or butterfly. The best proof is to give away the truth or not. You do have a guardian angel that is watching over you. You're too narcissistic to see that, I think. It's like a chess game, isn't it? One mystery after another. Gives a man purpose. Solving puzzles make one feel worthwhile in a way. But one day you will find there is no purpose. Everything is a random series of unconnected coincidences."

"But what about Ian Noone? The med student. And those two guys who beat me."

"Guilt is a wasteful emotion. Don't you think, baby boy? Any person who finds a way to expel guilt from their conscious is a specimen of evolution. Or is that person a psychopath?"

"What are you getting at?"

"I want you to know how sorry I am for all this. Collateral damage, though. You were meant for better things. You should have never come here. Now. I guess now she might use you. She wrap you around her fingers like she wrapped me and tricked me and used me and now I'm just a slave. And you will be soon enough. Blackmail can destroy an entire life. Did you know that? And you are forced to sit there and watch your entire life slip away from you. And there's nothing you can do. Just make do."

"So you admit it. You are guilty then."

"Guilty? I'm guilty of nothing. Like I said already. Guilt is a waste of time. My only confession is that I can no longer see the difference between light and dark," Ringo sighed. "When in Rome, baby boy. And when in Rome you sometimes lose your soul."

"Why are people like you always so evasive? Why can't someone give me a straight answer?"

"Where's the fun in that, Jimmy?"

"Ringo I know you know something. Tell me what you know. Help me connect the dots. What happened to Ian Noone? Who are the masked men who beat me? Emilio is connected. Isn't he? I know he is. He's everywhere Where is Jasmine? Is she alive? Is she dead? At least tell me that much."

"Why don't you ask Jasmine herself?" Ringo said as his eyes looked past me at someone else.

I glanced behind me. Jasmine was in the kitchen wearing nothing but a long white t-shirt. And Victoria's Secret red/black panties. The iPod switched to Judy Garland singing another song: "Smoke Gets in Your Eyes." Ringo smirked.

"Jasmine? What's going on—"

"There she is, Jimmy. The girl of your dreams. The fantasy of your life. The maker of all your nightmares. That's what you wanted, right?"

"What are you doing here, Jazz?" I asked Jasmine.

"Jimmy. What happened to you? You don't look well."

"I'm so confused right now. I feel sick all of the sudden."

"Yes. You look rather feverish, baby boy," Ringo said. "But maybe she's got just what you ordered. Am I right, Jazz? Just what your ordered."

Jasmine wrapped her arms around me and we circled slowly to the Judy Garland song lost in our mutual embrace.

"I don't feel well, Jasmine."

"Come with me. I'll take care of you," Jasmine said. She glared at Ringo who looked down immediately at his feet as if ashamed by what he had said. She leaned over to whisper something at Ringo. I couldn't make it out but I was also not myself at that moment. I was so relieved to see Jasmine that I didn't care about anything else. The only thing that I cared about, at that moment, was Jasmine. And that might have been one of my biggest mistakes.

Ringo shook his head as if disappointed by whatever Jasmine whispered in his ear and then sat down in a chair next to Norm.

Jasmine lead me from the kitchen through the living room and into an empty bedroom. All that was in the empty bedroom was a mattress, a small lamp on the floor, and an open gym bag with clothes scattered all around it. The walls were very clean and the room smelled a little like paint. As if someone had recently painted the walls.

"Here. Lie here. And relax. I'm here Jimmy. I'm here."

13

I lay down on the mattress feeling like I had betrayed myself in some way. However, I suppressed this conjecture after Jasmine laid her sexiness next to me. She wrapped her arms and exposed legs around me. Almost the same way she had done last night. I felt a sudden rush of heat run all through my body. She kissed me a few times on my flushed forehead and rocked me back and forth. I felt a convoluted feeling of contentment while lying there with Jasmine next to me. She commented on how warm my body and forehead felt to the back of her hand and suggested I might be running a fever. But she didn't let go of me.

My head lay in her soft bosom. Her bosom was like an excuse or invitation to withdraw from whatever I thought I was or whatever I thought I should be. Or whatever people thought I was and should be. I was able to let go of this collection of cancerous thoughts. And briefly yield to the unsentimental passion Jasmine offered me. And she did so without doing much of anything. Strange. Which also made me begin to hate her a little as much as I felt like I needed her affection at the same time.

"Jasmine. Did you get any of my texts? Or my voicemails? I've been—"

"Shhh, now. Calm down, Jimmy. You're not well. You need some rest and relaxation. Relax."

"But —"

"Look. My cell phone was stolen after I left you. It was a crazy day. Crazy day. And I was so busy I didn't have time to find a replacement. I'll go tomorrow I think and get another."

"Oh that explains—"

"Yes."

She then moved to kiss me on my lips. Her lips were chapped and cold. But I didn't mind.

"Cigarette?" Jasmine asked me.

"Yes."

Jasmine grabbed a nearby pack of cigarettes. She took two of them out and lit both of them in her mouth at the same time and then put one of them in my mouth. Jasmine placed an ashtray on my chest. A burning question emerged in my mind as we smoked our cigarettes.

"Lookit. Jasmine. A little bird told me that Jasmine might not be your real name?"

"My real name? Why do you think I have another name?"

"Someone told me that Jasmine is not your real name. Is it true? Is Jasmine not your real name?"

"Are you looking for my life story? Here's the summary: big dreams and small conclusions."

"So is it true or not?"

"It's true. Jasmine is not my given name. But it is my legal name."

"What do you mean?"

"I don't want to talk about it. Beside I think you should rest. You might be running a fever, Jimmy."

"Sorry. I'm just curious. After everything I've been through today. I feel like I deserve to know."

"Oh really? You think you're entitled? Deserves got nothing to do with it, baby. One day you'll find out no one deserves anything. They get what they get because that's how it is."

"Maybe so. But I really think I deserve to know something."

"You've had a bad day. That's all. And you want some sort of assurance that it was worth it. But prepare yourself for a big letdown. Again, none of what you went through was worth it. Sorry to be the one to give you the bad news, baby."

"It was not one of my better days. I mean, Norm is... Oh! I can't believe I forgot about Norm. We better go check on him."

"Don't worry about Norm. He'll be fine. We left him with Ringo. Remember?"

"Yes. That's what worries me.... what are you doing with Ringo, anyway?"

"Ringo is like my confidant."

"Do you love him?"

Jasmine seemed to hesitate a bit after I asked this question.

"Love is a word used too easily by people in this world. All four-letter words are. So to hell with it all I say. The hell with it. The hell with everything. Anyway. You're barking down the wrong tree, Jimmy. You need to calm down and relax. You need to forget about what you think you know. Forget about what happened to you. Shit happens. You know? Shit happens."

"So, you don't love him?"

"Ringo and I don't screw each other. If that's what you mean, Jimmy. It's strictly platonic. But with all the affection I require, excluding sex."

"I could be that for you. And more. You know that."

"Out of all the losers I have had to deal with in my lifetime I think you could be right. But we'll never know. We'll never know because that's the way things are."

"Why do you say that?" I whimpered.

"It just is. That's the world. A big empty promise. And I'm not going to contribute to that lie. Promises aren't worth keeping. They'll always get broken."

"Hollow at the core."

"Like I said."

"Who are you really, Jasmine? Who hurt you? Someone must have burned you really bad. I know you have a story to tell. Everyone has a story to tell. And the people who don't are the real fools. In my opinion."

"I'm whatever I want to be. And who are you, Jimmy Rodriguez? Who the fuck are you?" I couldn't answer her. At that moment I didn't want to bullshit her anymore. She was right. I didn't know who I was. I tried to take the things around me and utilize them in a way to help define me. But that didn't seem to work anymore. It seemed like I've wasted most of life trying to figure out who I am. Jasmine tried to wait for me to answer. She eventually burst out in laughter calling me a ridiculous silly man. She finished her cigarette and took my nearly finished cigarette from my mouth. She disposed of both of the cigarettes in the ashtray and then put the ashtray on the floor beside the mattress. She then counted the cigarettes left in her cigarette pack and closed her eyes memorizing the number. She touched my forehead.

"You're still warm. Poor baby. Jasmine is going to take care of you," she laughed.

"Is this how our world will end? Together but not together?"

"Life is very long, Jimmy. Maybe yes and maybe no. Stop being so overly dramatic."

"Alive but not alive."

Jasmine stared at me a moment with pity in her eyes. She tenderly stroked my cheek like a mother would stroke her own baby. She seemed transfixed on some thought spinning in her head. Only the ghosts of badly treated women knew what she was thinking. I could only imagine.

"Jimmy. You should go. But you can't now. But you should go. I don't want you to get into any more danger. You don't need the kind of problems that follow me around."

"What kind of problems?"

"I'll tell you one day after we're both dead and gone."

"I hate you sometimes. As much as I love you I hate you."

"The feeling is mutual, baby."

"Is that your way of saying I love you, too?"

"There's that word again. Love." Jasmine shook her head in disappointment. "What do you want to do?" she asked.

"I want to stay here with you," I said.

"But you can't. You can't stay here. Don't you see that? Not as long as I think you want to stay."

"Then if I can't stay maybe *I* can help you."

"Help me? How can you help me?"

"I don't know. But I can try. In any way I can. I want to help you."

"I'm beyond help. At least the kind of help you could offer me."

"You mean help from those two men?"

"What two men?"

"You know. Those two men who beat me up when they were looking for you. They were not very nice to me. Why were they looking for you? I think I deserve to know after what I've been through."

"Fine. I'll tell you. What difference does it make now? A long time ago when I was very young I married an older man who promised to take care of my family and me. Well, not only did he not take care of my family he used me like a punching bag and cheated on me with a countless number of women. I was so naïve then. I should have known better but I didn't. I wasn't always as strong as I am now, Jimmy. I wasn't always as sure as I am now," she then paused for a moment. She took a deep breath and continued.

"Then one day he came to me," she began, "He beat me, and then he forced himself on me. Yes. He forced himself on me. After he finished it was like someone had cracked open a window in my brain. I decided I would escape. But I knew if I escaped he would search heaven and earth to find me. Escaping a man like him is not an easy thing. You see me leaving him would only hurt his pride. Even if he knew I was unhappy with him and that was the reason for my escape him and that horrible life we shared. It didn't matter to him. To him I was just an object. A trophy. I knew he would never let me go and would punish me severely after he captured me. So, one night…. I planned it out so well. One night I killed him in his sleep and ran away. I changed my name and worked here and there until I thought I had settled. Until I thought I had finally escaped. What I did not consider was his two sons would go after me to avenge their father. They caught up with me a few times before but each time I was able to get away. And then for a while it seemed like they had both finally decided to leave me alone. So I stopped looking behind me. I relaxed. This time I was sure I had covered all my tracks. How silly of me? But life catches up with us all one day. So that is why I need to run away again. I need to escape. I might leave the country this time. Maybe go to Europe and work in some burlesque show. Who knows? And when I found out my ex-husbands two sons had found you when they were looking for me it was too close for comfort."

"But, that night when you came to my apartment. Weren't you already running away from them?"

"I wasn't running away. Or maybe I was. Something else had happened. It clued me of the eventual arrival of my ex-husband's moronic offspring. I was doing what I had to in order to survive. And I wanted someone to comfort me. I needed you. I also wanted to say goodbye to you. I wanted to give you what you always wanted before I left you forever. You must believe me when I tell you I never wanted this to happen to you. This is bigger than you or me. And you can't save me. Only I can save myself."

"Don't be so sure," I said.

"You should rest."

"Not before we do something first?"

"What did you have in mind?"

I reached over to kiss her and let my other hand explore her body. We kissed for a while as Jasmine lay on top of me.

"You're so warm. So very warm."

"And you're so cold."

"I know."

"Let me keep you warm."

The light outside began to fail. As blackness took over, the wind picked up, and so did the dust with the ash. And it screamed outside through all the emptiness and everything cooled. I found myself lost in my thoughts and within a very plain and boring room. The pain of the world would not go silently into the night. But for now I was with Jasmine. For now, she was my world and I was hers. Forever. And however long it would last it would remain an eternity in my memory. And even with her I felt a kind of loneliness I felt once long ago. Long ago when I was a very young child. Loneliness we both shared through our vast wounds and through the world's dark beauty.

We kissed again. The more we kissed the more we tricked each other into believing in a foolish dream of fairy dust and make believe. The more I wanted to be her knight in shining armor rescuing her from all the pain and suffering she carried deep within her soul. I wanted to protect her from all the villains and monsters. It was in that moment I knew I would make love to her one more time. I knew we would be closer together than we were the last time we were intimate.

"Maybe you can help me."

"I'm all yours."

She smiled as she pulled off my tattered clothes and kissed every bruise on my body three times. Her kisses on my bruises were harsh and sweet. I pulled her up toward me to kiss her some more and also include her neck. I helped her take off the t-shirt she was wearing. It seemed like we would never stop kissing each other as she began to dry hump me making my cock rock hard. I felt up her body and caressed her dark skin. I hugged her tightly. Her large naked breasts smashed against my bare chest. I felt her nipples harden.

"Don't get too excited now," she said. "You need to put that in me before you're finished."

"Don't worry," I lied.

I maneuvered to be on top of her as she took off her Victoria Secret panties. When we were both naked we held each other close and tight. Kissing and smelling and sniffing each other like wild animals out in the open plains. It was as if we were somehow both afraid to let go of each other.

My body heat increased substantially from the added heat of her body. Her heat was a dangerous welcome to my hopeless lust and my desire to make love to her and my desire to be in love with her. She was too smart to really let me into her world. As close as we were in this moment of sexual release I somehow knew she would eventually pull away from me. I had fallen in love with someone who was too lost for me to save. Maybe I could save her from all the horrors the world provided. Then again, I could let her go far from me after this night. I knew better, but like I said earlier, she was like an addiction. Or like the song says: she was my favorite mistake. And I was her willful victim.

Jasmine treated my body with such care. As much care as I treated her when my turn came to return the favor. Either she really loved me during this moment or she was that good of a seductress. No matter. She had me the first moment she and I laid eyes on each other at The Fish Bowl that rainy Sunday those few years ago. She had toyed with me. She had played with me. And I had hated her for it. But I kept coming back. Each time I came back I suppressed more and more of my desire for her. Yet now I realize she saw through my silly façade.

"I wish we could be like this forever," I said.

"Shhh, baby. Don't talk. You'll ruin the moment. Our moment. And our moment is now."

We kissed. Our tongues in each other's mouth. Her long sharp tongue wrapped around my smaller tongue. This made me tingle inside. Her tongue then let go of my tongue and she pulled away from kissing me. Then she looked into my eyes. She did not stop staring at me as our eyes met. I felt completely vulnerable. Tears began to swell up in her eyes. I opened my mouth to begin to speak but Jasmine put her hand over my mouth shaking her head.

"Don't speak," she whispered in my ear.

We made love the rest of the night. Both of us were worn out. Especially me. And we must have tried every position invented in the Kama Sutra. At least, positions I had never tried before. She guided me through all of them. She was well versed in the art of making love. And I was her obedient student. She was like a sexual tyrannosaurus. After this night, I knew the next woman I made love with, if it wasn't Jasmine, would be impressed with my carnal knowledge. All accrued from the times I shared intimately with Jasmine. After we had exhausted the topography of intimate fornication we finally decided to sleep. We held each other's hand while sleeping. Of course, I didn't really sleep. I was very drunk with contentment.

I felt happy or something similar to happiness. With any feeling of elation came the knowledge that it would only be temporary. But sometimes when one is in the moment one doesn't think of those things. But I do. Except when I don't sometimes. But I do. And I didn't see the need to sleep and dream because I didn't have anything to dream about. My dream appeared to have come true, though in a different way. I suppressed all my negative thoughts. The state of Norm and his health came running into my head. But I ignored it. The question of Ian Noone and his disappearance then came in my head. But I also ignored those thoughts. The two men who attacked me for no apparent reason during their search for Jasmine. I suppressed all my logic to allow me sustain my happiness.

Jasmine woke me up a half hour later to tell me she was going to make me some more tea because I was apparently still warm. I told her I was fine now but she insisted.

She returned several minutes later with the tea and very naked. She told me to drink it slowly. But to drink all the tea because it was good for me. I asked her what made this particular tea so special. She told me it had a few special secret ingredients that would help me get better. I drank the tea. Jasmine waited patiently until I had finished all the tea. She then put the cup on the floor and lay me down. She pulled the blankets to cover me and then she lay on top of the blankets. She told me to close my eyes and try to relax and go to sleep. I complied. And then I was asleep again. I was very much asleep.

PART THREE

14

HEADACHE. A horrible, horrible, horrible headache welcomed me when I woke. Less like a headache and more like a migraine. Everything vibrated. I saw a shimmering aura. I had to blink my eyes a few time until the spots went away. I was feeling very drowsy and somewhat lethargic. My neck was sore. Possibly from sleeping in an awkward position. My eyes were a bit out of focus. Even after blinking several times. It took me more than a few forgotten minutes to return my focal point to a point of normality. When I finally was able to see without any trouble it was then I realized why I awoke sitting up and not lying down.

I was not lying on Jasmine's firm mattress anymore. I was not in Jasmine's boring bedroom with its freshly painted white wall. Or Ringo's house for that matter. I was in my father's Pontiac Firebird. I knew it was my father's car when after I looked up at the car's interior ceiling and noticed Maria de Guadalupe starring down at me.

I wasn't even naked anymore. I had clothes on, but they weren't my clothes. The clothes were clean. They smelled like they recently had been retrieved from a cleaner's. They had their near perfect pressed creases. I was wearing a black shirt and black pants. My trusty aviators were with me stationed on my forehead. And I never wear my sunglasses on my forehead. I have always stored my sunglasses in the middle of shirt collar or hanging out of one my pants pockets. My fingers were decorated with multiple gold rings. The rings didn't fit my small fingers. Numerous gold necklaces hung from my neck for some reason. However, the same silver necklace my father had given me a long, long, long, time ago. With its silver crucifix my father was hanging around my neck undisturbed. The only necklace that actually belonged hanging from my neck.

I was not alone. Two people, who appeared to be sleeping, were with me in my father's car. In this car. This familiar car. This Firebird. *El Bambino*. This car with the same faint misty smell that reminded me of my father. Yes. This was my father's car. I was in my father's car. It had been cleaned to near mint condition. This car was never this clean when I drove it or even when my father drove it into eternity. I looked around for the *Bambino*'s car keys, and of course, they were missing. The car's interior smelled polished and foreign. I was able to smell the history of my father through all the sanitation. I remembered the hot days when he sweated through the back of his shirt and it left a moist depression on the driver's seat. Or maybe his memory overcame all the other sensations. Reality was less important than the things I remembered or how I wished the past to be remembered.

I realized the sleeping person next to me in the passenger seat was my friend, Norm. I moved my right arm to scratch an itch on my forehead when I noticed my right arm's wrist was handcuffed to Norm's left arm. Strange. I tried to shake Norm awake but he didn't stir. My instinct kicked in and a horrible feeling swept through me. I decided to check Norm for a pulse. No pulse. His body was cold and rather stiff. Rigor mortis perhaps. I stroked the side of his face. If there was a God, he never gave my friend a chance, I thought.

His eyes were closed. He looked rather peaceful. He didn't smell bad yet. He was close enough where I could make that much of a conclusion. But something did reek of major proportion. It smelled like a skunk or garbage left to cook in the sun. Or road kill that had been left on the road for a few days. I looked around the inside of the car hoping I would discover the origin of this unwanted smell. It didn't fit with the car's cleanliness. I wanted to dispose of it somehow.

A body.

I discovered lying in the back seat was a body. And the body was none other than the person who I had taken upon myself to search and hopefully rescue. It was Ian Noone. The med student I met the other night at The Fish Bowl. And he didn't look like he was sleeping. No. He looked very dead. The odor emitting from his body confirmed my hypothesis. Yeah, I guess he was asleep all right. The big sleep. The long goodbye. Dead. One of his arms was stretched out as if it was reaching toward the sky. Or reaching at Maria de Guadalupe. That beautiful mural of the so-called mother of Mexico, or so my father told me one time when I was a kid. A kid who believed anything his father told him.

The mural looked down on me and with my free hand I caressed the cracks and crevasses of the painting. I always do this when I see the mural. I started doing it when I was a kid and I continued to do it up to that fateful day when I attempted to abandon my father's car. When I attempted to leave him and all the bad memories the car conjured. My father was a good man. But he was an unhappy man. I had inherited his unhappiness. He wanted more. I wanted more. We both wanted more. We wanted the promise of the American dream. We wanted the freedom to pursue happiness without any restrictions.

I sighed. I didn't know what else to do. I had had a feeling Jasmine and/or Ringo would betray me. But I never thought like this. I never thought they would take it this far. Maybe I was in shock but for some reason I didn't freak out. I sat there and sort of accepted my fate. I felt numb. I knew I was screwed no matter what I tried to do. Especially after I noticed where the car was parked.

The car was parked near a police station. It was very early in the morning. The sun was rising. Any minute now the police who worked the night shift would be returning. And the police who worked the day shift would show up to get their briefing before they started working. It was only a matter of time before one of them would walk by and notice me in my precarious situation. What an absurd affair.

"Well this is a fine mess you've gotten yourself into," Clint said.

"Clint. You're back?"

"Only to tell you how much shit you're in."

"I know. I really messed up this time."

"You've let me down. You've let Steve down. I mean he's so mad he decided to not see you. He's not sure he wants to talk to you anymore."

"Well, there's nothing I can really do about it."

"In this world there are two kinds of people. People with loaded guns and people who dig. You are neither."

"Then what am I?"

"I can't tell you, kid. Now, remember, things look bad and it looks like you're not gonna make it, then you gotta get mean. I mean plumb, mad-dog mean. 'Cause if you lose your head and you give up, then you neither live nor win. That's the way it is."

"I'm not really mad. I'm... I don't know what I am. In shock?"

"You've been in shock most of your life. Haven't you?"

"What are you? My psychiatrist?"

"I'm trying to help, kid. If you don't want my help then I'll leave."

"Fine! Go! You're not helping me anyway with your silly pedantic advice."

"What did I say about using words I don't understand!"

"Oh, by the way. I know that shit you told me isn't your own words. Those are things you've said in your movies."

"Don't blame me for your lack of imagination. You are the one imagining me right now."

"Okay. Then I imagine you gone. Go! And don't come back."

"Don't test me. I might do that."

"I shouldn't be talking to an imaginary friend anyway."

"Hey kid. Uh-huh. Don't be so mean," Elvis Presley said. Suddenly everything was getting a lot more cramped. The King himself was sitting next to Clint. He was dressed in a glittery white jumpsuit. The kind he was famous for wearing during his Las Vegas days. His hair stood large on top of his head accented with a giant set of sideburns. He wore his classic golden-framed large sunglasses. Only Elvis Presley could pull off wearing such obnoxious binoculars. He snapped his finger a couple times as if he was trying to get through a new song in his head. The neutral position of his lips was with the upper curled up on one side of his mouth. Each movement he made seemed like he was one step or two steps away from shaking his hips and legs. Followed by dozens of screaming teenage girls squealing for his attention—that never materialized.

"Dammit! Now Elvis is here?" I said.

"Hey-uh-watcha mean?"

"Are you going to try to give me advice now?" I said.

"Imma do what? Looky here. You ain't nothing but a hound dog. Cuz, you-a-cryin' all the time. Got me? *Viva la vida*[27], baby."

"Ha! He's not making any sense. Is he?" Clint laughed.

---

[27] English translation: "Live life."

"Woah there nelly." Elvis said. "We should rope this drama to high noon. No what I mean? Heeeyah! Rawhide! Hang 'em high! Get a rest and be a whole-lotta better. Uh-huh."

"I was never in *High Noon*. That was Gary Cooper," Clint said.

"What? Oh, whatever. Imma uh just sayin'. You better shape up, kid. It's a jailhouse rock out there. Know whatta mean? Get your blue suede shoes on. Act like a tiger and not like a teddy bear. And don't be greedy. Know whatta mean?"

"No one knows what you mean!" Clint laughed.

"Uh, don't be cruel. Cool it baby. Cool it. I've been a cowboy before. I was pretty convincing at it. I uh, think so. Uh-huh."

"Can you two take this argument somewhere else? I'm a little preoccupied at the moment."

"Later," Elvis said.

"Elvis has left the car," Clint stated.

"And you are here. Funny. I thought I told you to leave," I said.

"I'm gone. I'm gone," Clint said.

Tap. Tap. Tap.

I looked outside. A police officer was standing outside tapping on my driver side window. He was tall and had a set of deep piercing blue eyes. He looked awfully young to be a police officer, which means he must have been a rookie. His head looked like it was shaven this morning. I could tell by how shiny and smooth it looked. Being that he was rookie also meant he was probably going to be very full of himself. I sighed. I rolled down the window.

"Problem, Officer?"

"What exactly is going on here?" the police officer asked.

"Well, I'm handcuffed to my dead friend and there's a dead guy in the back seat."

"I see. Please step out of the car."

"Okay. But like I said. I'm handcuffed to my dead friend. And he's a big guy. So, it might be a little difficult."

"Open the door and step out of the vehicle, sir."

"Sure thing."

I opened the unlocked the door and did my best to step out.

"Step out of the vehicle, sir"

"I'm trying."

The rookie cop lost his patience with me. He pulled his pistol out of his holster and pointed it at me. He held the pistol in both hands and made the proper posture he probably learned several weeks ago at Police Academy.

"Did I tell you I'm handcuffed to a dead guy?"

"Sir. I'm going to ask you one more time. Step out of the vehicle, or I'll—"

"Or you'll what? Shoot me? Come on, dude. I'm unarmed. Can't you call for back up or something?"

"Hank! Goddammit! Put your gun away. Goddam rookies. What's going on here?" An older police officer said as he ran up to us. He was a bit overweight but held himself well. His gut hung over his belt. He looked like a jolly blue giant compared to the skinny rookie cop.

"Put my gun away, Sergeant Matlock? Seriously? There are two dead people in this suspect's car. I mean, they look dead."

"Is this true?" Sergeant Matlock asked me.

"It's true. And I'm handcuffed to one of them. And he's a big guy. Almost as big as you. So, I'm having a difficult time getting out of the car. I'm not going to be any trouble. Scout's honor." I held my hand up and did the Scouts salute with two of my fingers.

"I see. Goddammit Hank! I said put your damned gun away. Go help that boy."

"But what if he makes a sudden move or something? Shouldn't we spray him with mace, Sergeant Matlock?"

"Are you going to cause us any trouble, son?" Sergeant Matlock asked me.

"No sir. I believe I'm already in a world of shit."

"See, Hank. He said he's not going to give us any problems. No go over and help that boy out of those handcuffs."

"I don't trust him. We should—"

"Dammit Hank! Do as your Sergeant Matlock says. Or I'll sight you right here and now! This is only your third day at this precinct from the academy and already you're running around like you're a super cop or something. Damn rookies. Every one of them is a damn pistol whipping fool."

Hank finally complied. He crept over to me very cautiously. "No sudden moves now," he said to me in a very stern voice.

"Don't worry about me."

Hank then slammed me against the car as he examined my handcuffs. "Well, this will make sure you don't give me any problems." Before I had the chance to even respond he dug his shoulder into my chest. And it was hurting me and making it hard for me to breath. Hank pulled out his handcuff keys and with the handcuff key freed me from the handcuffs. By this time my wrist was rather red and sore. Hank then threw me to the ground now shoving his knee into my crotch and jumped on top of me. Having Hank's knee shoved into my crotch made me feel even more uncomfortable. He pulled out his own set and handcuffs from his police utility belt. And handcuff both my hands together behind my back. Then he stood me up pulling on the chain between the cuffs. I wobbled a bit as he spread my legs apart. I was feeling somewhat disoriented from Hank's abuse of my personal rights. The jewelry I was wearing jingled with each mean-spirited tug or shove Hank thought it necessary to bestow upon me.

"All right. All right, Hank. You've had your fun. Ease up now. Now son. Tell me. Why are you in this here car with two dead people?"

"Honestly, I don't know. I was asleep somewhere else. And then when I woke up I wasn't there. I was here. I know it's hard to believe but it's the truth, officer. I do not intentionally handcuff myself to dead people. And I don't usually keep dead people in the back seat. In fact, I make it a rule to stay as far away from death as possible."

"Hmmm. I think I believe you. But, we gotta take you in. Sorry kid. You're under arrest for suspicious activity and possibly murder."

"I understand."

"Okay. Hank. Read him his Miranda Rights and let's get going. I'll call a paramedic and forensics to get here ASAP. Damn shame. I tell you what. I was hoping this would be a quiet day. Oh well."

Hank walked me inside the police station telling me my rights. The older cop waited outside for the paramedic and the forensics team to show up. Hank sat me down near an empty desk and re-handcuffed me to the chair.

"Wait here. I'm going to process you. Which means I'm going to get your information. Fingerprint your sorry ass. I'll take you to get a mug shot, and then we'll have you talk with one of our detectives. And don't try anything sudden. You're surrounded by cops now. We don't fuck around. You get the picture, punk?"

"Okay. I understand. Like I said earlier. I promise to behave. But I do want to ask you something. Can I get a cup of coffee while I wait?"

"I'm not your waiter. I'm a fucking police officer of the law. I serve honest people and protect them from scumbags like you."

"Sorry," I said.

Not a minute later, did another older cop with a balding head yell at Hank for yelling at me. I was beginning to see the development of a pattern. "Hank. Get the boy a cup of coffee. And while you're at it get me a cup, also. I'll process him."

"But he's my tag, Willy. I tagged him. You didn't."

"One thing you need to learn Hank, is patience and to watch that temper of yours. There's no need to get all worked up about nothing. And another thing. I'm a Lieutenant Detective. You'll address me as Lieutenant. The first word of out your mouth, when addressing me is: Lieutenant, followed by one of two words: 'Yes' or 'No.' Do we understand each other now?"

"Yes, Lieutenant." Hank walked off looking embarrassed and quite defeated. I felt like I had shared with Willy a small victory. A victory in etiquettes.

"Christ boy," Willy said. "Don't you look like shit? And a bit silly. I'll never understand why some people like to wear all the jewelry."

"Yeah. Well I feel worse. And trust me. I don't usually dress like this."

"I bet. So, why did Hank drag you in this early in the morning?"

"Shouldn't I wait to speak with a lawyer before I say anything else?"

"Oh. Yes. Sure. We'll lawyer you up soon enough. First I need to know some things. Like what do you call yourself, son?"

"James Luis Rodriguez. But everyone calls me, Jimmy."

"Well Jimmy, I'm Lieutenant William Theodore Jones. But everyone calls me Willy. Nice to meet you Jimmy."

"Nice to meet you, sir."

"Isn't it good to exchange these niceties instead of having to go through un-pleasantries? I hope this will make everything between us go very smoothly."

"Don't worry about me, sir. I'm happy to cooperate."

"Willy. Call me Willy."

"Uh, Willy. I'm happy to be of any assistance I can."

"All right. That's what I like to hear." Willy smiled.

"I do want to tell you. Whatever they pulled you in for, guilty or not, the fact you are already asking for a lawyer will instantly raise suspicion."

"I know I'm innocent. But I also know my rights. I'm not worried. By the way, I believe I'm being charged with suspicious activity and possibly homicide. But I assure you I'm innocent."

Willy cocked one of his eyebrows and then questioned me. I answered every question I felt was required of me to answer without the presence of a lawyer. They fingerprinted me. They took my mug shot and explained I would be registered permanently in their system. A system that was connected to all the states in the country. A system that even the FBI could access if they wanted. Later I asked when I would be assigned a lawyer. They told me I would get a lawyer very soon. I explained to them that I really wanted to answer all their questions. But would feel more comfortable answering them with the presence of a lawyer.

A few hours passed as I sat handcuffed to a chair. The cops went through their day quite immune to the insanity coming and going throughout their building. Drugged out hobos. Screaming mothers. Misbehaving teenagers. Repeat offenders. Old ladies filing complaint after complain after complaint. Another hour passed and by this time I ran out of things to think about. I tried counting the tiles on the ceiling but that only made me tired. Every time I closed my eyes a cop would bump me to wake up and tell me either politely or impolitely that sleeping was prohibited.

Boredom soon took over and I wondered what it would be like to try to escape the police station. This proved to be a good diversion. Sometimes I liked to calculate multiple outcomes using game theory. I wasn't too far from their desks and I wasn't too far from the lobby where the main door of the police station occupied. After I freed myself and based on how quick I was capable of moving. And based on the distance from where I was to the door. It made me think it was mathematically possible. All I would need was a couple of paper-clips and I am positive I would be able to pick the lock on my handcuffs. Everyone was so preoccupied with the business in front of them. I would have to time it right. And consider the cops nearby and how they might react to my potential escape. But it was possible. I would be able to walk out the door without any problems. A mad dash for freedom. It would be so easy.

Willy showed up when I was in the middle of this thought with a sandwich in one hand and a can of soda pop in the other. He told me to eat it and thanked me for my patience. They were in the middle of deciding what to do with me. More hours passed until I could see the sun setting outside through the windows. An entire day wasted with me sitting and waiting and wondering. I wish I were back in my bed and in my crappy bat-infested attic apartment.

Willy returned again to inform me that I would be spending the night in a cell in the police station. Tomorrow I would meet my lawyer, and then I would be questioned. After some more questioning they would decide whether or not to press charges against me. They asked me if that would be okay. I asked what the cells were like. Willy told me the cells were set up for a single person. So I would be alone. But at least I would have a bed to lie on. I agreed with their offer. Not that I really had a choice. Of course they really couldn't hold me I think. But then again I was not in the mood to fight them. Things would happen as they happened. If I could change them I would try to do so tomorrow after a good night's sleep. I did, however, inquire why it took so long to find me a lawyer. They informed me that someone, who wished to remain anonymous, was somehow familiar with my predicament. This someone had offered to hire a lawyer on my behalf. And that lawyer was out of town at the moment but would be able to see me by tomorrow. I was surprised word of my incarceration had spread so quickly.

15

I was able to see a little of the sky from my cell's small rectangular window. This gave me the opportunity to look at something more natural and complex instead of the cold dull square cell in which I was imprisoned. My cell reminded me a little of the somewhat vacant bedroom I shared with Jasmine last night. Both rooms shared a strange need to be restrained. The sun was descending and disappearing giving the sky a glaze of extra colors. With my hand I tried to trace the different colors wishing I had learned to be a talented enough to paint like my father. Each stroke I twirled with my finger scattered the clouds into tiny little misshapen puffs of cotton. The sunrays pierced through the clouds and I thought of Maria de Guadalupe and the shiny golden rays my father painted behind her.

I lay on my cell bed and continued staring at the sky. I tried to go over everything that happened the last few days in my head again and again and again. I was incarcerated even though I had committed no crime. I was being punished for the actions of others who I had neither aided nor abetted. At least I think so. I was more a victim than anything else. I waited and waited to see if Clint would appear to keep me company while I ruminated over my quandary. He never did. Nor did Steve or anyone or anything else for that matter. I was truly alone in this moment. My imagination would not provide me a brief intermission from these unhappy vicissitudes.

The police had taken all the jewelry I was wearing when they processed me. I convinced them to let me hold on to the necklace my father had given me. Some of them laughed when I insisted the jewelry was not mine. Some of the cops complained I was some sort of poser pimp. I wanted to protest but I remained vigilant through their accusations and through their ridicule. My good behavior, according to Willy, was the only reason I was allowed to wear my father's necklace.

I fiddled the silver crucifix with my fingers. I felt its grooves from its tiny carvings. The silver Jesus face was rather plain. Whoever carved Jesus carved him without any eyes. Only two depressions that gave him shadows where his eyes should be. His size was too small for such detail. Jesus looked almost like a face without a face. Eyes without eyes. Eyes without a face. As if to suggest there is no conclusion. Like one more bad dream after feeling all out of hope. "I'm all out of hope… " I began to sing to myself. Then I laughed. I couldn't help but laugh. This tiny figure meant so much to my father and to my grandfather. And yet I could go to any pawnshop and inquire to its monetary value. In the real world this was not priceless, but simply a piece of jewelry.

If there was an afterlife was my father floating somewhere starring down on me? The idea of living in another dimension, where the ghosts of my ancestors have the power to watch over me, while being powerless to help me, particularly bothered me. I could see now why in some ancient cultures there was the need to worship one's ancestors. For it made more sense to ask them to help than assume they were only watching and not in any way participating. And my father wasn't one to let himself be reduced to exclusively observe and let things happen. All the angels in heaven would be needed to hold him down from trying to intervene on my behalf.

I kissed the crucifix like my father had taught me to do so when I was a child. I did not believe it would change anything that was happening or was going to happen to me. I did not think it would bring me any sort of good luck. I did it more out of nostalgia and as a way to honor the memory of my father. I wondered what they had done with my father's car. Earlier, right before I entered my cell, Willy told me that they had discovered most of the engine was missing when they tried to start the car. Which he assured me would help my story somehow. Even though I had not really told them my story as of yet. I refused to talk anymore about my situation. I knew it was better to be safe rather than sorry, especially with the murder of two people hanging over my head. At the moment I was their only suspect. It was better not to think about the possibility of being blamed for these murderous deaths. Night was coming. No, it was better to force myself to stare at the sky and wonder at the cosmos. And the billions and billions of stars that would soon glitter, dazzle and amaze.

The jail was rather quiet that night. Not that I had any other night in the jailhouse to compare it with. I could hear everything outside. But nothing inside save for the consistent humming of the ventilation system. I heard every cricket's chirp. I heard the flapping of a moth's wing vibrating staccato. The origins of a tornado or a hurricane. I heard the strange hoot of a nearby nocturnal owl. In the distance I heard what sounded like a dog or a wolf momentarily howl. I heard every tiny sound that occupies the night in different intervals. I heard them all at once. All at once the night creatures created an orchestra for me to listen. I even heard my heartbeat. My heartbeat was controlled and steady. I felt very relaxed and calm. Again, I think I was in shock. My heartbeat was pumping blood without any great stress. My heartbeat was like a rhythmic drum to the chorus of the twilight fiends. And it bounced from my chest to my throbbing head. I breathed heavily through the throbbing. Throbbing then soon enough subsided.

You can't always get what you want, I thought.

My father was a big Rolling Stones fan. One of his favorite songs was "You Can't Always Get What You Want." He would explain his interpretation of the song to me over and over again. Normally after he had a few beers streaming through his system. He believed the song was saying that even though things don't always work out the way we plan we should try to be thankful for what we have. Thankful for what we have. I was staring down a hole with very little for which to be thankful. I am so very thankful. It seemed like another lie fed to me when I was a child. All I had was his necklace. He was gone and he could not save me. He could not help me or offer advice or disturb the wind to let me be. I could lose my life over this. Sometimes being the only suspect is enough to make one guilty. And I was guilty.

I was guilty of letting my optimism get the better of me. I was guilty because I let myself believe in the unobtainable notion of true love. Which caused me to trust the last person in the world I should have trusted. I was guilty of not living up to my potential. I was guilty for blaming the world around me for my troubles. I was guilty for letting myself participate in this world's absurd circus. Distractions. There were too many distractions. I had been letting myself be sidetracked by inconveniences. I had allowed myself to succumb to the idea that life had a predetermined meaning. When in truth there was no ultimate meaning or message. It does not necessarily mean the origin of predetermination is wrapped within some omniscient message. If I had a purpose I had to find it. I had to finally decide that something was my purpose.

My dead friend Norm deserved better than to die the way he did. It robbed his life of a chance of redemption and made his existence seem rather superfluous and hollow. If I am sentenced to death it would be the result of a life wasted. Perhaps the possibility of my termination would be a justifiable result to my missed opportunity to make something meaningful out of my rather absurd life.

I once thought of death as a great adventure. Now I realized that a better adventure would be to live my life; meaningless or not, but with absolute freedom. I was going to live my life if I was given a second chance. Not many people in this world get second chances. Usually the insight comes later after a lifetime of mistake after mistake. Everyone makes mistakes. Some people make more mistake than others.

Then again, how could I find value in being alive after all that had happened to me? I wondered. Every attempt I made to create purpose had thus far proven futile. My father conveniently found his meaning through my existence, he often claimed. He would vicariously share all of the academic achievements I obtained throughout my life. Brag about me to any person who would listen. Luckily he did not live long enough to see me fail. To see that I would prove him wrong and show him that all my accomplishments were nugatory. My father was the lucky one. He died believing he was right, at least I think so.

The temperature dropped a little in my tiny cell. The change in temperature must have been from bad ventilation or bad insulation. I stretched my arms and realized I could touch two walls with both my hands at the same time while lying on my cell bed. If I could push the walls away. Push them far, far, far, away from me.

I pulled the covers on the bed open and slipped underneath them and propped the tiny pillow up in an attempt to sleep more comfortably. I then closed my eyes to sleep but my body wasn't quite ready for me to sleep. So I lay there with my eyes open. Eventually I would grow tired and my body would be forced to shut down for sleep.

Either way I wasn't going to get much sleep tonight. I would prefer to sleep through this entire experience and awake somewhere much more practical and convenient. Like on a beach with sand stuck between my toes. I thought about sleeping for a thousand years or thousands of years.

I could really use a cigarette right now, I thought. The sweet taste of tobacco followed by an insufficient buzz might be the trick to calm me enough to sleep, or at least close my eyes. Even though when I looked at my hand it was steady. My heart rhythm balanced. My breathing regular. My mind, however, was racing through every thought imaginable. My thoughts cycled through my childhood, my adolescence, my college years, and the recent endless months of my life. I imagined by now they had either fired me at Paper-Clips or had at least made a half-ass effort at inquiring on my location and condition. I might even get a promotion after I return when word got round of my experience. That would be the logical conclusion to the surreal fallacy that encompasses corporate retail. Or maybe it was more wishful thinking. I needed to let go of that and focus on getting through this thing if I hoped to sustain my sanity and dignity in this fool's game.

There is no dignity in being made to look a fool. There is no dignity in betrayal. Only more confirmation that we are all alone. Trust no one… never completely. Never let anyone totally into your heart. If you do they will use it against you someday. The evidence was clear before me. And yet we all make this mistake and so we all suffer. We all must endure. The fact that I was incarcerated was a way for the world to display me as its fool. I wondered how many more thoughts I would have under this same thesis. If I am sentenced to a life behind bars, perhaps I could write a sociological research paper on it. Though I found I was often bored with writing research papers. And there was the cliché. Another Mexican named James Luis Rodriguez behind bars. I didn't wear bandanas on my head, or shirts with only the top collar button buttoned, or call people *esse* or *homes*[28]. Yet say my name and most would not be surprised I ended up here in this cell and this very uncomfortable cell bed.

I was bored. Some hours had passed and I could not sleep. With nothing to do and being unable to sleep I remained stationed in limbo. So very bored. Of course, in jail it didn't matter anymore that I was broke. At least in here the jail provided me with free room and board and free food. All at the expense of the taxpayer. Then again, if I'm found guilty of these murders I might be sentenced to death. I felt like a hypocrite to start praying for redemption now from something invisible. If God is all knowing and all seeing like they say he is then he would more than likely see through me. It was better to be true to my convictions and myself. Should there be an afterlife, and if God is a forgiving God then I might be okay. If, however, God is a vengeful God and he may decide to punish me for my lust, my greed, my sloth, my wrath, my envy, my pride, and my apathy…. to name a few.

What if I didn't remain here under lock and key? What if I tried to escape? If I escaped I would always be running. I would turn myself into the greatest chameleon. I would turn myself into the greatest pretender. Like Harrison Ford in *The Fugitive*. Perhaps that is the ultimate freedom: The freedom of invention. I could determine any action or reaction I make without restraint. For, whenever anything tries to confine me I would change. I would change my personality. I would change my name. I would change my face. I would change my accent. I would change my language. I would become whatever I wanted to be at that moment and when convenient to me. I could leave people I found annoying or pursue those I found appealing. Whenever it pleased me. Again, there would be no restraints. I could be as bad as I want to be. Or I could be

---

[28] English translation: Spanish slang for "brother" or "friend" or "bro"

as good as I can pretend to be. It would be the ultimate act
of selfishness. I wanted to romanticize the version of
freedom some more but instead I shrugged it off like a
world that burdens only those who let it. I do not believe
this is a reality I would like to occupy. There is no virtue in
selfishness.

    The lights went out. All of them. Darkness.
Absolute darkness. My only light came from the faint
luminous moon. I wondered if there had been a power
outage. Perhaps the doors were now unlocked. No. That
can't be true. They're not connected.
    The darkness amplified all night outside. And I
dreamed. I dreamed while I was awake. I couldn't close my
eyes. There was no need to close my eyes because all was
dark. And then the moon would hide behind a cloud.
Whenever this happened during the night I was then in total
darkness. In absolute darkness my demons decided to
manifest before me.
    Horrible sickly visions materialized. I found myself
disabled by a sudden seizure that took control of my entire
body. All the fiends of my soul came at me with a vengeful
force. There was no remorse in their attacks. I was
paralyzed as these demons each took turns to visit me. Each
showed up, one after the another, more real than before. I
could not tell which of these visions were fantasies and
which was reality. My analytical spectrum told me they were
all illusions. But I was afraid to test this theory. I let it
happen. I let their memories torture me and pollute me.
    The cell floor changed from cement to dirt. I saw
my father's rotting corpse sticking out of the ground. He
was half covered in dirt and mud. Millions of worms
slithered in and out of his eye sockets, nostrils and mouth.
As worm after worm slid out of his mouth, my father's
mouth moved as if he was trying to say something to me. I
could not understand him because of all the slimy
earthworms sliding out of his mouth. And though his face

was covered in rotting flesh his fingers were all bones. He scraped the dirt off of him with his bone fingers. It seemed like he was saying I was not meant for this but I could not tell for sure.

Emilio, dressed in his best summer suit stood over my father's rotting corpse. He smoked a large Cuban cigar and wore his signature fedora. His cigar smoke snaked around him as he glared at me and puffed at me. Emilio then stepped on my father's bony fingers with great animosity. My father tried to cry in pain but could not. Then he said he was sorry for some reason. And then I saw Emilio get on his knees and pray to a deteriorating statue of Saint Mary, the mother of God, the Virgin mother. Tears of blood fell from her detailed round cheeks. And then they were all gone. It was silent and black for a moment. I wiped some of my sweat off my forehead.

Norm then appeared from the shadows. The moonlight reflected off his pasty zombie skin. He sliced his own head off his body. Blood was spilling everywhere. He cried, like a baby, as he tore his head off and looked at me as if it was my fault.

Ian crawled on top of me. He had no eyes but black holes where his eyes should have been. He grabbed my arm and squeezed my arm hard as he whispered, "I am no one. I am no one. I am no one," over and over again. I slapped him away, which made him disappear right before me.

I then saw Jasmine come toward me with a knife stabbing me over and over again. "Take that cocksucker!" she yelled while stabbing me. I saw my cuts from her stabs did not heal. Instead they opened more and more revealing my inner organs. My organs fell to the ground from my body one by one like lumps of rocks. I looked down and saw Jasmine, Ian and Norm eat my fallen organs like brainless zombies.

Tentacles snaked into my cell and grabbed my arms and my legs. The tentacles pulled and pulled at me until my arms and my legs torn off. And then.... when my seizure finally subsided and my breathing normal again and the sweating had ceased…. they were gone. And I was alone again in my cell. In the darkness with the moonlight.

I pulled my sweat drench covers off of me. I got up and went to the sink in the cell to splash some water on my face. The water's cool temperature temporarily reduced my panic attack. I let the water from the faucet run for a while. The flow of water was controlled and ordered. I cupped some of the water in my hands and then I drank some of it. I splashed some more water on my face and rubbed my eyes even though I could not see a damn thing. I felt around for a towel but could not find one. So I dried my face with my damp bed sheets. I pulled off some of wet sheets and lay back on top of my cell bed waiting for the next day to finally begin.

Dawn broke. I was starving. My long sleepless night had come to an end. I assumed someone would serve me breakfast sometime soon—somewhere—somehow. Or I would be taken to a place to consume my breakfast. Like a breakfast buffet with large quantities of various things to eat. I hoped it would be a full breakfast with buttermilk pancakes covered in maple syrup, sausages, biscuits and gravy. Or a Western omelet would also suffice. Waffles made fresh from one of those professional waffle makers. Juevos Rancheros or breakfast burritos and a cup of steel-cut oatmeal. Some yogurt and some strawberries to go with the yogurt. A tall glass of milk and a tall glass of orange juice. A cup of black coffee fresh ground and freshly brewed. A continental breakfast with everything I've already mentioned and more. I was really hungry.

16

WILLY introduced me to my lawyer, Jeffrey S. Dumont, III. He was clean-shaven. He wore a set of glasses with thick black frames. He was wearing a black suit with thin white strips made of some of the finest material I think I have ever seen. Around his neck instead of a regular necktie he instead opted to wear a bright red bowtie. He also fancied chewing tobacco. A habit he admitted picking up during his military service and was never able to quit. He refused to tell me who had hired him. My lawyer also assured me that his compensation would also be covered by this same anonymous benefactor. I did not protest. I felt a little relieved knowing I had a well-tested. And, according to Willy, well-respected counsel representing and advising me.

When we were finally alone I told my lawyer everything that happened from the night Jasmine came to pay me a visit. I told him about Jasmine's disappearance and note the following morning. I told him about the two ski-masked men who assaulted me the next morning, my adventures with Norm. I decided to leave the part out where Emilio shot and killed a waitress named, Tala. Although it did eat at me a little later. Sometimes we do things and we do not know ourselves why we're doing them. I told him about Ringo, also known as, Richard Starks. I told him about the car accident. The encounter with Ringo with Norm at my side. My lustful final meeting with Jasmine. And the morning where I awoke to find myself handcuffed to my deceased friend. And then I told him about Ian Noone. Who by this time I could no longer remember how he looked. Then I realized I forgot to tell my lawyer, Jeffrey, Ian's connection to all that I had happened. So I backtracked to the night where Norm and I encountered Ian at the Fish Bowl.

After all of the storytelling I asked my lawyer if he would get me a cigarette. My lawyer handed me a pack. He said he didn't smoke but always carried a pack of cigarettes with him just in case. After lighting the cigarette I smoked it in strides. I needed to save each drag and give the nicotine optimal time to work its magic and give me a buzz long overdue.

I chose to not tell him about Clint Eastwood or Steve McQueen. Or the security camera at The Fish Bowl, which was a very paranoid security camera, in my opinion. And I did not tell him that Norm had briefly changed into a monster made of tentacles and tried to strangle me to death. I also did not tell him about the nightmarish visions which paid me a visit last night in my cell. I had a feeling those details might hinder my chances at freedom. And I desperately wanted my freedom. I wanted to feel like I was in control of my destiny again. Even if it was an illusion.

My lawyer asked me to go over these details several more times as he made notes and chewed and spat his tobacco into a nearby paper cup. After the fourth telling my lawyer smiled. "Well," he said. "Golly. Looks like we have some consistency here—I'm happy to acknowledge. Oki dokie. Let me see. I think you will be okay. It really depends on whether or not the prosecutors agree. What did you tell the cops?"

"Nothing. My name and some very basic information. I told them I wouldn't say anything until I had consulted a lawyer."

"And they didn't press you for more info? No interrogation?"

"No. Not yet."

"Golly. They must like you for some strange reason."

"Willy told me I'm well-behaved and very polite."

"Yes. But that could also work against you. It may seem you are too calm. That you lack compassion for the deceased."

"What I feel inside is separate to how I appear to feel on the outside."

"Yes. Believe me. I understand. But appearances are everything sometime. What we have here is a case where you happened to be in the wrong place at the wrong time. Your story is strange. But the fact that you were handcuffed and found near a police station clearly suggests someone was trying to set you up. Now, if the police believe your story and they can find the person you believe is the guilty party, then we might be okay. As of right now you are the only suspect."

"So, I'm guilty till proven innocent?"

"Not exactly. It depends. They may dismiss the case for lack of credible evidence in the long run. Right now I don't know. But, I feel confident that you will be okay. Tell the police verbatim what you've told me. And don't worry. I'll be sitting right next to you."

"Damned if you do and damned if you don't."

"All right. I'll ask for the detectives to join us now. Don't worry. You'll do fine."

Willy and another investigator whose name I can't recall joined us. Willy was cordial from the very beginning. The other investigator sat and glared at me. He would impatiently tap his finger on the table while Willy asked me somewhat the same questions my lawyer had asked. Probably because the other investigator decided to not say anything might be why I do not remember his name. I assumed his presence was to offset Willy's agreeable demeanor. I found his tapping more distracting than intimidating.

After the questioning had concluded I was told they would let me know in an hour if I was going to be charged with anything. I asked them if I had to wait in the jail. They asked me if that would be problem. Before I could say anything my lawyer interjected that they could not hold me longer without any charges. I told my lawyer that it was okay if they could assure me, without a doubt, that it would be no longer than an hour. Willy agreed to my terms. And I returned to my cell to wait to find out if I was going to be charged with anything.

I paced around in my cell not because I was anxious. Not because I was deep in thought. I was very hungry, you see. It was near lunch and I was hoping I would get to eat soon before anything else. My stomach grumbled. The breakfast they served me was very bland. The breakfast consisted of a small can of fruit and a small box of cereal and a pint of milk and a prepackaged miniature muffin. This breakfast lacked taste and did not adequately fill my stomach.

Willy stopped by to see how I was doing. I asked him if they had made their decision yet. "We'll let you know within the hour," he sighed. He asked me if I was worried as he pointed out my pacing. I replied I was pacing only because I was really hungry and that breakfast proved less than appetizing. Willy laughed agreeing with me and left. And no lunch followed for a few more hours.

Later another cop finally appeared with a tray of food. Lunch! I received it in my cell and sat down immediately to eat whatever they had decided to serve me. It was a prepackaged sandwich, an apple, a can of soda, and prepackaged bread rolls. Yummy. I groaned at my continuing misfortune as I removed the sandwich from its plastic wrapping.

I chewed everything slowly so that it might fill me up better. I remember reading somewhere one time that if one eats their food slower it will cause them to feel full quicker—and not overeat. There was no chance I was going to overeat this meal. But I was going to do my best to not feel hungry again so much so later.

We returned to the interrogation room. Sitting next to me was my lawyer who handed me another cigarette and, of course, Willy. Willy told me that the people I named checked out. Ringo had been a person of interest for a long time. They checked out Jasmine and confirmed a Jasmine had worked at The Fish Bowl, but had not shown up to work the last three days. I asked them what they could tell me they knew about Jasmine and Ringo. Willy told me he was not at liberty to share that information with me.

I was no longer a suspect. I was now a witness. Only I wasn't. Willy explained to me that it would be hard to prove Ringo or Jasmine murdered Norm and Ian Noone. It was a situation that lacked evidence for them to do much of anything. I pleaded with Willy if there was anything else we could do. I didn't want my friend Norm to die in vain. Willy sighed that his hands were tied. He informed me that I should be thankful that I wouldn't be charged with murder. Then Willy shifted in his chair. He clasped his hands together and looked down at his papers.

"There's one more thing," Willy said.

"What?" I asked.

"Well. After we put you in our system… it turns out you're not really an American citizen."

"Wait. What? What do you mean? I've lived here all my life."

"I'm sure you think that, son. But the truth is your Social Security card is a forgery."

"But how was I able to use it for so long? I don't get it? Are you saying I'm an illegal immigrant?"

"That's what it looks like. I'm afraid in light of all that's happened it's been decided it would be best to deport you. Immediately."

"But didn't you tell me that I'm no longer a suspect? I have a college education. Doesn't that matter?"

"This is above my head. You see our system is connected to the FBI database. You can thank the Patriot Act for that. And when the FBI discovered you were an illegal immigrant.... Well, with the new tough immigration laws.... I'm sorry, son."

"I've lived here all my life. All my life. There must be some sort of mistake. Can you check again?"

"This is the world we live in now, Jimmy. No more amnesty. No nothing. If you're an illegal you're gone."

"Can we fight this?" I asked Jeffrey.

"I'm afraid he's right. We can't fight the deportation. At least, not right away. But we can work to fight to get you the right to return. But, I have to tell you, it will be a costly endeavor. I will have to check with your benefactor and see if he's willing to pay."

"I have a benefactor but I have to leave my country. This isn't fair. This is my country. I'm an American. Even if you can prove that I was not born here this is all I know. I don't know anything else."

"I'm really sorry about this," Willy said. "It's not right. But those are the rules now. If you're found to be an illegal then you have to go. No matter how long you have lived here."

"Calling someone illegal is like calling them a nigger," I said. "It dehumanizes a person."

Willy patted me on my hand while shaking his head in mutual disgust. We were all powerless to the laws that prohibited dignity in a nation that claims its foundation on the principles of liberty and freedom.

"Well. Do I get a week of probation or something? You know. To get my things and to say goodbye to my friends?" I asked.

"I'm afraid that's impossible, Jimmy. Homeland Security has decided that you are to be deported immediately."

"Don't worry, Jimmy. I'll get as many as your things from your place and bring them to you tomorrow," Jeffrey said.

"Wow. That's very kind of you, Jeffrey," I said.

"Well, if I could do more I would. Please believe me when I say I would do more if I could."

"This is a damn shame," Willy said.

"So I'm to stay one more night in my cell?"

"Yes. Sorry about that."

"Not as sorry as I am," I said.

We had only known each other for a brief moment. And yet we found a moment to embrace each other as if the struggle of being human had been something we had shared with each one another all our lives.

Knock. Knock. Knock.

"Who is it?" Willy asked.

"It's Hank, uh, Lieutenant," Hank said from the other side of the door.

"Hank, what do you want? We're a little busy right now."

"Can I come in?"

"It's okay," I said.

"Alright. Come in," Willy said to Hank

Hank came in holding a Styrofoam cup of coffee. "Need to tell you we are running low on space so we're doubling up on some of the rooms. Mr. Rodriguez is going to share a cell with a Mr. Clark Short."

"Mr. Short? Mr. Short? Dammit it all to hell! Who authorized that? The kid is being deported tomorrow. Can't we at least give him his own cell for the night?"

"The Captain made the authorization, Lieutenant, sir."

"Goddamit! Okay. Thanks for letting us know Hank."

"Sure thing," Hank said as he threw me a rather vindictive smile and then left.

"Willy. It's okay. In fact it might be nice to have someone to talk to tonight. I don't think I want to be alone tonight, anyway. I do have one question: Where is he going to sleep? There's only one bed in there right now."

"Oh. We've done it before. Your bed is stackable." Willy said. "I will do my best to see if you can at least have the cell to yourself or switch you with another individual."

"Oh. Again, it's not a big deal," I said.

"It should be. It's a big deal to me. Whoever this Mr. Clark is—and why he's sharing a cell with you doesn't make sense to me."

"Okay."

Willy threw his pen on the table muttering something to himself under his breath. I could tell he felt powerless to help me. I finished my cigarette and started another right away. Who knows if they will let me smoke when I return to my cell. Probably not. Jeffrey shifted through some paperwork and asked me sign something concerning his fee. I asked him if he was expecting me to pay him. He told me to not worry about it reminding me that everything had already been arranged. Then he asked me write down my address for him. I wrote it as neatly as possible with the knowledge I might never step foot in my apartment again. A place I had lived for over five years.

17

"I am a man of misfortune," Clark Short said. "I am for good but I am riddled with sin. I am told I should be ashamed but I'm not. I loved my mother and I loved my sister. I am not ashamed to admit loving two compassionate and caring women. I have loved others, too. Some don't believe in love like I do. Some call love taboo. But I have loved. I have desired. I have lusted. I am a sinner. And because of my actions I'm told to be ashamed. Luckily for me I have had everything I need in life. And I am thankful for that. I am not one to complain because I believe in a forgiving God. Because I often don't know what I do or not what I'm going to do. We are all really children of misfortune, Jimmy. You. Me. Them. Everyone. Everything. Last time I was in jail they were pretty mean to me. Not like you, Jimmy."

"This isn't your first time behind bars?" I asked.

"You seem surprised."

"Well. Yes I am. Maybe it's my bias, but you're wearing what looks like an expensive suit. You're very well groomed and your nails look like they are manicured. Maybe your crime is a white-collar crime. Right?"

"The last time I was in jail was really the first time for me. They were very mean to me. I didn't want to cause any trouble so I tried to be invisible. But every place I tried to stand one of these convicts tried to claim I was occupying his space. Anywhere else in the world and someone like me might be telling them the same thing. I guess this is the only place they had a sense of power. Whatever it may be. It did not give them the right to verbally abuse me the way they did. Granted, it was a very scary moment for me in my life. Luckily one of the convicts took pity on me. If it wasn't for that guy I might not be alive today. If it wasn't for his Christian compassion I might not be here talking to you. No, sir."

"What was his name?"

"You know. I don't remember. Funny, isn't it? I can't remember his name. But I've never stopped thinking of him. It's strange how life is. Don't you think?"

"So what are charged with?"

"The same thing I was charged with last time. The funny thing.... And I know I can tell you this because I know you're leaving the country tomorrow.... The funny thing is that they don't know that. I had that last charge dropped and erased from my record. And you know? I'll do the same thing again this time. Why? Because I can. God knows I'm sorry for my sins. God knows I have asked him for forgiveness. So there's no need for me to be punished anymore once I've confessed my sins to our heavenly Father. Don't you agree?"

"I can't say that I do."

"You don't believe in God's forgiveness?"

"I don't believe in God's compassion."

"Really? Wow. What caused you to second guess God?"

"It's a long story. But lately I haven't been sure there even is a God."

"Oh, there is a God. Believe me. I've spoken to him. I confess to him every day. And now I have a feeling that God brought me here to help you with your faith. I will do my best to help you with your faith tonight."

"Don't bother. The last thing I want is someone getting all evangelical on me my last night in the United States."

"You need to let go of all your hate inside. You need to let God work his magic on your soul."

"Like I was saying, no evangelizing tonight, please. So, did they arrest you for preaching the good word to people who didn't want to hear it?"

"No. I told you. My sin is love. I love too much."

"You love too much? Sounds like a bunch of horse shit to me."

"You know you shouldn't curse. It's a sin to curse. A minor sin, yes. But a sin is a sin. Sometimes small steps lead to bigger steps later."

"I'll ask for forgiveness later. I feel like you're being evasive now."

"Fine. Why was I arrested? I'll confess it to you. I will tell you. It doesn't matter if you know, right? You're going away. But you don't deserve my confession. Only God deserves my confession. But I'll tell you anyway. Maybe my action will rub off on you as an example of God's forgiveness."

"So, tell me."

Clark closed his eyes for a few minutes as if he was lost in prayer. Then he opened his eyes and began is if he was about to be his most sincere. "Well, I needed help. I was afraid. I have a wife and kid, you see. And in spite of these blessings I'm a troubled soul. I need to pray every day for forgiveness. I have little pictures running in my brain. Memories. They say I hurt that girl. I would never hurt someone intentionally. I'm not like that. But I saw her. She had such a pretty face. She had beautiful black hair. She lived in my neighborhood. She played with my kid. And then one day I saw her on her cute little bike. I was alone. She was alone. So I start talking to her. She wasn't afraid of me. She trusted me because she knew me. I asked why she was playing alone. She said her parents had gone to get some groceries. Her parents told her to stay inside but she wanted to ride her bike. So she disobeyed. I told her that maybe she should listen to her parents and stay in her house. That what she did was a bad thing. She was about to cry when I tried to stop her. I told her I have some Popsicles in my house. I asked if she wanted one. She nodded her head. So, we went inside my house. We were alone together. And I got her a Popsicle. While she was eating her Popsicle I told her she had very beautiful hair. I asked her if it would be all right if I touched her hair. She nodded again and didn't say anything. So I touched her hair. And it was innocent until it wasn't anymore. And my hand went from her hair to touching other parts. It was like my hand had a mind of its own. And then… and then… well. She—"

"I'll stop you right there. I don't think I want to hear anymore."

"But I have to tell you everything. How else am I to give you my confession if I don't tell everything?"

"No. I don't think so. I don't want to hear anymore."

"You hypocrites are all the same. You have to let go of your pride if you are ever to receive God's salvation and forgiveness."

"How many times have you done something like this, Clark?"

"Why do you ask? Why should I tell you? You stopped me right when I was about to tell the best and most revealing part of the story."

"Lookit. Answer my question first."

"Many times. The first time was when I was seventeen. My younger sister had a friend over. And well, you know? Each time though, I was sorry after it happened. I asked God to forgive me, and he did. But out of all the times I've sinned I've only been arrested twice. That's because God was watching. He knew I was sorry for what I had done. But sometimes God challenges us and that's probably why I got caught. This time and one time before. I'm a man of misfortune. But my misfortune here will be my fortune in the afterlife when God accepts me into his heavenly kingdom. Don't you see?"

"No. I don't. I think you're a sick pedophile psychopath who has found a pathetic way to rationalize his perversions. And I'm not your father confessor. I won't offer you any redemption or forgiveness. I only would offer you damnation."

"To each his own. To each his own. But you're the one who needs help, my friend. Not me."

"Lookit. I'm not your friend. You don't know me from Adam, man. Tomorrow I'm gone and the only part of that which makes me happy is knowing I will never see your sorry ass again."

"Why are you getting so hateful with me? I've been nothing but kind to you. Hating me for what I've done is no reason to hate me now. I've already told you I'm a man of misfortune."

"Why am I forced to share a cell with you on my last night in the America? Why? You know what? I'm tired now. All I want to do is sleep. Leave me alone. I'm going to bed. Good night."

"Fine. But I'll pray for you. I'll pray for you, friend."

"You'll pray for me? You know what? Don't bother. You're the last person I want to be praying for me. Your prayers would only hurt me. Not help me."

"Sticks and stones. And your words will not hurt me. For, I have Jesus on my side. He's my driver."

"Would you give it a rest, Clark?"

"You're the one who asked."

Later that night I awoke to the sound of Clark Short snoring in the bunk above me. He snored like he didn't give a damn. He snored under the assumption that he could do whatever he pleased as long as he asked God for forgiveness. He snored like a beast slumbering in a cage before being freed to attack while his victims sleep. Innocent of his true intentions. He was the monster who made things go bump in the night when they normally do not go bump. He was more of a monster than any person I have encountered in my lifetime thus far.

I waited. 2:00 AM approached with the coming and going of the vibrating ventilation system. I somehow knew that at 2:00 AM Clark Short would shed his human skin and reveal himself to me in his true form. I wagered my options when the moment happened. I wondered what I would do and how I would react. Nothing he changed into would change my animus toward him. The hostility growing inside of me only nurtured my abhorrence for Mr. Short. He was revolting. He was disgusting. And soon we may do battle. One way or another.

The bunk beds began to shake. I heard a deep groan from the above bunk where Mr. Short was sleeping. He was changing. He was turning to reveal beastliness underneath. This scoundrel of scoundrels. This low of lows. Who breathed my air. With which I was forced to share with a cell. No more. No more would I let him bother me or anyone else. I had to attack him after he had changed to his true form. Then he would be weakened. Then I might get the better of him. And destroy him.

The bed shook as if a demonic being was making it presence known. Much like that scene in *The Exorcist*. When the bed began to shake out of control while the two priests tried in vain to fight the demon who had possessed that innocent girl. That poor innocent girl. An innocent child, the victim of choice for Mr. Short. Scoundrel! You hateful, hateful, hateful thing!

I couldn't take it any longer. I jumped out of the lower bunk bed. The bed was shaking and bumping against the cell wall. I moved to one side of the bunk bed where the rails were. I climbed up a little to get a closer look at Mr. Short's transformation near his feet. I hoped I didn't disturb him in the wrong way. I'm not sure why I decided to do this. I wanted to peak to see what was happening to him. He was not a man. He was a sick disgusting creature who didn't deserve anything that had been given to him.

What I saw was worse than what I could have imagined. He was not changing into anything. Not at all. Horns weren't protruding from his balding head. Fangs weren't growing out of his mouth. His skin wasn't changing to scales. Even his eyes were very normal: they weren't red or lizard like. They were green. A very emerald green. But he did not take notice of me. He was transfixed in a moment of disgusting hyperventilation from some fantasy he was having. Drool fell from the sides of his mouth. He breathed in and out like a wounded manatee. Then I discovered the origins of the earthquake the bed was having.

He had pulled down his pants revealing everything below the waist. Both his hands were wrapped around his very erect penis. He was feverishly shifting his stick to the point of giving himself a rug burn. It was more disgusting than I thought. His balls looked rather swollen. All around his private area were clusters of inflamed papules and vesicles on the outer surface of the genitals. Resembling cold sores. I jumped off the bed and regurgitated the dinner I had eaten earlier. Now some of my puke was on the floor. I sweat a little after I puked and was momentarily overcome by a small fever. When my body temperature had stabilized I knew what had to be done. Mr. Short needed to die and I was going to kill Mr. Short, if it was the last thing I would ever do in my country, I was going to kill that man. That pedophile.

I grabbed the top sheet off my bed and began twisting it around until it took on a rope-like shape. From the intensified breathing and shaking I could tell Mr. Short was about to climax. I would rob him of that moment. With the twisted sheet I quickly wrapped it around his neck catching him totally off guard. He let go of his erect penis and reached up with both his hands trying to pull off the twisted sheet around his neck. The more he pulled at it the tighter I squeezed.

"W-W-What ... what .... are you d-d-doing?" He wheezed out through the asphyxiation.

"I'm killing you, Mr. Short. I'm killing you."

"Y-Y-You can't do this. Please ... stop!"

I ignored his requests for compassion and empathy. The only compassion and empathy I had were for Mr. Short's victims. And tonight I was Clark Short's judge, jury, and executioner.

"I have money. L-l-lots of ... m-m-money."

"You said it yourself. It doesn't matter what you tell me. Tomorrow I'm being deported. So, that got me thinking. It doesn't matter what I do to you. Because tomorrow I'm being deported."

"Please! Oh God! Please!"

"Mr. Short. I am the hand of God. I am the hand of vengeance. And tonight you will die for all your sins."

"No! Please! God! No!"

He struggled some more. I did not realize how long it would take to strangle him. I had to give it to him, he was a fighter. He would not go gently into the night. No one who is dying ever does. My muscles were beginning to ache and I began to sweat a little more. Eventually he struggled less and less until his body went limp. I kept a tight hold around his neck a few more minutes to ensure that he was dead. To make sure he was not playing possum, or something like that.

I let go finally having resolved he must be dead by now. I unwrapped the twisted sheet from his neck. With two of my fingers I checked for a pulse. I didn't feel one. But I wanted to be absolutely certain the monster of a man was totally dead. I remember seeing a bad guy kill another bad guy in a movie by twisting the dude's neck. I decided to attempt the neck twisting myself. I wrapped one my arms around his head and jerked it quickly. I heard a crack and I then I knew I had achieved my goal. Mr. Clark Short was dead.

I took a few breaths to collect myself. I looked around the tiny cell at the mess I had made. Some puke on the floor. The now deceased Mr. Clark lying in his bed with his pants down. His penis erect. That sick bastard remained aroused while I was killing him. And it remained erect after his eminent demise. Disgusting.

With the twisted sheet I used it to cleanup the puke. I laid the sheet, now drenched in my puke, over Mr. Clark. Then I pulled the rest of his sheets over him. I closed his eyes and turned his head to the side to make it look like he was sleeping. After doing all of that I went to the sink and splashed some water on my face several times.

Then I got back in my bed and went to sleep as if nothing had happened. Mr. Clark would never harm another child. I had done a good deed. Now I felt ready to face whatever next would happen to me.

18

ONCE again I was chained to a chair. But this time I was chained to a chair in an airport. I sipped my cup of coffee Willy had been kind enough to purchase for me. Willy sipped his.

"Damn. That's some good coffee, ain't it?" Willy said.

"Yes. It's really good."

"Yeah. That's Dunkin' Donuts coffee for you. But you know what also makes this coffee special? The folks who run this Dunkin' Donuts are Ethiopian. I got this book on the history of coffee my wife bought me for Christmas some time ago. I found out that the origin of coffee is in Ethiopia. My dumb ass thought it was South America. Wow. The things we assume. That's why we should always read. Anyway, best coffee, bar none. Ain't no comparisons."

The airport expanded while the walls remained compact. Spread throughout in dense waves were the airport's perfidious and always complaining patrons. Comprised of the middle-class vacationing avaricious passersby. The preoccupied children with their cancerous tantrums. And the bemused business travelers who all read the stocks with rapacious eyes from their crinkled newspapers. Only a few seemed to reluctantly take notice of me or looked through me as if I was invisible—as if I was inconsequential. I was unequivocally and severely invisible. I was an invisible man as far as the laws of the land of red, white and blue were concerned. I was easily disposed. Label me persona non grata. Label me no one.

So I was being punished. The punishment was based on decisions my father made on my behalf before I was even self-aware or capable to provide input. Those memories were like empty roads curving through a vacant desert in my mind. And they went nowhere. At the moment the only person who seemed to care was Willy. He had taken it upon himself to oversee my transportation and deportation. The representatives of the Department of Homeland Security wore blue jackets. They asked me to sign here and sign there. They brought interpreters because for some reason they didn't think I could speak English well or fluently.

Someone squeezed my shoulder.

"You think you can leave without saying goodbye, *hijo*?" Emilio said with his signature thick Latino accent.

"Jimmy. You know this man?" Willy asked.

"Yes. It's okay, Willy. Don't worry," I said.

"Can we have a moment, officer?"

"Well. I suppose it's okay. I'll sit over here. Give you some space. But I'll be keeping my eyes on you. Got me?"

We both nodded.

"You sure you want to be seen with me? I'm surprised you even want to talk to me after everything that happened," I said.

"Water under the bridge. You are in a much more serious situation. Mira. Here is a box for you."

"I'll need to inspect that box," Willy yelled from his seat at us.

"*¿Qué? Sí. Sí.* Sure. Sure." Emilio got up from the seat next to me. He handed the box to Willy. He had maneuvered far enough away where he couldn't eavesdrop but still keep watch over me without any trouble. Willy opened the box, shuffled through the boxes articles, and then handed it back to Emilio.

"*Gracias*, officer." Emilio then came back to me and handed the box to me.

"What's with the box?"

"I made a promise a long time ago to give this to you when I felt you were ready. I never felt you were ready. Even now I am not sure you are ready but now I see we don't have a choice. *¿No?* So, it is best to give you the box now."

"What are these things?"

"These are the things that used to belong to your mother, Jimmy. These are things that will tell you all about your mother."

"My mother? How can this tiny box tell me everything I need to know about my mother? What do you know about my mother?"

"Your mother asked me to look over you when she found out I was coming here."

"So, my mother is alive? Where is she? In Mexico?"

"*Sí. En México.* They're scattered things that belonged to her. So you can know a little about her, I guess. She was a very beautiful woman, Jimmy. All the men wanted to marry her. But your mother fell for your father. I'm sorry to tell you this. When your father came here he kidnapped you. What I mean is he took you without telling your mother. And after he left with you he never let her contact you again. She tried. Many times she told me she tried. She was even going to try to find a way to travel to the United States to find you. She was going to come with me but then she got sick. Sick enough that she could not travel. Some say she was sick with a broken heart. But I don't believe that. Maybe it was something in the water. You know how bad the water is in Mexico. And people are very superstitious there. But I knew your mother. I loved your mother very much, Jimmy. She didn't deserve to be abandoned like she was by the two of you. Maybe your father he was doing the right thing. Who knows? Really, who knows why people what they do? All I know is she made me promise to give this to you before I left. I never contacted her again, either. Maybe I'm as horrible. I didn't want to. When I found you I was afraid if I told her it would make her worse and even more depressed. So I did not tell her anything. I thought if I left her with a hope that I might contact her back it would be better. Because if I contacted her who knows what she would have done next? *No sé*[29]. And to this day I miss her, Jimmy. But like I said I can't go back to see her. Because I know she's not how I remember her."

Emilio's eyes began to water. He pulled out a handkerchief to wipe his eyes and blow his nose. I noticed Tala, whom I thought was dead, rush to sit beside Emilio. She wrapped her arms around Emilio in an attempt to offer him comfort. Emilio shoved her off.

"I told you to wait over there."

"I'm sorry Emilio. I saw you crying and I wanted to make sure you were okay." Tala said.

"I thought you were dead. I thought Emilio killed you?" I said.

"Theatrics are sometimes necessary I have found. I was only trying to scare you. But here we are now. Water under the bridge."

"You know. I don't care anymore. You're not dead. That's good. But I have many other things on my mind."

"*Sí, por supuesto, mi hijo*[30]. Everything you need to find your mother is in that box. At least I hope so. And when you find your mother you will find her family. I was told they visit her every day. They will take care of you. Trust me. Family means much more in Latin America than it does in the United States. Now, I must go." Emilio began to get up and leave then stopped as if he suddenly

---

[29] English translation: "I don't know."

[30] English translation: "Yes, of course, my son."

remembered something very important. "I almost forgot. Here." He handed me a piece of paper. "When you get in Mexico, go to this house, first. They will give you a room. Also call me at this number after you get there. It's a local number but it will connect to me here. Don't worry. Everything is arranged."

"Everything is arranged?"

"Yes. You are a smart kid. *Muy inteligente*. I almost forgot to tell you. I set up a job for you to teach English. We need more teachers. Don't you think? Like they say, the dream begins with the teacher. No? I think so."

"There's still something that bothers me which I hope you can help me with, Emilio?"

"And what is that, *hijo*?"

"Whatever happened to Ian Noone?"

"Oh. Him again. You still think I killed him?" he smiled.

"I don't care if you did or not anymore. I just want to know what happened."

"Bad luck. That is what happened to him. Let me explain. But first I must ask: What do you know about Jasmine?"

"The last night we spent together she told me about her past and how she's been trying to escape it most of her life."

"Yes. But she didn't tell you anything about Ian Noone?"

"Not a thing."

"Very well. Ian Noone was no one. He was nothing. He was someone who happened to be in the wrong place and at the wrong time. He was what he said he was. He was going to be a doctor and he was going to get married. But he also had a secret. We all have secrets. His secret was a little addiction to a white dragon called cocaine. I was not involved with this. You see he had the misfortune to make arrangements with Ringo, of all people. A very unstable and unforgiving person as you have recently learned. Apparently he owed Ringo a considerable amount of money. I think he was going to try to convince Ringo to give him more time to forgive him for his debt. But Ringo was going to make an example of him. He was going to have Big Ray break his hand and fingers so that he would have a difficult time being a doctor. Cruel. I know. I think he was studying to be surgeon. Anyway, that night was when Jasmine recognized him. At first she didn't know who he was but eventually she realized he was related to her ex-husband. So, for some reason she convinced Big Ray and Ringo to get rid of him. Fear makes sometimes brings out the worse in people. But those three idiots made a mess of things. They called me asking if I would help them clean their mess. I didn't want to but I have a soft heart for Jasmine. I agreed under the condition that Ringo leave town as soon as possible. Alas, he didn't listen. Don't worry, though. He is being taken care of as we speak. He won't be bothering another person again. So, by that time the son's of Jasmine's ex-husband had already discovered her whereabouts and heard about what they did to their cousin Ian Noone. But only Ringo, Big Ray, and Jasmine knew of Ian's cocaine problem. And the two sons of Jasmine's ex-husband decided not to tell the cops. They would let the cops figure it out themselves. Or at least that is what they hoped would happen. As for Jasmine, they still wanted only to pursue her. They wanted revenge for their father and revenge for Ian. Even though I don't think they really cared for Ian. So that is why Jasmine left. I am very sorry she did what she did to you but I also told you to never trust her."

"How do you know all these things?"

"I have eyes, ears, and noses everywhere. Everywhere!" he then looked at his watch and then said, "Look at the time! Your plane is going to leave soon. If you want to know more you can ask me later, but there is not much more to tell you. I must leave you now! *Ciao.*"

I waved goodbye to them both awkwardly. I had no more words to say and Emilio only squeezed my shoulder implying he understood there was no need for more words at this moment. He could not or would not hug me. Emilio then put on his white fedora and turned away looking sharp in his white summer suit. Tala wrapped her arm around his arm and they walked away like the end of some cheesy 1940's romance film with Humphrey Bogart and Lauren Bacall. Perhaps the beginning of a beautiful romance or friendship. Or something like that.

After Emilio left I opened the box to spend more time scrutinizing its inner contents. I found a picture of a young beautiful Mexican woman with long black hair. She had a big flower in her hair and a warm smile that evoked a sense of innocence and wonder. She wore a dated summer dress and looked to be no more than eighteen in the picture. I turned the photo around. Something resembling a date was written in pen on the back. But it was scribbled over so much that I could not figure it out. I found an envelope that was sealed shut. I opened the envelope and pulled out two folded sheets of paper. On the first sheet was an address. I wondered if that was my mother's address. Above the address was my mother's name: Esperanza Maria Valdez Lopez.

There were other pictures. Pictures of my mother with people who were probably her family. Pictures of my mother with people who were probably her friends. A photocopied piece of paper of my mother's High School Diploma, I think. The school was called *Nuesta Madre de …* something. I couldn't make the rest out. A small white glove with laces around the wrist area. I found another envelope marked with my name. When I opened it up I discovered it was a lock of what must have been my hair when I was a baby, maybe. A picture of my mother in a hospital bed holding a baby—probably also me. And a letter addressed to me written in Spanish, of course. I found no pictures of my mother with my father. There was a children's book also written in Spanish that looked like it was published long before I was born. I do not understand how these items would tell me all about my mother. Instead I found myself more curious and hit with a barrage of many more questions. Questions I hoped I would find the answers to after I entered my new country. Or my country of origin.

I closed the box.

The airport intercom echoed. Willy escorted me onto the plane to where I was assigned to sit. We began to exchange goodbyes. Willy took the handcuffs off me and undid my restraints.

His radio squirmed. Willy ear's twitched. He held the handheld radio up to his ear and listened to their garbled commands. Then he turned off the radio and placed it back in the holster on his belt.

"They think you killed Clark Short. You did. Didn't you, Jimmy?" Willy asked. I didn't say anything. "I knew a little about him. I knew enough that I don't blame you for doing it. Well, there's no turning back now. You were in the air before I could stop you."

"Why are you letting me go?"

"Jimmy. I've been a cop for a long time. A long time. When you've been a cop as long as I have been you see many things. Things you wished you had never seen. Things you wish you could erase from your memory but you can't. They say experiences are what make a man. After everything I've seen and some of the things I've done to protect and serve. I sometimes wonder what kind of man I am? I am supposed to represent good. I am supposed to uphold the law. And at what cost? The older I get the more grey I see and the less black and white things are. One of my first arrests was the arrest of a man, no more than twenty-one, who was accused of pedophilia. Well, I watched a rich man accused of one of the worst crimes a human being could conceive walk through our jail like it was some kind of revolving door. Not because he was innocent. He wasn't. I can tell when I man is innocent or not. All you have to do is look into their eyes. It's an unwanted talent you pick up after being a cop for as long as I have. I've looked into the eyes of pure evil. And that was an evil man. But because of his family and because of his money he got away. He was probably going to get away again if you hadn't... well, when I see you Jimmy I see a sad kid. I see someone who has had some bad luck. But bad luck and good luck doesn't tell me who you are. Its what you do. And you did the only right thing you thought you could do. They have taken everything from you. They have taken away your country. And despite all these things you could've let cynicism let that man go. But you didn't. You didn't. We all make mistakes but it's the people who get back on the horse who are the real heroes. It's the people who never let go of their hope in humanity. That's why I'm letting you go. I'm also letting you go because I know if I were in that cell alone with that man I would've done the same thing. And I do not hesitate when I tell you this: this world is a little better off with a man like that dead and gone. This world will be only a little better when all men like Clark Short are gone. Gone to never come back again. Gone to never harm another innocent child again. Gone to not hurt the people we care about. Like the one who hurt my little brother a long time ago. He was a good baby brother. Never deserved what he got. I vowed to get the man who hurt my brother. I never did. I never will. The man who hurt my brother could be dead of natural causes now. All I know is I got a little more justice in my heart knowing you stopped that man the same way I would. But don't take this as a get out of jail free card. No sir. This is an opportunity for you to improve... always improve. Be a better man. Always try to be a better man, Jimmy. And everything else will figure itself out."

"Take care, Willy," I said.

"You take care, Jimmy. Remember; don't lose what faith in yourself you have been able to keep inside."

"I'll try."

Willy left. I had a window seat, which gave me a view and a distraction. And I went to sleep knowing I would wake up somewhere foreign and empty to me.

PART FOUR

19

THE airplane cabin hummed. My seat was reclined. I licked the peanut salt off my fingers. Then I wiped my hands with a small paper napkin. I pulled out the SkyMall catalog that always reminded me of the Brookstone stores in the mall. I shifted through the pages wondering what a so-called "ultra sonic dog deterrent" that looked like a birdhouse would be like. Or the water bowl built to resemble a toilet bowl for cats and dogs. I thought how ridiculous to buy a $50 water bowl shaped to resemble a toilet bowl.

"You know, I never did like peanuts that much. They kind of leave a bad after taste. If you know what I mean? And they stick to your teeth and everything," said Clint Eastwood.

Clint was sitting next to me in the middle seat. And sitting in the aisle seat was none other than Steve McQueen. Both were drinking whiskey on the rocks in lowball glasses. Steve was wearing a burgundy turtleneck and one of those sport coats with the elbow patches. Clint was dressed in a casual white shirt and regular jeans.

"That's why I always have something to drink afterwards," I said and pointed to my plastic cup of Coke.

"Ah, yes. But then again if you always have to have a drink to wash away the taste and debris of the peanuts, then what's the point of eating the peanuts? Protein? Give me a bag of trail mix any day over a bag of salted peanuts. Kid, let's cut to the chase. We're here to say goodbye. It's been fun but we must part ways from this point forward." He grinned without showing any teeth and squint his eyes. A squint which made cowardly men flee and brave men admire.

"You guys are not coming with me?" I said.

"Nope." Clint said.

"That's too bad," I said.

"We are such stuff as dreams are made of. Rounded out with a sleep," Steve said. "We are all drivers on our own roads. Sometimes we need help with directions. But in the end we all arrive at our destination. Alone."

"It's going to be hard not having you guys as my imaginary friends. I had become quite fond of having you guys around from time to time giving me advice and yelling at me."

"Well. I ain't one to get sentimental. But I'll be missing you too, kid. Our mission is done here, though," Clint said.

"It's logical. Everything ends. Everything has a cycle. Stars are born and then die like everything else in the universe." I said.

"But something always comes out of the leftovers. What's that thing you like to say about stardust, kid?" Steve asked.

"Oh yeah! We are made up of leftover pieces of stardust."

"Ain't that the truth? Fairy dust. Stardust. Smoke and ash. We rise, we fall. Continuity. Shit. Did I make a haiku?" Clint said.

"No. I don't think so," Steve asserted.

"So. What are you going to do now, kid? It's a fresh start. You get to start a new life in a new country and live the dream and not dream the dream," Clint said.

"Live life how you want. Become a new star out of an old fading star," Steve added.

"I don't know. I haven't really thought of that. The future seems more uncertain to me than ever before. The only thing I really want to do first is maybe find my mother. Maybe I'll quit smoking."

Clint and Steve both looked at each other. They seemed lost in a telepathic conversation since they were staring at each other for a long time and would take turns nodding and shaking their heads. I assumed they were speaking telepathically so I could not hear what they were saying about me. I felt like a child not understanding what his parents were talking about. I soon resolved I had enough of their head nods and head shakes and threw the ice left in my plastic cup at both of them.

"That wasn't necessary," Steve said.

"Christ, kid!" Clint yelled.

"Sorry guys. I got tired of waiting for you to talk to me again."

Clint, Steve and I discussed the many shenanigans we had all been through together. Most of which I cannot recall anymore. We laughed and we cried and we hugged and we punched each other as if we had always been the closest of friends. They were my dream mates. Things I had conjured up when I was bored and had nothing better to think about.

In the end perhaps it was all boredom's fault. I felt for a long time I had nothing particular to do with my life. I had lost interest in almost everything. And I was bored by the grey surroundings that occupied Ohio. After my father passed away I became really depressed. I was depressed for a very long time. And then I realized one day everything was meaningless to me. I wanted out but did not know how to get out. I wanted a way to be free and fly into the sky and become as cool as Clint Eastwood and as hip as Elvis Presley and as relaxed as Steve McQueen. I wanted to become more than I thought I was because everything and everyone around me was all so boring. And there I deferred myself from my father's dream. And then I drifted. I drifted away like a boat cast to sea without anchor and without captain and without destination.

Steve stood up at one point announcing he had to pee and promised us he would be right back. The seatbelt sign went on in the plane. I knew Steve would never come back and I was okay with that. Some people can't handle goodbyes. Clint tried to give me some more broken advice and some more cowboy wisdom. But he was fairly drunk by now. I told Clint I hoped to meet the real Clint Eastwood one day. Clint tilted his head for a moment.

"Anything can happen, kid. Why, I once met Humphrey Bogart. He was something of an idol to me. Everyone thinks my idol was John Wayne. Hell! He was all right but he was no Bogie," Clint said then gulped down the last of his whiskey.

My eyes were growing heavy. The cabin pressure was doing a number on me as the onslaught of a massive headache soon took over. I thought nothing of it but decided I would close my eyes for only a moment. So I closed my eyes. And when I opened my eyes time had passed again. I had lost time. And Clint was gone. It was me with two strange men who looked Mexican. One was watching an inflight movie while the other was reading a book written in Spanish with Oprah Winfrey on the cover. I wanted to punch both of them. I wanted them to go away and leave me alone.

I felt awful again.

20

I was dreaming. I was sure I was dreaming. Maybe I wasn't dreaming anymore.

When I got off the plane and after I went through customs and after they had processed me the Mexican authorities let me go. I entered the country of Mexico left to my own devices. I did not know where to start. Everything smelled different and everything felt different. I found a payphone right outside the airport and dialed one of the phone numbers Emilio had given me. No one answered. I waited an hour near the phone. I watched everyone walk by speaking a language I was having a hard time comprehending, even after my recent studies. I thought by now I would understand better but most seemed to be speaking in a dialect with which I was not familiar. Now I had no choice. I was going to learn to speak Spanish whether I liked it or not.

Everything was crazy outside. The street vendors sold everything from empanadas to lemonade to fruit to candy to plastic Mayan temples. And dolls dressed in Aztec clothing. Cab drivers yelling at me to see if I needed a ride. Groups of people waiting outside for their loved ones to meet them after leaving the airport terminal. In the distance I thought I smell sautéed onions that made me realize I was also a little hungry.

I called the phone number again, dialing collect from a collect phone card Willy had given me. I had to figure out a way to leave a message. After several more minutes of waiting, and trying to breathe through Mexico City's congested smog, the payphone rang. I answered the payphone and on the other end was Emilio. He asked me where I was. I told him I was at the airport but outside sitting near this payphone not sure what to do next. He told me that I would have to sit there and wait. He promised me that someone would arrive soon enough to pick me up and take me to the place Emilio had set up for me. I asked him how long I would have to wait. He told me that in Mexico everyone is always late. I would have to find a way to get used to waiting. He advised that in order for me to survive in Latin American I needed to erase the words "wait" and "late" from my vocabulary. So I waited deciding the best way to pass the time was smoking a few cigarettes.

Smoking was like an international peace sign. Every now and then some fellow smokers would sit with me sharing a smoke or asking to bum a drag. Small talk came along with the inhaling tobacco. I did my best in my broken Spanish to contribute in the small talk. No one seemed surprised I was American. Paranoia made me worry that someone might try to steal my bags from me or beat me up and take my money. That never happened. It was an unnecessary fear. I however, remained cautious for I was the outsider after all. Wasn't I?

Several hours passed before a rusted and beat-up Volkswagen Beetle swerved near the median. It stopped right near where I was sitting. I man who looked like he was in his forties stepped out holding a sign with my name on it. He was wearing a New York Yankees baseball cap. The green t-shirt he was wearing looked like had been wearing that same t-shirt his entire life. I raised my hand and told him it that I was the man for whom he was looking. He looked at my blankly. So, I said the same thing, again. Only this time I did it in my best broken up Spanish. He smiled and laughed and grabbed my bags. I got in the car. It smelled like armpit. He turned up the car radio. I would soon find out his car radio played nothing but salsa music. If I tried to change the station he would yell at me. My driver told me him his name was Hector and I told him it was nice to meet him, in Spanish, of course. After that we both listened to salsa music in silence the entire hour and a half drive sweating in the hot Mexican heat. I fantasize learning to dance salsa and merengue. Or any other dance I could learn during my permanent banishment from the United States.

A small town soon appeared over the horizon. Hector exited off the highway into the town and then turned right into a street of narrow houses. They looked like someone had squished them together. My driver got out and took my bags out of the car. He then waited for what I assumed was a tip. I had not exchanged my dollars to pesos so I handed him a US twenty dollar bill. I figured he had deserved it after such a long trip. He jumped at the sight of Andrew Jackson. He pointed at one of the houses. Then bounced back into the Volkswagen Beetle and drove off. The smell of smog somehow followed us from Mexico City to this small nameless town. I remember seeing a woman walking on the side of the street, carrying some groceries, and wearing a surgical mask. I remember thinking either she was crazy or really smart.

I walked to the door and knocked waiting for someone to answer. I was greeted by a young woman dressed as a maid. She had big cheeks and was always smiling. I held up the sign with my name on it and motioned at my bags sitting next to me. She said nothing but nodded her head and then closed the door. I stood there waiting for what must have been fifteen minutes before someone else opened the door. Emilio was right about all the waiting.

An older woman, dressed in a modest dress greeted me in broken English. She knew who I was and showed me the room where I was going to be staying. She told me her name was Maria. I thought Maria was too common of a name in Latin America. After I had placed my bags inside the room she pulled me into the kitchen where I was introduced to her little daughter, husband and tiny dog. I'm not sure what kind of dog they had. It looked like a mix of some sort.

We all ate dinner together speaking through broken Spanish and English. However, Maria's husband Rigo spoke English very well. He even knew some American colloquialisms such us hey brother and what's up? and whatever. After answering what seemed like a million questions about America and my education Rigo took me with him alone to his office. He asked if I smoked I said yes and told him it had been a while since I had a cigarette. Yes, it was a lie but nicotine had proven to be a reliable sedative from all the stress in my life. I promised myself I would quit someday—whenever someday comes. Rigo pulled out a pack of smokes and we sat in his office smoking cigarettes and downing shots of tequila. Rigo was a professor. He was probably the connection Emilio needed to get me that teaching gig he claimed he had procured for me. He told me I would teach English at a private for-profit institution. It teaches only English to any Mexican who applies and can pay the bill. Since, many Mexicans want to go to the United States, there were many private English schools offering English classes. Rigo told me, even though I would not make much money, in Mexico I would make enough to be their version of middle class.

I asked Rigo when I would start teaching. He told me he was going to have me wait at least a month before he would allow me to start teaching. He said he didn't want to throw me in there blind with those pack of wolves. He said first I needed to get used to Mexican culture, the food, and go over the lesson plans for the English classes I would eventually teach. I found myself suddenly very excited to be teaching. I was excited to be in a new country. I was excited that I would get the chance to start over.

That first night in Mexico I did not sleep a wink. I was excited. I heard different sounds at night in Mexico over the sounds I might hear in the United States. I also heard familiar sounds. I heard them like I never heard them before. I felt a strange sense of calm take over me. That night I did not think of all the bad things that had happened to me. I did not think much of anything of the past. Instead I thought about the future. I thought about the chance to start a new life. The chance to start a new career. The chance to meet a beautiful Mexican woman and marry her. And have children with her. And grow old with a big Mexican mustache and I thought about being called Don Rodriguez one day. I thought I could save my money and buy a ranch somewhere in Mexico and sell cattle to Texas. And I did not care if I ever returned to the United States. If they didn't want me then they would never have me again. I was a son of Mexico now.

I now imagined myself plucking the string of a twelve string Spanish guitar with my fellow Mariachis. We would sing in unison. Random Mexican women would dance a lustful dance to our crooning. They would throw themselves at me, tearing off our clothes, exposing their beautiful brown skin. Their large breasts and round asses. I would charm them with my loner *machismo* persona which always resulted with me yelling *¿POR QUÉ?* at the moon followed by the raising of only one eyebrow. That would make the women go even crazier. I would take shots of tequila between songs and between bathroom breaks. Bathrooms were not bathrooms. Bathrooms were now *baños*. Beers were no longer beers. Beers were now *cervesas* with limes in them. Friends were not friends. Friends were now amigos who called you *cabrón* and hombre. Women were not women anymore. Women were now *chicas* and *bellas*. I would grow my black hair long so I could look more like Antonio Banderas did in Desperado. And sing that song which goes something like this:.*Aye, aye, aye .. aye, aye, mi amor ... ay, mi morena de mi corazón*[31]

---

[31] Los Lobos and Antonio Banderas, "Canción del Mariachi" ('Morena de Mi Corazón')" *Desperado: The Soundtrack*, 1995.

21

It took me a few weeks to get used to the lay of the land. At the moment my Spanish was not that great but it was getting better. I discovered no matter where I went I was told I spoke Spanish with a gringo accent. The locals found it amusing because even though I looked Mexican as soon as I opened my mouth they realized I was really a gringo.

One time I was very thirsty and made the mistake of drinking water out of a nearby faucet. Why I did this I don't even know? Perhaps I was delirious from the heat. A few hours later I was throwing up everywhere. I was then quarantined to my bed for nearly two weeks, delaying me further, from my first teaching job. At one point I was worried I was never going to get better or that when I did the job would no longer be available. Rigo told me not to worry. He took it upon himself to come see me after he returned home from work to go over the lessons plans I would have and the Spanish I would need to know as a teacher. Maria doted on me as if I was her son, caring for me and feeding me. I was not used to all this attention. Maria, Rigo and I grew so close during my illness that Maria declared I was now her adopted son. Rigo smiled and patted me on the head like I was some kid who didn't know any better.

Emilio would call me from time to time to get updates on my progress. He was like a devoted father offering advice and laughing at my stories of culture shocks and unintentional mishaps from my many adventures through Mexico. I asked him when he was going to visit me. He always told me someday... someday. I knew someday never came. It saddened me a little knowing this. However, I was finally realizing that life is full of loss along with its many gains. I had to find a way to not meander on the negative and focus instead on the positive. I thought about what it would be like to finally meet my mother. I decided after I was better and after I was employed and after I had grown more accustomed to Mexican culture and to Spanish, I would then be ready to find her and visit her. It would be perfect then. She would see me and would be so proud at what I had achieved not only as an American but also now as a Mexican.

I had lost a considerable amount of weight from my stomach virus. However it did not take long before I was at my regular weight again. Maria and Rigo fed and fed me. Mexicans don't glamorize skinniness like we Americans do. Maria and Rigo also took it upon themselves to fatten me up by purposely feeding me fattening food. I was all too eager to let them do so. I don't believe I ever ate this much food and such quality of food before in all of my life.

Nights were always the same. After dinner Rigo and I would retire in his office drinking whiskey or tequila and smoking cigarettes or cigars. We would talk about politics and philosophy and women and literature. Rigo took it upon himself to explain to how to deal with a Mexican woman. Rigo seemed to enjoy my company telling me it was nice to have another man around the house and talk about what only men can talk about. He confessed he sometimes felt outnumbered by having two women in the house. Rigo began to lend me books to read. Sometimes he would lend me two copies of the same book: one in English and the other in Spanish to help me along with my Spanish.

I grew particularly fond of the poems of Pablo Neruda. I asked Rigo how I could repay him for all his generosity but Rigo waved me off. He told me Emilio had arranged everything on my behalf. I was so touched I immediately felt guilty of any past negative thought I had of Emilio. I also decided that when I finally met my mother I would tell her how good Emilio was to me. Or maybe she already knew? Either way I would tell her everything.

When Rigo was away other nights were spent with his wife Maria and any friend she had over and wanted me to meet. Maria and her friends would sometimes give me much needed dancing lessons. There was always a friend who was planning on going to the United States someday and wanted my advice. Maria would also inform me of the proper way to speak to a Mexican woman. I learned that Mexican women appeared to talk more than American women. They talked and talked and sometimes they talked all at once sounding like a flock of birds. CACKLE! CACKLE! CACKLE! And sometimes it seemed like they were all screaming at each other and on the verge of committing bloody murder on one another. My fears were put to rest afterward when they all kissed and hugged each other as if they were all the closest of friends. And they were.

When we went to restaurants for lunch we would spend hours at a restaurant. After we sat down it seemed to take a decade before a waitress came to take our orders. Another decade passed before we were served our drinks. A millennium passed before we were finally served our meal. And then we spent what seemed like a century talking and drinking and talking and drinking.

A few more months passed and I had not started any work at the English School. Rigo admitted to me he didn't feel I was quite ready yet. I was growing more and more anxious—luckily Rigo and Maria were very good at keeping me occupied. I must have been introduced to dozens of single Mexican women. They all seemed to giggle in delight at a potential romance with an exotic gringo. I dated many of them. I soon found Mexican women were less shy about sex than American women. I was having more sex with different women than I had ever before in my life. And yet I felt nothing for most of them. I was entertained with their company but I had not felt a connection to one of them as of yet.

Partying or celebrating a holiday also took a while for me to acclimate. When Mexicans celebrated a holiday it would go on for days and days and days. Every holiday was like a festival. The whole town would stop and participate. Work was always secondary to them. I had a very hard time keeping up with them during these parties, celebrations and festivals. At one point after partying for a day and a half I was forced into a conga line marathon. I was so tired that the people in front and back of me had to hold me so I wouldn't fall over on the floor. They all laughed and made fun at how I so easily tired. Or how few shots if tequila it took to get me very drunk. They would give me shots of tequila and refill it the within seconds after I had finished gulping it down. My liver threatened to strike but was ignored by the rest of my organs and me.

When Rigo had some of his *amigos* over, they would teach me Spanish slang and curse words. They also taught me some Spanish customs and gestures which Rigo made me promise to never tell Maria.

Then there was the time we saw a group of mariachis playing on the street. I thought again about my fantasy of me as Antonio Banderas in *Desperado*. Rigo, Maria and his little daughter stopped to listen and dance. Some nearby attractive woman grabbed my hand and before I knew we were all dancing and kicking our feet into the air. I never saw the woman who I was dancing with again. But that's how it was in Mexico. People enjoy life or they try to take more moments to enjoy life and fewer moments are spent worrying about the future or worrying about other trivial things.

Everything felt like an endless vacation or an endless party and I was happy to participate. I began to think less and less about the United States. I did not care to be American any more. I was born a Mexican and I would die a Mexican. A true son of Mexico. And like my adopted Mexican family I worried less about future plans and spent more time living in the present on the ride I was on and I felt so damn happy spinning around and around everything around me like an inconsolable fool. I was an inconsolable fool with my life walking along with me and not ahead me.

I was now having so much fun I found myself somewhat afraid. I was afraid it would all end after meeting my mother. She was still a complete stranger to me. I knew I would find her soon enough but not yet. Not yet. It didn't feel right. I had to enjoy myself for a while. I never had the chance to really enjoy my life and now I was beginning to enjoy life. Now it seemed as if the nightmares of my past life were finally behind me and the dream of my life now would begin and stay with me. Now and forever.

22

Soon enough I realized teaching English was an excellent occupation for an American ex-patriot to have in Mexico. I am not speaking of monetary awards. The Mexican women seemed to adore my gringo-ness to a certain extent. I had a good number of relations with many of the female students. Since this was a private school that focused on only one subject: English—most if not all of the students were over the age of eighteen.

Of course, I tried to never have a relationship while the object of my desire was my student. I preferred to wait until afterward. I also did this to avoid any unnecessary assumptions or perceptions by my other students. Like favoritism or something like that. I would choose the ones I liked and based on what I learned from Rigo, Rigo's amigos, and Maria about Mexican women I would plant seeds throughout the course to lead them to me. And then I would wait to make my move after the commencement at the course's end by inviting them to dinner to "celebrate" her graduation.

The women here loved it when I talked to them about America or did something only a gringo would do. They found it charming. Sometimes, I would lie to a girl and tell her that one day I might bring her back to the United States with me. Of course I never told them the truth: I would never return to the United States because I had been deported. And I was also probably wanted for murder. Anyway, it did not matter that they didn't know that. I had grown accustomed to not keeping the same girl around too long. I was not looking for love. I was only looking for some fun and a good time.

Making love to a Latin woman was much more complex than with an American woman. I hate to sound like I am generalizing. And this is all based on my limited experiences with American women. At first, some of the Latin women were very critical of me. And at first some were very hurt by how I made love. They felt like I was insulting them or making fun of them. Eventually I learned from my mistakes and became the Latin Lover I knew I was always destined to be. It was all about passion. A passion born from a love of life and being alive. It was about becoming creatures capable of magic. It was about entering another dimension. Sex with a Latin woman was never boring. Never. It was always animated and marvelous and focused.

Rigo loved to hear me talk about my sexual conquests each night after dinner in his home office. Even after working a while in my job as a teacher Rigo and Maria insisted I stay. They said in Mexico there was no need for a man to live alone. People think men who live alone must have something to hide. So I was told I would not be allowed to move out until I found a woman to settle down with and marry. I did not protest. It made sense. Perhaps it would be better to wait till I was married before I met my mother? It would be reassuring for her to know her son had not only been successful in America and Mexico, but was also now married to a beautiful Mexican woman and would someday start a family. After all, Rigo and Maria were good to me. And Emilio continued to send them money to cover my cost. At one point I tried to convince Emilio to stop but he told me if he stopped helping me it would rob him of any evidence that he was a good person. I told him he was a son of a bitch. *Mí cabrón.* Emilio laughed.

A few months passed. Subsequently I began to speak Spanish with more confidence and less hesitation. I even began to pick up the colloquial phrases and mannerisms. It was my hope that by this time I did not stick out like a sore thumb so much as when I first arrived in Mexico.

They say we usually find the love of our life when we're not looking. Then I suppose that is what happened to me. When I first met Inés, she was another one of my students who wanted to learn English and dreamed about coming to the United States one day. But there was something different about here. I cannot quite put my finger on it. She had a rare quality which caused me to sometimes hesitate when I spoke to her. I was nervous around her and when I was close to her desk. I tried to hide it. However when she would smile at me I knew she saw through my charade. She was the first and only student for whom I broke my rules. I would ask her to stay with me after class to talk alone. At first she was understandably reluctant. Then one day she said yes. And we began to speak to each other after every class. And everything blossomed.

When I was with her I felt like I was with an angel. She made me feel like I was the most important person on earth. She asked me more questions about the United States than any one had ever before her or after her. She was very curious and very smart and very pure, in a way. She said she wanted to go to the United Sates to go to a university and then have a career in the United States, or something silly like that. She had a tint in her eyes that whispered to me an eternity of bliss.

We soon moved from meeting after class to meeting for dinner. I had other dates with other women I had planned in advance to meet but I cancelled them all to be with Inés. With her I thought long term. With her I thought about destiny or other silly things like that. Eventually she introduced me to her family and eventually I invited her over to meet Rigo and Maria, my adopted family. In my head I began to plan the wedding and the honeymoon and a life together on a ranch and many, many, many children. I was in love. I was sure I was in love. I was sure this time it was really real.

We would take long walks together during the evenings and Inés would tell me more of her dreams and I listened half-heartedly. Her indescribable beauty blinded me. I pulled her aside one night and told her that if heaven existed she must be its personification. She blushed then kissed me on the cheek. It made me only love her more so I pulled her against me and we kissed as if tomorrow would never come. Sometimes I wish that were true. When I kissed her I felt complete. I started to listen to every silly love song I used to make fun of before. Now they all made sense. I was enraptured with Inés. She had me wrapped around her rose thorns. I felt not a prick but a poke. Sometimes I would send her Pablo Neruda poems, she always assumed I wrote them for her myself, even after trying to explain to her I didn't. She preferred to believe I was the poems' original author.

Time passed and I started to look for a house to buy for Inés and myself. I looked for a while without telling Inés. I wanted to surprise her. I imagined her jumping up and down in then leaping into my arms and thanking me a million times with a million kisses. I realized in Mexico I would be expected to marry her before she would even consider moving in with me. So then I began wandering into jewelry shops looking for an engagement ring. I searched and searched all over town until I found the one I knew would make Inés scream in excitement and jump in pure joy. I also imagined it would be a great story to tell my mother when I finally met her.

One night we had dinner together in Rigo and Maria's house. Rigo and Maria were gone to some party. I felt that was the perfect opportunity to propose to Inés. So after we had finished dinner I told her to stay where she was sitting and I got on one knee and I pulled out the ring and I proposed her. She screamed like I imagined. She jumped in joy and kissed me as I had imagined. Everything was perfect. Too perfect.

Inés sat back down in her chair exclaiming how happy she was to marry me knowing I would take her with me back to the United States.

I sat back down and stared at the table while Inés went off talking about all the things we could do together in the United States. She stopped halfway through her fantasy asking me if I was sick because I looked worried. I lied and told her I was fine. I knew I wasn't.

Nothing was fine.

We made love for the first time that night. Before we made love Inés told me it would be okay for us to have sex before being married because we were going to get married anyway and she knew in her heart we were destined to be together forever. She had promised herself she would only sleep with the man who she married. We made love the whole night. And when we woke the next morning I took her to a friend's house because she didn't want her parents to know she had stayed the night at my house.

23

EMILIO called me after I'd returned home that morning. He was very frantic and even sounded angry.

"*Hijo*. How long has it been since you have been in Mexico?"

"Almost a year now, I think. Why?"

"Why have you not gone to find your mother?"

"Oh. I don't know? I will. I promise I will. I just want things to be perfect before I met her. You know what I mean?"

"I told you about your mother. I gave you that box."

"Emilio. Lookit. This is a small town. Why hasn't she come to look for me? It's not like most of the people don't know who I am or about me by now. She must then know I'm busy. She must know I am waiting for things to be perfect before we meet. Right? It has to be perfect, Emilio. It has to be perfect."

"The next time I speak to you I want to hear that you went to see your mother or her family, *hijo*. If I find out you didn't I will not be happy. What kind of son are you? Remember, Jimmy. I have ways of finding out. Good Bye!"

I found myself flustered by Emilio's call. He was obviously angry with me otherwise he would not have threatened me. I went to my bedroom and lay down thinking about Emilio's words. I tried to remember all the things he told me that day at the airport. How Emilio described my mother as a very beautiful woman. How Emilio claimed my father had kidnapped me from my mother when he smuggled me into the United States. And how my mother became sick from a broken heart. I remembered how sick I got when I drank some Mexican water. Though I got better after a while. How my mother did not deserve to have been abandoned by my father and me. I am not sure how I was at fault. I was too young to have remembered any of this. How Emilio did not contact my mother because he was not sure what she would have done next. Implying she might have become inconsolable with grief. Or something like that.

I pulled out the box of my mother's things from underneath my bed and looked again at its inner contents. I looked at my mother's picture again. I thought she looked like an angel. She looked perfect. She looked pure. Then I noticed something I had never noticed before. My mothers face looked exactly like the face of the Maria de Guadalupe my father painted in the Firebird. My father had reimagined my mother as a saint. Or he was honoring her. This realization made me feel even more perplexed. I looked for the piece of paper where an address written on it. I was a horrible son. I felt dreadful. So I cried.

I cried for my mother. I cried for forgetting about the woman who had given me life. I cried for not meeting her right away. I cried because my father had hurt her. I cried because now I realized that though he hurt her, he never stopped loving her and never stopped asking for her forgiveness. And every time he prayed to Maria de Guadalupe for guidance he was praying to my mother.I cried because I knew the woman who I had finally fallen in love with would leave me after she found out I could not take her to the United States. I cried. I wrapped myself in my covers and went to sleep knowing I would have to go search for my mother the next day.

The next day I set out to find my mother. Rigo let me borrow his car. He asked where I was going. I didn't want to tell him or Maria so I lied and told them I was doing something else. I drove all over town getting lost most of the time. Apparently I had not figured out the town, as well as I thought. I drove asking people where they thought the address was until I finally found myself on the other side of town almost where it stops. This did not make any sense to me. According to the address and the input of each person I had asked I was where I was supposed to be. But the neighborhood was nearly abandoned.

I drove through the street of a ghost town and squatters. The people who lived in this village made poverty in the United States look like paradise. There were cinderblocks of unfinished buildings occupied by people hardly dressed in tattered clothes. They all lived in little apartments no bigger than a bedroom. They looked at me as if I did not belong there and maybe they were right. The place reminded me of that Brazilian movie, *City of God*. A group of young kids ran by me throwing things at Rigo's car. I sped up a little hoping I would lose them. Luckily something else caught their eye and they luckily lost interest in me.

I finally found what must have been the address written on the piece of paper. I got out of the car for a closer inspection. There was no one inside the apartment when I opened the door. Only the remains of the things of people who had lived there a long time ago. I searched around to see if there were any clues I might be able to find. I searched through everything and instead found nothing.

When I stepped outside I felt the urge to cry again. Then I felt angry. I wondered why Emilio had guilted me into a wild goose chase which resulted in a futile conclusion. However, while I was leaning on Rigo's car feeling sorry for myself, that same group of kids from earlier, had returned. By the time I realized they were near they had surrounded me. I will never forget their eyes. It was indescribable. There was so much hate there. As if they had never known what love was because no one was around to love them. One of them yelled something at me in Mexican slang before brandishing a knife. One of the skinny ones pushed me and then a couple grabbed both my arms. The one with the knife grabbed my shirt and then pressed his knife against my neck. I felt its cold hard steel break into my skin.

I wondered if this was how my life was going to end? Would I die here in a place God had seemed to forsake? Would this be the conclusion of everything for me? I want to fly away.... in the sky.... high above the rest of the world and listen to the conversations.... I want to see everything so that I might never be bored. Maybe being dead would be better because I would never have anything to worry about again? Who has ever heard of the dead complaining?

Sirens screaming in the distance—growing louder and louder. This made the kids jump. They let me go and ran away. I grabbed my throat searching for my new open wound but could not feel a wound. I got back in Rigo's car and looked at my neck in the rearview mirror. All I saw was a part of my neck's skin reddened from the knife agitating it.

When I returned Rigo and Maria asked me about the place I lied to them about. For some reason I decided to confess to them where I really went. After I told them Rigo grabbed my arm and asked me to come with him. We got in his other car, a much nicer than the one he let me borrow, and we left the house together in his car. I asked Rigo where we were going and Rigo told me he would tell me when we got there. I told him I thought he was being rather dramatic and Rigo told me that was not his intention.

We drove around for a while. Rigo remained silent as I told him about my father and Maria de Guadalupe and my mother. Every now and then he nodded as I spoke to him about my father and my mother and the box and her various pictures. Rigo continued to respond to anything I said with silent nods as he drove us to our unknown destination.

Then he parked the car and we got out. I followed him as we walked into a cemetery. Rigo and I walked deep into the cemetery until he stopped at a very small grave. He bent down at one of the gravestones and wiped some debris that had collected in front of it. He then pointed at the name.

"That is your mother, Jimmy."

"My mother is dead? Why didn't anyone tell me?"

"We thought you knew. But I guess you didn't. You were going on like you knew because you never asked us about her. So, like I said, we thought you knew."

"I was waiting for everything to be perfect. I wanted to surprise her with good news. I didn't want to tell her only bad things about me, like my deportation, and the people who hurt me, and betrayed me. I want her to be proud of me when she met me. I was waiting for everything to be perfect. But then Emilio yelled at me to go find her. He said he wanted me to meet her family."

"Emilio loved your mother but your mother loved your father. They say your mother died of a broken heart. I don't know if that's true. But they say she had given up living. Some things are inexplicable, Jimmy. We liked having you around. You are like a son to me now, Jimmy. And you seemed so happy with us. I-I didn't want to ruin that. Maybe I was also lying to myself. I'm sorry, Jimmy."

I waited a moment to speak. I had a million things to say. I had a million things to ask. Instead the first thing I said was, "Where is my mother's family?"

"They live in the next town."

"Take me to see them."

Rigo nodded and we left my mother's grave and we got back in his car and drove into the next town into the evening. Rigo decided to remain silent. I turned on the radio to try to get my mind off of everything. I felt incomplete again and disoriented by the disjointed emotions I was having. I was disturbed.

We arrived at a small modest house. Rigo and I walked up to the door together. An older woman who resembled my mother in eyes and in nose answered the door. Rigo told her who I was. She screamed in delight and wrapped her big fat arms around me exclaiming to me that she was my great aunt, or my grandmother's sister. Rigo asked if I wanted him to wait outside in the car. I told Rigo that would not be necessary.

I was introduced to another woman, who I was told was my grandmother, and all four of us sat in their living room talking about my mother. They asked me many questions and I was afraid to answer any of them. My grandmother and great-aunt lived together because both their husbands had already passed away. They spoke over each other and loudly like most Mexican women. The only difference being they were of relation to me now. Rigo and I could not get a word in edgewise. I was overwhelmed with everything. Uncontrollable tears ran down my cheeks and all of us cried together.

My grandmother made some coffee that we all drank. The coffee was very delicious. I do not think I have ever had better coffee in my life. They then proceeded to tell me about my mother. They told me my mother had health problems her entire life. I asked them what sort of health problems. They said tuberculosis and then finally cancer, which ended her short life on this earth. They postured that my mother's illness might have been one reason my father kidnapped me and left my mother alone in Mexico. They told me my mother might not have been able to survive the journey. Yet they were still quick to condemn my father for taking me away from my mother. I told them taking a baby on such a journey was just as dangerous. But my great aunt told me that babies are very easy to hide and care for. I decided to not argue that point any further.

They told me my mother lived out the rest of her life as a local seamstress in the town. She made clothes and helped the tailor whenever he was overwhelmed. But she spent the rest of her life in poverty. She refused the advances of all men. Even wealthy men who offered her an escape. She never remarried. She preferred it better to be single and not risk having her heart broken again. Neither was aware of my mother's plan to visit me. I wondered if what Emilio told me about my mother at the airport was true. I concluded it would take a long time to separate the legend and the truth of my mother.

They told me told the one thing that made her feel good was the knowledge I was doing better in the United States. Of course, knowing I was away from her and knowing she might never see me again, also made her sometimes depressed. She was known to weep in silence days at a time. And during these times of depression no one was able to console my mother. My great aunt told me she thought my mother held out hope she would someday see me again. Even after she learned she would never be able to visit me due to her illness. Then my grandmother confessed it saddened her that my mother had passed away before I returned. She then cried while rocking back and forth in her wooden rocking chair. My great aunt nodded in agreement with while shedding her own share of tears.

They then showed me a picture taken of my mother not long before she had passed away. From the picture it appeared that the years of her ongoing illness and harsh life had brought millions of wrinkles all over her face. Her hair was all gone. Probably due to the cancer. I wondered if Emilio ever tried to help her. I wondered if my mother refused his help. I wondered if she could have been saved of such a life filled with grief. She wasn't even that old when she had passed. But life had quickly aged her. In the last picture taken of my mother, she no longer looked anything like the young woman in the photograph in the box that Emilio had given me. To me it seemed the idea of her having a broken heart was very true. Even if all her life she had been dealing with an illness. She looked defeated.

And yet I felt relieved to finally know the truth. She was not only a good person she was better than I had imagined. No wonder my father painted my mother as the Mother of God. Now I had a place where I could speak to her even though she would never speak back to me. I could see how wonderful a person she was through my grandmother and great aunt's eyes. Even though she was often sad and often struggling with her health she seemed content and never gave up hope that she would someday see me again.

I did not stay there that night. I decided to return with Rigo to his house. When Rigo and I were back at his house I said nothing and went straight to bed. I was so tired. However, I knew I would return soon enough to find out more information about my mother and my family.

The next day I called Inés and asked her to see me. She told me we should go to some hill where an old colonial church was built on top. According to Inés, the top of this hill had a great view of the town. It was a beautiful day and she thought it would be romantic. I agreed.

We bought some ice cream that was being sold nearby and brought it with us to the top of the hill. Inés pulled out a blanket she had brought with her. We sat on the blanket and ate our ice cream while looking over the town. The church bells in the tower began to ring.

I wanted to tell Inés everything. I wanted to tell her about my father and about my mother. I wanted to tell her about my friend Norm and how he died for nothing. I wanted to tell her about the friends I had at the Fish Bowl and about karaoke. I wanted to tell her about Ringo and Jasmine. I wanted to tell her about the murdered Ian Noone, that no one seemed to care about, and died because he was unlucky. Who died because he was no one. I wanted to tell her about Clark Short who revealed himself to me in his true form... a monster. I wanted to tell her how I killed him my last night in jail for the good of humanity. I wanted to tell her about Detective Willy and his unusual display of compassion for me. I wanted to tell her about Emilio and how he probably loved my mother more than my father ever had. Or that my mother might have died of a broken heart and lived the rest of her life unmarried and missing me. I wanted to tell Inés everything, but I didn't. And we sat there together on the hill and I tried to clear my mind. I didn't want to think about the future. I didn't want to think about the past. It was hard to do because all Inés wanted to talk about was going to the United States someday very soon.

A small breeze blew. I tried to exhale the pressure away from my brain. I turned my head to gaze at Inés' unadulterated beauty. She had now grown quiet. I could tell she was getting sleepy. She laid her head on my lap and then she closed her eyes. I sighed an empty sigh. Another festival was about to begin and I could see people hanging decorations far away. And then I heard the echo of a voice I once thought I had known at one time or another.